REAL MURDER

A LOVERS IN CRIME MYSTERY

By

LAUREN CARR

REAL MURDER

Published by Acorn Book Services

For information call: 304-995-1295
or Email: writerlaurencarr@gmail.com

Designed by Acorn Book Services

Publication Managed by Acorn Book Services
www.acornbookservices.com
acornbookservices@gmail.com
304-995-1295

Cover designed by Todd Aune
Spokane, Washington
www.projetoonline.com
Image provided by Arman Zhenikeyev/www.fotolia.com

ISBN-10: 0989180492
ISBN-13: 978-0-9891804-9-8

Published in the United States of America

To My Family and Friends
in Chester, West Virginia.

It is true. You can take the girl out of the small town,
but you can't take the small town out of the girl!

REAL MURDER

MURDER

A LOVERS IN CRIME MYSTERY

Cast of Characters

(in order of appearance)

Bart: Bouncer at Dolly's Gentlemen's Club.

Larry Van Patton: Bartender at Dolly's Gentlemen's Club.

Bianca: A slender redhead who wore her hair in thick waves down to her shoulders. She's one of Dolly's girls.

Ava Tucker: A redhead whose girl-next-door quality made her a good choice for new members at Dolly's Gentlemen's Club. Friday the Thirteenth is not her lucky day.

Congressman Roderick Hilliard: United States Congressman from West Virginia. On Friday the Thirteenth, his private plane slammed into a moutainside, killing him and two of his assistants.

Congresswoman Rachel Hilliard: Roderick's widow. Friday the Thirteenth was her lucky day. After her husband's sudden death, she became West Virginia's new congresswoman. She is known as the Ice Queen.

Joshua Thornton: Hancock County Prosecuting Attorney and former JAG lawyer. Widowed father of five. Now his children are growing up and leaving the nest, which allows him the freedom to fall in love with Detective Cameron Gates.

Tracy Thornton: Joshua Thornton's older daughter. A gourmet chef, she is studying at the CIA.

Deputy Mike Gardner: Hancock County sheriff's deputy. Joshua's childhood friend. He disappears on Friday the thirteenth. Joshua Thornton is the last one to see him alive—except for his killer.

Dr. Tad MacMillan: Chester's home town doctor and Hancock County Medical Examiner. Used to be the town drunk and womanizer. Married to Jan.

Jan Martin MacMillan: Editor of *The Review* newspaper in East Liverpool, Ohio. Tad MacMillan's wife. New mother to Tad Junior.

Donny Thornton: Joshua's youngest son. Sixteen-years-old. Last baby still left in the nest.

Woody: Donny Thornton's friend. The only working out he does is his thumbs on video games.

Lieutenant Miles Dugan: Cameron Gates' supervisor at the state police barracks in Pennsylvania.

Detective Cameron Gates: Pennsylvania State Police Homicide Detective. Joshua Thornton's bride of forty-five days.

Sheriff Curt Sawyer: Hancock County's sheriff.

Hunter Gardner: Mike Gardner's son. He took Tracy Thornton to prom. Accepted to the police academy, he plans to take his father's place in the sheriff's department.

Belle Fontaine: Hunter's mother. Mike's widow. She remarried as soon as her first husband was declared legally dead.

Royce Fontaine: Hunter's step-father.

Irving: Cameron's Maine Coon cat. Irving has issues, not the least of which is the human male who married his woman. You'd have issues, too, if you looked like a skunk.

Admiral: Joshua's Irish Wolfhound-Great Dane dog. Irving's friend. His only issue is climbing up onto the furniture when he thinks no one is watching.

Douglas O'Reilly: A student at West Point. Legend says he drove his Mustang into Raccoon Creek after finding out his girlfriend was pregnant. Is that really what happened?

Eleanor O'Reilly: Douglas' mother. She refuses to believe her son committed suicide. Unfortunately, the police refuse to investigate a case that isn't a real murder.

Cynthia Gardner: Mike's mother, or is she?

Dolly Houseman: The kindly blue-haired old lady who lives across the street from the Thorntons. Al Capone was her Uncle Al.

Lorraine Winter: The neighborhood's nasty old woman. Donny says the snakes avoid her yard.

Colonel Henry MacCrae: West Virginia State Police Superintendent. He makes a special trip to Chester from Charleston to investigate Mike Gardner's murder.

Philip Lipton: Head of the state crime lab in Weirton, West Virginia.

Virgil Null: Murder Victim. His first night with Ava Tucker was his last.

Russell Null: Virgil Null's older brother. He is on the board of county commissioners. He now owns and manages Null Landscaping, family business for more than fifty years.

Flo O'Reilly: Douglas' sister. After his death, she is left behind to care for her family.

Anthony Tanner: Convicted murderer suspected of being up to his old tricks once again.

Tiffany: Pole dancer who is taken hostage.

Dirk (Slim) Reed: Once the main insurance guy in the Ohio Valley. Now he is in his nineties and has a memory like a bank vault.

"The idea that everything is purposeful really changes the way you live. To think that everything that you do has a ripple effect, that every word that you speak, every action that you make affects other people and the planet."

Victoria Moran, Author

PROLOGUE

Friday the Thirteenth, February 13, 1976
Dolly's Gentlemen's Club, Newell, West Virginia

In the upper tip of West Virginia's northern panhandle, the tiny town of Newell has two claims to fame—Homer Laughlin China Company, whose wares are used in restaurants and fine dining all over the world, and the Waterford Race Track. Folks travel for miles to see the Thoroughbreds race for the finish line.

Off the record, Newell also had another claim to fame in the Ohio Valley. It was located a half mile off Route 208, the first left beyond the race track—Dolly's Gentlemen's Club.

On a lazy weekday afternoon, one would think that the huge white antebellum house with a wrap-around porch and verandah off the second story, all nestled behind two huge willow trees, was simply the grand home of a gentleman farmer.

Those not in the know would assume the young women living there were some lucky farmer's lovely daughters. The local law enforcement told people that the establishment

13

was a boarding house for women—who happened to throw big parties on the weekends.

There was no sign out front because Dolly didn't have to advertise. Some of the richest and most powerful men in the Ohio Valley knew where to go for the most private of entertainment.

Fridays were always the club's busiest nights. After a long week of wheeling and dealing, the valley's male movers and shakers would swing into Dolly's for a drink or two or three or four, and then go upstairs to one of the private rooms for some personal entertainment.

Or, if there was a particularly sensitive issue that needed to be discussed in top secrecy, Dolly's parlor was available for a private meeting with all the necessary ambiance, which included a fully stocked bar and a lovely bar maid.

By one o'clock in the morning, the bar would close up and the men would be sent home to their families. Bart, the club's bouncer, would sometimes have to help a customer who had had too much to drink to his car.

On this Friday, the thirteenth, Bart was in a hurry to get home to his wife. During the day, he worked as a bank security guard. On the weekends, he earned extra cash under the table by taking care of Dolly's girls. A faithful husband, he could be counted on to take care of the women whom he protected like a big brother looking after his little sisters—all eight of them.

Since the grandfather clock in the grand foyer now read an hour past midnight, it was technically the fourteenth—Valentine's Day. Bart anticipated giving his wife an early present of roses and champagne when he got home.

The bartender, Larry, came in from the store room behind the kitchen. "Well, I just had to chase another one out."

"Another what?" Bart asked, hoping it hadn't been a persistent journalist looking for dirt on one of the politicians who regularly patronized Dolly's.

"Nosey wife looking to see where her husband goes on Friday nights." Larry went behind the bar. "I found her in the kitchen. She saw me and skedaddled out the back door like a bat out of hell."

"Whose wife was she?"

"How should I know?" Larry replied. "She was an ugly old biddie with shoulders like a linebacker and long gray hair tied back in a bun like some old schoolmarm. No wonder her husband, whoever he is, hangs out here."

"The party meeting in the parlor is all done, Bart." Bianca, a slender redhead who wore her hair in thick waves down to her shoulders, carried in a tray containing two brandy snifters. Even in her high heels and tight red leather mini skirt, she strode in with the grace of a dancer, which she was. She was one of the most popular dancers in the lounge. "They left a half an hour ago." She sighed. "What a snooty tramp— you'd think since she used to be one of us … I'm tempted to make an anonymous phone call to her husband to let him know exactly what he's married to." Grumbling, she took the glasses back to the kitchen.

Sitting at the bar, Bart admired her sexy stride to the back of the house until he caught sight of Jaclyn's client coming down the stairs and going out the front door.

Only one more left. That tall skinny kid who went upstairs with Ava.

As a security guard, Bart prided himself on his powers of observation. He managed to keep track of the time each client went upstairs, which girl he went up with, and what time he left. Bart considered his powers of observation to be a necessary talent.

He checked his watch. This last john had gone up with Ava at ten-twenty. Since the client looked barely old enough to drink, the bartender had carded him. A redhead who possessed a girl-next-door quality, Ava was a natural choice for him.

After the couple went up the stairs to Ava's room, Larry joked with the bouncer about it being the kid's first time. They rarely saw johns so young and nervous. A private club, Dolly's catered to a much more sophisticated clientele.

Give them another five minutes. Even so, Bart was anxious to go home to his own woman and get away from the cigarette smoke and flowery perfume smell.

"Hey," he called out to Jaclyn when he saw her start up the stairs after wishing her client, one of her regulars, a sincere good-bye. "Can you tell if Ava is done with her gentleman?"

Jaclyn frowned. "I didn't know she had one up there."

"She took him up there before ten-thirty," Bart said. "He hasn't come out yet."

"Maybe they fell asleep," Jaclyn said. "The light's off in her room." She paused. "But then, the music is on."

Each of the girls had a stereo in her room to play music in order to drown out the noise of other girls and their gentlemen. The music served as a signal that the girl had a client and was not to be disturbed.

"She's not allowed to let him spend the night." Bart stood up.

The two of them went upstairs to the room at the end of the hall.

The bouncer banged on the door. "Ava! Wake up! It's time for your gentleman to go home. Wake him up."

They waited.

"Ava!" Jaclyn wrapped her robe around her. "Wake up, Sweetie. You know men aren't allowed to spend the night. You don't want to get into trouble with management, do you?"

The other girls on the floor strolled out into the hallway. A few whose clients had left earlier were dressed in their real nightclothes, which included terry robes. Others had night cream on their faces.

They all listened for Ava to respond.

"Ava!" Bart tried turning the doorknob. The door was locked. As loud as they were, Ava should have been answering the door. Then he was worried. *Had she overdosed? Did she even use drugs?* He didn't know Ava well enough to know if she did.

He took the keys he had for the bedroom doors out of his pocket. As a guard, he had the keys in case any of the girls got into trouble with a client, or, as in this case, possibly had a medical emergency.

He unlocked the door and forced his way inside. The lights were indeed off. The girls crowded in the doorway to see what was preventing Ava from answering the door.

Bart flipped on the wall switch to bathe the room in light.

In unison, the girls screamed at a variety of hysterical pitches.

The stereo was set to repeat the song "Stairway to Heaven" by Led Zeppelin.

Ava was in bed. Her last client lay next to her. Both of their hands were tied behind their backs. Duct tape covered their noses and mouths to stifle the cries for help they had tried to make while being killed in silence.

Friday the Thirteenth: September 13, 1996
Allison's Diner
Carolina Avenue, Chester, West Virginia

"It was twenty years ago today that West Virginia Congressman Roderick Hilliard was killed when his private plane, which he was piloting, crashed into the side of a Blue Ridge mountain during a flight to Washington, DC. Two passengers in the plane, the congressman's lawyer and his assistant, also died in the crash," the newscaster reported from the radio that provided background noise in the small diner. "Congresswoman Rachel Hilliard recalled her late husband today in a speech to a group of veterans—"

"Dad, why does Murphy always get the last fry?" seven-year-old J. J. Thornton objected when he saw his identical twin brother going after the last fry on the plate set between them at the booth. "I never get the last bite."

"You do so," Murphy said.

"When?"

"Last night," Murphy said. "You finished the popcorn."

"Did not," J. J. countered, "Tracy got that."

"Point is I didn't." Murphy reached for the fry only to discover that his sister, two-year-old Sarah, had snagged it while they were arguing, smashed it in her little hands, and shoved it into her mouth to create a nasty mess on her face and everything she touched.

"Dad!" the twins called out in unison.

"What?" Joshua Thornton found it difficult to keep the exasperation out of his voice when he looked up from the reports in the file he was reading. Even though he had been sitting at the table during the ordeal, he had managed to block out their squabbling. It was a talent he had developed while working his way up in his navy career as an officer, and as a lawyer, with a growing and rambunctious family.

Such a skill was not a great marital attribute, especially when your wife was trying to organize a move halfway across the world while keeping four children, all under the age of seven, in line. Joshua tried to help his wife as best he could, but that was difficult when he got his first assignment at their new post in Naples, Italy. A navy officer was accused of raping a fellow officer. Joshua Thornton was expected to lead the investigation as soon as he arrived.

How did he prepare for a major court martial case while moving a family of six halfway across the world? Carefully.

Joshua had agreed to take the kids out for lunch at the downtown diner on the main drag of Chester while his wife, Valerie, and his grandmother finished the last of the packing.

"Sarah ate the last fry." J. J. pointed a finger of accusation at her. "It was supposed to be mine."

"It was mine," Murphy said.

"Why don't I ever get the last fry?" Five-year-old Tracy refused to be left out.

"Because you never call dibs," J. J. answered.

Murphy told his father, "You said I could have the fry."

"No, I didn't," Joshua replied.

"You did so say so!" This irritated Murphy more than losing the fry to his sister. He went on to recount in detail that while they were eating he had asked if he could have the last one, to which his father had replied, "Uh-huh."

Considering that he was in the midst of reading a witness account and not necessarily paying attention, Joshua hated to admit that Murphy's statement could be true.

"Josh?"

With a smile of relief, Joshua looked up to see a young man dressed in the uniform of a Hancock County Sheriff Deputy making his way from the door to their booth.

Even with his red hair cut short into a military cut, the curls at the ends of his locks were evident. The laughter in his blue eyes projected his good-natured personality. "That is you!" the deputy grinned widely at Joshua. "How have you been?"

"Mike … Gardner?" Joshua stood up and greeted the muscular police officer with a warm handshake that turned into a hug. "How are you?" When he pulled back, he looked the muscle-bound man up and down and let out a whistle. "Look at you."

"Me?" Mike gestured at the booth filled with children. "What about you? Are these all yours?"

"Yeah." With a wicked grin, Joshua explained, "I travel a lot and my wife gets lonely."

"Is that a real gun?" Tracy pointed at the gun on the deputy's belt.

"Yes, it is." Mike grasped the weapon to protect her from reaching for it while draping his other arm across the back of her seat. "And what is your name, pretty lady?"

"Tracy," she replied. "And this is my baby sister Sarah. She's two-years-old. I'm five." She held up her hand to show him all of her fingers.

"Well, Tracy, my son is five-years-old, too," Mike said.

"What's his name?" she asked.

"Hunter."

"Does he have any brothers or sisters?"

"Not right now," Mike said. "But we keep hoping to give him a little sister."

"You can give him mine," Tracy said. "I won't mind. Mommy always tells me to be generous with those who have less than me."

"That doesn't apply to your siblings," Joshua interjected.

"I'm Joshua Thornton Junior," J. J. told Mike. "I was born first. This is my brother Murphy. I'm seven minutes older than him."

"What's your name?" Murphy pointed at the police officer to demand the information.

"Deputy Mike Gardner," the officer replied. "I grew up with your father. We lived one block apart and went all through school together." He turned to Joshua. "I had no idea you were back in town."

"We're on one month's home leave," Joshua said. "Tomorrow morning we're on our way to Naples."

"Italy?" Mike's eyes grew big.

"For three years," Joshua said.

"Well, you always wanted to see the world."

"And that's what I'm doing." Not wanting to brag, Joshua steered the conversation back to his friend. "What about you? I thought you were still out West." Taking note of his uniform, he added, "I see you've made it through the police academy."

"After college and doing my time with the marines," Mike said. "I've only been with the sheriff's department for about six months." He looked around before lowering his voice. "Working on my first murder case."

"Really?" Joshua asked. "Interesting?"

"I'm going to meet my CI out at the park."

"What's a CI?" Murphy asked in a loud voice.

Mike shushed the boy while Joshua answered in a low tone, "Confidential informant."

"Man," Mike told Joshua with a shake of his head. "I wish you weren't going tomorrow. I could really use your help in this case."

"What type of case is it?"

"A murdered prostitute." Mike's eyes got a far-away look in them. "No one seems to care about finding out who killed her ... but I care."

"That's what matters," Joshua said.

When the server interrupted their conversation to give the deputy his lunch in a take-out bag, Mike refused to give Joshua a chance to get away without finishing his thought. His eyes were bright when he suggested, "Hey, Josh, maybe you can come with me to meet my CI. You'd know what to ask him. You could help me figure out if what he's telling me is the truth or not. You always had a good sense—trusting your gut, you used to say—"

"I can't, Mike," Joshua said with a shake of his head.

Saying nothing, Mike stared at his childhood friend.

Guilt washed over Joshua. "I can't."

"I could really use your help, Josh. This case is important to me. It would only take a few hours."

"I'm leaving for Naples at six o'clock in the morning." Joshua held up his watch to show him. "That's in less than twenty-four hours."

"I understand." Mike flashed him a smile. "I guess I'm just a little nervous." With a hasty good-bye, he hurried out the door.

Joshua slapped the folder down on top of his other papers. "Anyone want dessert?"

Four hands went up.

That was when Joshua noticed the mashed fried potatoes on Sarah's hands and face. He was wiping it off when J. J. declared his intention of eating a hot fudge sundae with nuts and cherries. Murphy put in his vote for a hot fudge brownie delight with extra whipped cream and chocolate ice cream instead of vanilla.

The server arrived at the table with extra napkins. "Everyone save room for dessert?"

In a voice one decibel over the children's, Joshua said, "Two single scoops of vanilla ice cream. Two single scoops of chocolate, and one hot fudge brownie delight with whipped cream, nuts, and cherries for me."

J. J. and Murphy's faces fell while the server walked away. "No fair!" J. J. cried out.

"It's very fair." Joshua looked out the window to the passing traffic on Carolina Avenue. He watched Mike climb into his police cruiser and pull out into traffic. Behind him, a black Bonneville pulled out to fall in and follow him. Unable to make out the driver through the smoky window, Joshua felt his stomach twist into a tight knot.

"Mike," Joshua heard the name climb up out of his throat while his breath quickened. Suddenly, he was out of his seat and running for the exit. He burst out the door, onto the sidewalk, and into the street to see the cruiser and the black Bonneville disappear into traffic.

That was the last time anyone saw Deputy Mike Gardner.

CHAPTER ONE

Eighteen Years Later
Tomlinson Run Park
New Manchester, West Virginia

"Would you like another breast, Tad?"

Dr. Tad MacMillan studied the last two bites of white meat on the chicken breast in the middle of his paper plate before answering the robust woman standing over him with a foil pan in one hand and a pair of tongs clutching a fried chicken piece in the other. He was already on his third piece.

"Come on, Tad." His wife, Jan, urged him from across the picnic table. Her attention was divided between her husband, their three-month-old son fussing in the baby carrier on top of the table, and her long blonde hair that had abruptly become too hot on her neck. "You know you want it. That's what church picnics are for. Eating until you bust." She clenched a hair clip in her teeth and gathered her hair together with both hands.

Entertained by the funny looking object sticking out of his mother's mouth, Tad Jr. giggled.

Tired of waiting for his response, the woman plopped the plump breast onto his plate and moved on to the next table to foist the remaining chicken on other picnickers.

"I'm trying to save room for Cameron's hot fudge lava cake," Tad said while searching the parking lot for his cousin and his wife, "if she ever comes."

After taking the clip out of her mouth, Jan continued to make funny faces at the baby, who giggled harder. "Not to mention the ice cream that Josh is supposed to bring."

"Where are they anyway?"

"Cameron got a lead on a murder case she was working and took off this morning." After securing her hair up on top of her head, Jan picked Tad Junior up out of the carrier. "Josh decided to work on an opening argument that he's giving tomorrow. He didn't want to come without her."

"Just like newlyweds." Tad dove into the next piece of chicken. "I remember when you refused to go anywhere without me at your side.

"Now I don't even notice when you aren't there," she confessed. "I never thought we would get this old and settled."

"Can you really picture me being settled?" Tad let out a laugh before peeling the crispy skin off the chicken piece on his plate.

"I just hope T. J. takes after me instead of you in that regard," Jan said.

"You're not the only one."

While hugging their son, Jan looked across the picnic table at her husband, Dr. Tad MacMillan, the town doctor and Hancock County's medical examiner. His salt and pepper hair brought out his blue eyes heavily framed with laugh lines. They may have been old and settled, but his laid back style and charismatic ways still caught her off guard sometimes.

Taking in their friends and family that littered the park for the church picnic, Jan found it hard to believe that less than a decade earlier she had resigned herself to the fact that she would never marry, let alone have a journalism career, and a fussy baby, who just threw up down the back of her shirt.

While the older members of the church congregation were helping themselves to seconds and thirds of the picnic fare, the younger and more athletic picnickers were racing paddleboats across the park's lake. Joshua Thornton's sixteen-year old-son Donny, the only remaining child at home, was included in that group. The boys were racing the girls.

"Faster! Pedal faster!" Donny yelled at his friend Woody.

"I'm going as fast as I can!" The chubby teenager, who rarely exercised anything except his fingers while playing computer games, was put out with being coerced into this activity in the first place. At least since he was partnered with Donny, a linebacker on Oak Glen High School's football team, he stood a chance of winning the race.

"Beat you!" the girls squealed from the shore where they turned their craft around.

With a curse, Donny kicked at the pedals and sat back to let the sun shine on his face.

The paddleboat rocked when Woody leaned over the side to peer into the water. "Hey, what's that?"

"What?" Donny replied without opening his eyes.

"Down there."

"Down where?"

Woody nudged him in the arm. "In the water. It looks like a car."

Opening his eyes, Donny sat up. "So someone tossed their old car into the lake. Happens all the time."

"Do the police dump their old cruisers in the lake, too?"

Joshua Thornton pulled his SUV into the Medical Center parking lot in Beaver, Pennsylvania, and rolled into the space next to the state police cruiser, which he recognized as belonging to the district chief.

Good. Someone who'll be able to tell me what's going on.

Thinking about the most likely possibilities of why he had received a call from the state police barracks that Cameron was in the emergency room, his heartbeat quickened along with his pace through the hospital entrance.

She'd been shot. Can't be too bad though. If that were the case, they'd have sent a police officer to come get me. They wouldn't have made a vague phone call.

Joshua didn't see anyone he knew in the emergency room reception area, He was like everyone else who walked in. It was a big difference from the East Liverpool City Hospital in Ohio, which was on his side of the state line, or rather closer to his area of West Virginia. There, someone would have been waiting at the door to fill in Hancock County's prosecuting attorney.

But at the Medical Center in Beaver, Pennsylvania, Joshua Thornton was simply another nervous family member of someone who had been brought in by ambulance.

"Excuse me." He rapped on the glass window at the reception desk. "I'm looking for a patient. Detective Cameron Gates with the Pennsylvania State Police?"

"Are you family?"

"I'm her husband."

Saying those words still sounded strange to him. It had been less than ninety days since Cameron had accepted his marriage proposal. He had concealed the diamond ring in the bottom of a hot fudge sundae. After licking off the fudge, she slipped it onto her finger and hadn't taken it off since, except to put on her wedding band.

"She's in emergency room three. Through those doors and to the right." The receptionist hit a button to release the security lock on the door and let Joshua into the ward.

He spotted Lieutenant Miles Dugan in the hallway on the other side of the door.

"Joshua …" The lieutenant rushed forward to clasp his hand. "She's going to be fine. They're giving her an MRI right now, but she's been conscious and talking. The doctor says it's a concussion."

Joshua tried to concentrate on his words, which were being drowned out by the moaning and calls of pain in the next room, where a man was handcuffed to the gurney. Nearby, a uniformed police officer was watching an attractive nurse set the man's broken leg.

"Crazy bitch! Police brutality. I'm suing! I get a call to a lawyer, don't I? That crazy bitch almost killed me!"

"What happened?" Joshua tore his eyes from the cursing man to the police lieutenant, who was guiding him into the next examination room. The empty gurney showed signs of having been occupied.

"I'm sure Cameron told you about a case she'd been working on—the rapist who killed a woman in front of her four-year-old daughter?"

Joshua nodded his head. "One of those cases that's been keeping Cam up at night. Those are the ones that get to you."

"They should be bringing Cameron back soon." Lieutenant Dugan gestured for him to take the chair in the corner next to the gurney.

Joshua recognized the brown spring jacket folded up in the chair. When he picked it up to move, the bright light overhead caught on the shiny gold of his new wedding band.

"This morning," Dugan was saying, "Cameron got a lead on where her prime suspect was." Aware of the suspect in the next room, the lieutenant lowered his voice. "She was after a jilted boyfriend who had disappeared off the grid right after the murder. One of his old pals, looking for the reward for information about his whereabouts, called to say that the suspect was staying with his new girlfriend at an apartment complex up on the North Side. Cameron went to check it out. She knocked on the girlfriend's door and as soon as she flashed her badge, the perp bailed out the bedroom window and went down the fire escape. The girlfriend tried to hold her back. By the time Cameron reached the window, he was on the ground and running across the parking lot." A smile broke across the police lieutenant's face.

"What happened?" Joshua asked. "What did she do?"

Lieutenant Dugan laughed.

Fingering the gold band on his left ring finger, Joshua imagined what Homicide Detective Cameron Gates would do if she were on the second floor watching her perp getting away. "Are you telling me that she jumped off the second-floor fire escape to bring him down?"

"Witnesses say she landed right on top of him. They both hit the pavement like a ton of bricks and were unconscious when the uniforms got there." Dugan gestured at the examination room next door. "As you can see, he broke her fall."

Not believing Dugan, but knowing his new wife, Joshua realized it was entirely possible and shook his head. "She's crazy." He was torn between being as amused as her boss and being scared for his wife's safety when she behaved so recklessly.

"That's what makes her so good," the police lieutenant said.

"Well, it's about time my silver fox got here!" Cameron sang out when the nurse brought her into the room in a wheelchair.

Trying to appear serious, Joshua fought the grin that came to his face when he saw her dressed in her brown slacks with a teal polo shirt. She had a scrape across the width of her forehead and a gash on her right cheekbone.

"This is my handsome groom that I was telling you about," Cameron told the nurse who insisted on helping her out of the chair and into the bed.

"Congratulations," the nurse said to Joshua. "When did you get married?"

"Forty-five days ago." Recalling how beautiful Cameron looked while standing at the pulpit in his church, and seeing how beautiful she was grinning at him from where she was sitting on the edge of the gurney, Joshua smiled.

After assuring them it would take about an hour for the results of the MRI, the nurse left. At the same time, the lieutenant moved on to the next room. "I'm going to see about getting our murder suspect released and down to the station for processing."

Once they were alone, Cameron turned to Joshua. Her auburn hair curled and waved in every direction to where it fell at the bottom of her neck. The green specks in her hazel eyes seemed to flash at him. "Go ahead." She flashed him a wink. "Let me have it."

Sighing, Joshua stood up. Imprisoning her between his arms, he towered over her in the bed. She gazed up at him while he leaned over to kiss her tenderly on the lips. "I'm glad you're all right."

"So am I." She ran her fingers through his silver hair that fell in a wave down to the top of his shirt collar. His face was so close to hers that his breath feathered across her cheek. It tingled the open wound.

"I'd order you to be more careful if I thought it would do any good," he said.

"I'm as careful as I can be," she said.

"What if you had missed when you jumped off that fire escape?"

"I didn't."

"What if you did?"

"But I didn't."

He sighed again. "Cam, I buried one wife. I don't think I could go through burying another."

"Same here," she replied. "Losing my first husband almost killed me—and I'm not only talking about emotionally. I'm not going to let you go through that, and I don't intend to go through it again myself."

He kissed her aching forehead. The touch of his lips on her wound both excited and hurt her. "I guess this means we'll have to make a pact to go together."

"Works for me." She pulled him down to kiss him fully on the lips. With her arms wrapped around him, she felt the vibration of his phone, which was clipped to his belt. "Let it go to voicemail," she whispered when he pulled away to answer it.

"It might be Donny," he said. "I was in such a hurry to get here that I didn't bother calling him at the picnic." He read the caller ID. "It's Tad." He pressed the phone to his ear. "Hey, Tad, what's up?"

"Are you home?" Tad asked him.

"I'm with Cameron," Joshua said.

"Are you coming to the picnic?"

Joshua checked the clock on the wall overhead. It was midafternoon. By the time they got to the picnic, people would be leaving. "I doubt it. Why? Is there chicken left over? You can send it home with Donny." He flashed a grin at Cameron who fell back onto the gurney with her fingers laced behind her head. "Cameron and I will eat it."

"I think you better get over here to the park."

The serious tone in Tad's voice jolted Joshua. "Why?"

"The kids found a car at the bottom of the lake," Tad said, "and there's a body in it. Josh, it's a police cruiser—the police have already determined that the license plate matches the cruiser Mike Gardner was driving when he'd disappeared."

Joshua felt as if he'd been kicked in the gut.

Seeing the expression on his face, Cameron rose up onto her elbows when he promised Tad that he would be right there before hanging up. "Josh, what's wrong? Is Donny hurt?"

"Donny's fine," was all Joshua got out before Lieutenant Dugan and the doctor stepped into the doorway.

Lieutenant Miles Dugan introduced the doctor to Joshua and Cameron before turning over the reporting to him. "Detective Gates, we did a thorough MRI of your head and couldn't find anything."

Joshua choked back a laugh.

Cameron jerked her aching head toward him. "Don't make me hurt you."

The doctor continued, "We found no intracranial bleeding. That doesn't mean that you have none. You could have some slight bleeding that didn't show up. You were unconscious and you did have memory loss. You do have a concussion, and we recommend that you take it easy for a few days, maybe up to two weeks."

The doctor directed his attention to Joshua, "You'll need to watch her. She'll want to sleep while her brain heals. Keep checking on her, and if you see any trouble waking up or memory loss get her to the ER."

"That's easier said than done," Joshua replied.

The lieutenant added, "The doctor has recommended that with this type of injury you take two weeks sick leave."

"Weeks?" Cameron squawked.

The police lieutenant was firm. "You have the time. We can't have you out there in the field if you've got a potential brain injury." He gestured at Joshua. "You only took a couple of days off when you got married. Go home. Take a honeymoon. Enjoy being a newlywed."

"And don't go jumping off any tall buildings," the doctor added.

Cameron waited until they were in Joshua's SUV before asking the question that had been on her mind ever since he had taken the phone call in the examination room. "What's going on? Why do you have to go running over to the park? Is someone in trouble?"

"Something like that," Joshua answered while staring at the SUV's dashboard without seeing it. "A guy I grew up with … we were friends. Mike had a son the same age as Tracy." His face contorted as he recalled it. "She went to senior prom with him. Hunter." He turned to her. "His dad was a deputy. Hancock County."

She reached out to grasp his hand resting in his lap. "What happened?"

"He disappeared eighteen years ago," Joshua said. "We were shipping out to Naples and had come home to see Grandmomma. The day before we left, I ran into Mike. He said he was investigating the murder of a hooker and asked me to go with him to meet a CI. I blew him off. When I saw him driving off, I got such a bad feeling about it—but it was too late. He was gone …" He looked up to gaze out the window. "No one ever saw him again. I didn't even know he had gone missing until nine months later when Tad mentioned it in a letter. When I found out that the last time he'd been seen was that day, I contacted the county sheriff—from Naples. I called all the way from overseas to ask about the disappearance and they had no idea what dead hooker I was talking about. According to the sheriff, there had never been any prostitutes in Hancock County, dead or otherwise."

"Did they find his body? Is that why Tad called? They found his body in the park?"

Staring straight ahead, Joshua nodded his head without saying a word.

She reached up to cup her hand under his chin and forced him to look at her. "You do know your friend's murder is not your fault, don't you?"

"I blew him off, Cam."

"You were moving overseas," she said. "You were preoccupied. You had kids and a wife and a lot of responsibility."

"Not so much that it gets me off the hook from being a friend," Joshua said. "Mike asked me to go with him. He must have sensed he was in over his head and was asking for my help."

"If he was in over his head, he should have backed off." Cameron sighed. "That's in the past. There's nothing you can do to change what happened. The question is what you're going to do now."

She stared at him until she drew his eyes to her. When he turned to peer into her brownish-green eyes, his expression softened. She leaned across the seat to him. "I'm off for the next two weeks," she said. "You know what happens when I get bored."

He answered with a soft kiss on her lips that grew in intensity until they were startled by a sharp knock on the windshield.

"Hey, Thornton, can't you at least wait until you get her home?" Lieutenant Dugan ordered with a laugh.

CHAPTER TWO

In Tomlinson Run Park, Hancock County Sheriff Curt Sawyer met Joshua when he pulled off the road to park in the grass along the lake. It wasn't hard for Joshua to find where the cruiser had been dumped. The road blocked off by police cruisers and crime scene vehicles, as well as the medical examiner's SUV, was a clear giveaway. Picnickers who had been celebrating the beginning of summer only hours before refused to leave so that they could watch the police and tow truck work down by the lakeshore.

"We're just about to pull him up," the sheriff told Joshua, who moved in closer to see for himself. "The diver says he's strapped in the driver's seat. As bad as the decomp is, we'll need dental records to determine if it's him."

When he saw Cameron get out of the passenger side of the SUV and come around to grasp Joshua's arm, the sheriff greeted her with a nod of his head. Then he noticed the bruise across her forehead and cheek. "You look like you've had a good day, Detective."

"I got one more killer off the street," she replied.

"That always makes it a good day," he agreed.

Joshua was so focused on the police cruiser slowly being pulled up out of the water that he barely noticed the red

Mustang that swerved around the road block to tear up the grass before screeching to a halt not far from them.

Stopping him with a hand to his chest, the sheriff intercepted the young driver when he jumped out of the car and tried to run down to the lake's shore. "Hunter, you shouldn't be here."

"Is it him?" the young man demanded to know while trying to dodge the sheriff who, while notably shorter, was much stronger and experienced. "Someone sent me a text that it was a police cruiser. Is it Dad's? Is he in there?"

A mirror image of his father, the young man stepped around the sheriff where he encountered Joshua, who grasped his arm to hold him back. "Hunter, you don't want to be here."

Tad had come up from the lakeshore to block the young man's access to the scene. "Hunter, if that's your dad, you don't want to see him, believe me."

"Then it's not a rumor," Hunter said. "It's a cruiser and there's a body in it. It must be him."

"We don't know that for sure," Joshua said.

"I'm not an idiot! How many cruisers disappeared in the area in the last twenty years?" Hunter held up his index finger. "One. And my dad disappeared with it. There's no one else it can be."

Hunter attempted to wade through the three men blocking his way to the lake to get a closer look, only to be held back by Joshua and the sheriff while Tad attempted to reason with him. "Listen to me. If it's your dad, I can tell you with certainty that he wouldn't want you to see him like this."

The missing deputy's son paused.

Tad continued, "Remember him the way he was. If you see him in the condition his body is in now ..." The doctor shook his head. "Keep your memories of him the way he was."

The young man swallowed while blinking back tears in his eyes. "That's the problem. I was five years old when he went missing. Most of my memories of him are now gone."

Her eyes also filled with tears, Jan touched his arm. "I remember him, Hunter." She clasped her hand on his shoulder. "The place you need to be now is with your mother. I'm sure word has gotten to her already. She needs you. I'll go with you. As soon as they know something, Tad and Josh will let you know."

Hunter hesitated before allowing Jan to guide him back to his car. He slid into the driver's seat and drove off. After loading Tad Junior into their car, Jan followed.

Cameron stepped up to where Sheriff Curt Sawyer was watching to make sure the dead deputy's son had indeed left. A former police officer with the marines, Curt Sawyer had hung onto his military bearing.

"Did you know this missing deputy?" Cameron asked him.

"I'm afraid not," Curt said. "I know a lot of people in this town who did. Mike Gardner was a good man. Not an enemy in the world. Hunter takes after him. He's going into the police academy this fall. Did you know that? Just got out of the army. Did a tour in Iraq. Will be a fine deputy when he graduates."

"Josh said he grew up with this … " She knew Curt had just said his name. She wondered if Joshua had told her. Cameron searched her memory. *Why can't I remember? Curt just said it.*

"Gardner," the sheriff told her. "Mike Gardner was his name."

"Josh said he was investigating the murder of a hooker."

"I looked into it when Josh first moved back here," Curt said. "I wasn't sheriff back when Gardner disappeared, so what I know is not first hand. There were no murder cases involving a prostitute, dead or otherwise, back when he disappeared." He shrugged. "I wish I could help." Seeing that the cruiser was out of the water, the sheriff excused himself to go down to the lakeshore to join Joshua and Tad in examining the vehicle and the dead body inside.

"Hey, Mrs. Thornton!"

It took a full moment for Cameron to realize Woody was talking to her when he broke through the crowd to join her.

His round cheeks were red with pride when he smiled at her. "I found the car!"

"Good for you, Woody," she said.

"Donny said it was just an abandoned junker, but I saw the lights and knew that it was a cruiser," Woody said. "I thought, why would the police dump one of their cruisers in the bottom of the lake? Then I knew that it was something suspicious. Maybe I have what it takes to be a great detective like you, Mrs. Thornton."

"Actually, it's Gates," Cameron said.

"'Huh?" Woody asked.

"I kept my maiden name," she explained. "It's Gates, not Thornton. You can call me Cameron though."

Woody blushed even deeper.

"What happened to you?" Donny came over to ask when he saw the cut on her cheek and the bruises.

"I jumped off a second-floor fire escape," Cameron said.

"What were you doing jumping off a second-floor fire escape?" Donny smiled in anticipation of her response.

"I was chasing a killer," she said.

"Did you catch him?" Woody asked.

"Yes," she said, "he broke my fall."

"Good for you." Woody bumped fists with her.

Joshua was walking slowly when he came up from the lake. Cameron broke from the group to join him. "Is it him?" she asked.

"They found a badge pinned to what is left of his clothes," Joshua said. "We wiped off the gunk and found his badge number on it. We'll need dental records to confirm it, but it's Mike."

"Cause of death?"

"Body is badly decomposed, but Tad might be able to determine it," Joshua said. "His gun isn't in his holster. It might be in the car under all the mud, but since it's not in his holster I think he was disarmed." He looked down at the lake. "This was no accident, Cam. No way he could have lost control of his car and ended up this far off the road and all the way over in that lake. Someone dumped it—most likely in the middle of the night after the park was closed." He turned around to take in the thick woods surrounding them. "Lots of places around here to hide the cruiser until dark when no one was around." He turned to her. "Someone killed him, and I'm going to find out who."

She took his hand and gazed up into his blue eyes. "And I'm here to help."

CHAPTER THREE

"Sawyer doesn't know of any murdered hookers in the area," Cameron said more to break the silence in Joshua's SUV than anything else. After all, the sheriff had already told her that Joshua had looked into the case after his wife had passed away and he had returned to Chester.

"I know," Joshua responded.

Cameron rubbed her forehead while resting her head in her hand on the side window in the front seat.

They were on their way to Belle Fontaine's home. Mike Gardner's widow had remarried shortly after Mike had been legally declared dead. Royce Fontaine, Belle's second husband and an executive with a pharmaceutical company in Pittsburgh, had moved his wife and stepson to a luxurious house on Woodland Avenue that looked over the town and Chester Bridge crossing the Ohio River.

Cameron pointed out, "You know, most hookers I've encountered don't exactly list their occupation as 'prostitute' on their resume. Maybe he was looking into the murder of a woman who was a hooker but posing as a masseuse."

"We don't have any masseuses in this area," Joshua said. "I did think of that. Didn't get any leads." He pulled the SUV around the end of the cul-de-sac and parked in the street in front of a French country, white brick home.

Cameron recognized the red Mustang parked at the end of the driveway as the one from the park. "Nice car." She hesitated in front of the sports car. "Expensive."

"Would you believe he paid cash for that car?"

"If you told me he was a drug dealer."

"Not Hunter Gardner." Joshua slowly shook his head. "He has always been a very responsible young man. He started mowing lawns as soon as he was big enough to push a lawn mower. He bought a junker when he got his license, but he always wanted a shiny, fire engine red Mustang and that's what he put his money away for." He nodded his head toward the beautiful sports car. "That was a present he got for himself after coming back from his second tour in Iraq."

"You don't see young men like that every day," Cameron said, as she noticed a silver BMW sedan parked in front of the garage.

"Personally, I believe there are a lot of young people like that," he said. "It's just no one talks about them."

Royce Fontaine opened the door for Joshua and Cameron before they had the opportunity to ring the doorbell. Without pausing to offer any greeting, he pelted Joshua with a rapid barrage of questions. "Is it true? They found Mike? Jan Martin just left because that baby was getting fussy. We were hoping Tad would have called her to let her know before she took off. Is it really him?"

"We don't have a positive ID yet." Joshua looked around Royce to where Belle was sobbing while her son comforted her in the living room. "But the body in the cruiser was wearing Mike's badge and it was his cruiser." He introduced Cameron.

She tried not to judge people by their handshake. Possibly, Royce was more focused on his wife's distress than greeting his visitors. Shaking his hand was like shaking a dead fish.

After one pump, Royce released her hand to pursue Joshua, who was on his way into the living room. "Belle really isn't feeling well right now. This has been a terrible shock to her—to all of us."

Even though Royce was approximately the same height as Joshua, his slight frame and stooped-over posture, which accentuated his flabby stomach and pear shape, made him appear much smaller. His pasty complexion added to his unattractive appearance.

In contrast, Belle was a stunning brunette—attractive enough to make Cameron feel a tinge of jealousy when she jumped off the sofa to throw her arms around Joshua, hug him tightly, and sob into his chest.

"I'm sorry, Belle," Joshua whispered while rubbing her back. "I am so sorry."

"I always wondered … I thought I had grieved and was over it … but when Hunter told me … it's like it's started all over again." Clutching him by the arms, she pressed her face into his chest and cried.

"His cruiser was in the lake?" Royce asked while prying his wife out of the other man's arms.

"At the bottom of the lake," Joshua said with a nod of his head.

Royce grasped Belle's arm. "He must have had an accident. Lost control of his cruiser and ended up crashing into the lake."

Cameron's eyes met Joshua's. *If it was an accident, how did Mike lose his gun?*

"Considering how far into the lake the cruiser was, I don't think so," Hunter said. "Someone killed my dad."

"Now, Hunter," Royce said, "don't go upsetting your mother." After easing Belle back to the sofa where she sat down, he handed her a fresh tissue.

Joshua and Cameron sat on the love seat across from them. "Before we start investigating this case, we do need to get a positive ID," Joshua said. "Tad will do a dental record comparison. Assuming it is Mike, Belle … I asked you this before, but I have to ask again, on the off chance that you remember something—When I last saw Mike, he mentioned something about investigating a murder. The victim was a prostitute."

Belle was already shaking her head. "I have no idea what he could have been talking about. You must have misunderstood him, Josh. Mike was a deputy. He was a patrolman. He wasn't a detective. He didn't investigate murders."

Even while Belle was objecting, Cameron noticed Hunter sit up in his seat. At first, a questioning expression crossed his face and his eyebrows furrowed in deep thought.

For the first time since they had come into the Fontaine home, Cameron observed the young man sitting next to his mother. His face was filled with concern. His expression was one of serious contemplation.

A wave of recognition washed over her. *Where have I seen him before?*

Joshua noticed the suspicion on Hunter's face as well.

Royce was on his feet. "Josh, now is really not a good time to be asking Belle all of these questions. Believe me, we have been over Mike's disappearance forward and backward and never have we ever turned up anything. Frankly, if Belle knew anything, I think she would have remembered it by now." He ushered them to their feet and toward the door.

"Actually," Cameron said, "it has been my experience that families of victims often remember, or are able to piece together facts better, after some time."

"There's nothing to put together. Mike had a horrible car accident. That's all." Royce opened the front door and gestured for them to leave.

After the door slammed behind them, Cameron and Joshua looked at each other.

"He seems rather insistent on Mike's death being nothing more than an accident, don't you think?" Joshua asked.

"Extremely." She let Joshua take her hand and lead her to his SUV. "Hunter knows about the dead hooker. Did you see his face?"

"Yes, I did." Joshua opened the door for her.

"Why didn't you ask him about it?" She slid into the passenger seat.

"I don't have to ask him," Joshua said. "He'll tell me … when his mom and Royce aren't around."

"Why did Cameron jump off a second-floor fire escape?" At the refrigerator, Donny turned around from where he was getting a drink of milk when Joshua escorted Cameron into the kitchen.

They had finally made it home to their three-story stone house on the corner of Rock Springs Boulevard and Fifth Avenue in Chester, West Virginia.

It seemed like Donny thought his dad wouldn't notice him drinking straight from the milk jug if he directed his attention to Cameron's latest stunt.

"It was one of those cases where you had to be there." Joshua took the jug out of his hand and put it back in the fridge.

The sixteen-year-old boy, who at six feet and four inches was two inches taller than his father, looked down at Cameron who had slipped into the first chair she encountered in the country kitchen.

"Okay," she said, "I admit it was a little foolish to jump off a second-floor fire escape—"

"A little?" Donny laughed.

"But when it comes to catching bad guys," she said, "we tend to be so focused on how dangerous it will be for the next guy our perp runs into that we don't notice from how high up we're jumping." She didn't want to confess to how tired she had become during the drive to the park, time on the lake, and the visit to the Fontaine home.

Sensing that his mistress had had a rough day, Irving, Cameron's Maine Coon cat, leapt into her lap and rubbed his face against her chin.

Cameron had inherited five grown children from Joshua's first marriage, as well as Admiral, a Great Dane-Irish Wolfhound mix. Joshua had inherited Irving, a twenty-five pound Maine Coon cat who prompted screams from the neighbors. The long-haired cat was black with a white stripe from the top of his head down to the tip of his tail. At first glance, he was identical to an oversized skunk. Even though everyone on the street knew about Irving, there was still occasional screaming on Rock Springs Boulevard when he was out—especially from a neighbor who had a tendency to drink a few too many beers in the evening.

With an odd personality that was more canine than feline, Irving held a strong resentment toward the human male that was taking up so much of his female human's time. Since moving into their new home, Irving had tolerated Joshua. Granted, the three-story home with a rolling front and backyard with lots of things to explore and a dog who had become good buddies with the cat was nice, but it wasn't enough to compensate for stealing his mistress' attention.

"Anybody hungry?" Donny asked. "You must be since you didn't get to the picnic. After what you've been through, don't worry. I'll take care of dinner."

"I'm too tired to eat," Cameron said.

"What are you going to make?" Joshua asked his son with a knowing smile. Donny only cooked two things: hot dogs and microwave French bread pizza.

"I was going to order pizza to be delivered," Donny answered.

"I don't want any." Cameron was already on her way up the stairs with Irving in her arms. "I'm going to take a hot bath and go to bed."

"Sounds like a plan to me," Joshua replied.

"Dad …" Donny stopped him before he could follow Cameron up the stairs. He held out his hand. "Credit card for the pizza?"

"Didn't you get enough to eat at the picnic?" Joshua took his wallet out of his pocket.

"That was four hours ago," Donny said.

"So this is not about getting dinner for us, but about you." Joshua slapped the credit card into his palm.

At the same time, the phone rang.

"I'll call them, place the order, and answer the door when they come. What do you want on it?" Donny checked the caller ID. "It's Tracy." Without bothering to connect the call, he held out the ringing phone to his father. "I'll go call from my cell." He raced up the stairs to his bedroom.

Taking the phone, Joshua pressed the button to connect with his older daughter. "Hey, Tracy."

"Dad, is it true?" she responded in a breathless voice.

"Is what true?" Climbing the stairs to the master suite, Joshua tried to piece together what would have his daughter so anxious that she would be calling him from New York. *Is something happening with one of the kids that I've missed? Something I've neglected to stay on top of since meeting Cameron?*

The churning in his gut told him that he was not as focused on his children as he used to be, and should be, since falling in love a second time around. In rationalizing the situation, he told himself that with four of them living away from home and having their own lives, the last thing they wanted was Dad sticking his nose into their business.

"Hunter's father," Tracy replied to him. "Someone sent me a text that they found Hunter's dad at the bottom of the lake in Tomlinson Run. Did they really? Is it him? Was he murdered, or was it an accident?"

Joshua opened the bedroom door and stepped inside. He could hear the water running in the claw-footed tub in the bathroom. Sitting on the bed, Cameron had stripped down to her black lace bra and panties. She looked exhausted.

"First," he replied to Tracy, "Tad has to compare the dental records to make a positive ID. Then he will need to examine the body to see how he died. Third, forensics has to examine the cruiser and scene to determine if it was a car accident or murder."

"What do you think?"

"I don't think anything until I get all the pieces—"

"I'm not the media, Dad," Tracy said. "I'm your daughter, and Hunter is my friend. What do you think?"

"Based on the conversation we had …"

"I'm coming home," Tracy said.

"Honey, you don't have to come home." Joshua noticed Cameron's head jerk up to look at him. "There's nothing that you can do. You have your internship …"

"I finished that for the semester," Tracy said. "I've already taken all of my finals. Summer break started Friday. Hunter is my friend and he needs me. Besides, I haven't seen Cameron since the wedding that you two didn't have. I think it's time for your new wife and me to get to know each other." Vowing to call the next day with her travel arrangements, she hung up.

Joshua gazed at Cameron, who was wordlessly looking up at him. "Tracy is coming home."

Without a word, Cameron stood up and went into the bathroom. When he tried to follow, she closed the door.

"Is that a clue that you aren't happy about this?" he asked through the door.

"I'm tired," she called out to him. "I have a headache."

He could hear the water splashing when she climbed into the tub. "Does Tracy coming home have any impact on your headache?"

"No."

Joshua tried the doorknob to discover it was unlocked. He went in to find Cameron in the tub. "You just lied to me."

"No, I didn't." She closed her eyes and sank down into the water until it was up to her chin.

He pointed a finger of accusation at her. "There, you did it again. When you lie to me your voice goes up two octaves. What's your problem with Tracy?"

"The real question is what's Tracy's problem with me?"

Joshua closed the toilet lid and sat on the seat. "Tracy doesn't have a problem with you."

She opened her eyes to glare at him. "Now who's lying?"

"I'm not lying."

She narrowed her eyes into greenish-brown slits. "Look me in the eyes and tell me that Tracy and J. J. don't have any problem with me—with us."

Joshua leaned forward. Resting his elbows on his knees, he gazed into her eyes. "Tracy and J. J. have no problem with you or us."

"You're looking me in the eyes."

"That's what you told me to do."

"Which proves you're lying." She sank down into the hot water.

"How does that prove I'm lying?"

"If you were telling the truth, you'd be looking at my breasts," she said. "A naked woman is lying right in front of you and you're looking into my eyes instead of at my breasts. Why? Because you want to convince me that you're telling the truth. If you were telling me the truth, it wouldn't be so important for you to cover up your lie by looking me in the eye. So you would be relaxed and stare at my breasts at will. Instead, you were focusing on my eyes. That tells me that you're lying."

"I've been looking at your breasts for months," Joshua said. "Maybe I decided to look into your eyes for once."

"I guess this means the honeymoon is officially over."

"What makes you think Tracy and J. J. disapprove of you …" he asked, "besides my looking into your gorgeous eyes instead of at your sexy breasts?"

"Josh, I live in this house." Cameron picked up the wet sponge and wrung the water out of it. "I hear your side of the conversations you have with your kids. Tracy and J. J. objected to you marrying me—" She threw up her hand to point a finger at him when he started to object. "Don't you lie to me again. I've heard them. Everything was fine until we got married, and suddenly—"

Caught, Joshua sat back in his seat on the toilet and crossed one leg over the other. In silence, they eyed each other until she backed down by closing her eyes and dropping down into the water. Under the water, she rubbed her scalp with her fingertips before sitting back up.

"What do you want me to say?" Joshua asked her while she pressed the excess water from her hair.

She dropped back against the end of the tub. "There's nothing you can say," she said with a miserable tone. "I guess—"

"They're problem is not you." Joshua startled her by sitting forward and leaning his elbows on his knees. "Do you want me to tell you what their problem with us is?"

"What?"

"That we didn't have a wedding," he said. "They're upset that we didn't have a big celebration with bridesmaids and groomsmen and guests and the whole nine yards."

"Be serious."

"I am serious," Joshua said. "J. J. and Tracy took it personally. Murphy and Sarah don't care. But Tracy and J. J. feel like we shut them out of this new chapter that our family has transitioned into."

Cameron lifted her eyes to peer at him through her long eyelashes. "What did you tell them?"

"That it was my decision," he said. "We had all the big weddings and white gowns and parties and all that when we were young. Now we're older and we didn't need it, and I didn't want to wait for all of them to arrange their schedules so that they could all be home at the same time to have a wedding. We wanted to get married and move on with our lives."

"You took the blame," she said.

Joshua grinned at her. "I'm a man, I can take it. That's what husbands do."

Moving over to the side of the tub, she folded her arms across the top and rested her head on the crook of her arm. Her glare had been transformed into adoration. "And you do it very well."

"Of course," he said in a husky voice, "I do expect certain privileges for blame taking."

"Well, big boy, why don't you just slip out of those clothes and come on in and talk to me about what payment you want from me in exchange for doing your husbandly duty."

CHAPTER FOUR

As the doctor had predicted, Cameron was sound asleep before the sun set.

Out of what had become habit, Joshua turned in with her. Unable to fall asleep so early, he read a deep and intriguing mystery on an e-reader.

Irving took his spot at the foot of the bed—on her side. Admiral was stretched out on the floor. The great dog used to sleep on Joshua's side of the bed, but since Cameron had moved into their lives, he preferred sleeping next to her. She had a softer touch for pettings.

Joshua wasn't quite certain when he had finally fallen asleep. He had rolled over and was holding Cameron's body close to his when he woke up. She smelled like the vanilla bath oils she had put in her bath water. Her cinnamon colored locks were tickling his nose while he dreamed about them going away, alone, with no cat, no dog, no kids—the two of them—when—

Donny banged on the bedroom door. "Dad, someone is here to see you."

"What?" Cameron's arm came flying up. Her bony elbow collided with Joshua's nose. "Where am I?"

"Coming." Holding onto his throbbing nose, Joshua got twisted in the covers while reaching for his bathrobe and the edge of the bed.

"Dad, are you up? Did you hear me?"

"What's happening?" She grabbed her head with both hands.

"I'm here, honey." He grabbed her hands and kissed her on the forehead. "Donny says someone is here. I have to go. I'll be right downstairs."

"Josh?" She rolled over and reached for him.

He turned to her. "Yes, dear?" He shrugged into his bathrobe and tied the belt.

A soft smile came to her lips. "Can you bring me a cookie and glass of milk when you come back up?"

Even though he was certain she would be asleep seconds after he left the room, he kissed her on the forehead. "Anything you want, darling."

He was not surprised to find Hunter Gardner waiting for him in the living room. After apologizing for waking Joshua up, he explained, "I needed to wait for Mom to fall asleep before coming over here. She was really upset about all this coming back up again. Royce gave her a sedative."

Gesturing for Hunter to sit down on the sofa, Joshua sat in the chair across from him. "I could see by looking at your face that you knew what case your father was working on. Why didn't you want to say anything in front of your mother?"

"She doesn't think I know," Hunter said. "Maybe that's why she's pretended all this time that she had no idea what you were talking about when you asked her before. Talk about denial. Actually, I don't know really, but when you said 'prostitute,' I thought that if Dad said he was going to be investigating a hooker's murder, maybe ... "

"What is it, Hunter?" Joshua asked.

"My father was adopted," Hunter said. "It's a family secret."

"Must be," Joshua said, "because I knew your father my whole life and this is the first I heard anything about it."

"The only reason I know about it was from listening to relatives talk when I was a wee little kid," Hunter said. "I'd be real quiet, and they wouldn't notice me in the room. I heard some aunts and uncles talking about how my grandmother had a younger sister who ended up becoming a prostitute—you know, the official family black sheep. Once, I asked my mother about it and she got really upset—saying that no one in our family was ever a hooker and how dare I even suggest such a thing. Then she ordered me to never say anything to my grandmother, Dad's mom, about it." He tapped his temple with his finger while winking at Joshua. "That told me that there was something to these rumors I was hearing. Not only did I overhear relatives saying that Dad's aunt was a prostitute, but I also heard that she was Dad's mother and my grandparents had adopted him."

"Was this family black sheep murdered?"

Hunter shrugged his shoulders. "I really have no idea what happened to her. But my grandmother should know." He squinted at Joshua. "Thing is, since you mentioned it, it makes me think that if Dad was going to investigate a prostitute's murder on his own, wouldn't he dive right into this case if the victim was his mother?"

"Knowing your dad," Joshua said, "I have no doubt that he would."

"I should have gone with him," Joshua said into his brandy before taking the first sip. "We were friends. I remember when we were six years old. We built a raft, handmade, out of plywood. Since we were too young to use a hammer and nails, we tied it together with baling twine. Then we took it down to the river. That thing actually floated—until we were in the middle of the river. Then it started to sink. Luckily, some people heard us screaming for help. The police and fire department and everyone in town came out to rescue us."

Joshua tore his eyes from where he was staring into the fire he had built in the study's fireplace to look over at Irving, who was perched with his front paws tucked under his black body in the wing-backed chair across from him. His emerald eyes bore into Joshua like an accusation.

"I let him down, Irving." Joshua sat forward in his seat with his elbows on his knees. He looked down into the brown liquor in the snifter he held in his hand. "But I was in the navy. I was on my way to Naples. I couldn't not go. I had orders to be there."

Meow.

"His murder wasn't my fault. Who's to say that if I had gone with him that we both wouldn't have been murdered—that both of our bodies wouldn't have been in that cruiser? Or maybe his murder had nothing to do with the case he was working on."

"If it wasn't your fault, why are you kicking yourself over it … whatever it is?"

Joshua jerked his head around to look over at Irving, who was still eyeing him.

"You forgot about my milk and cookies." Cameron came in from where she was leaning in the doorway to slip her hand over the top of the chair to his shoulder.

"Sorry."

"How many of those have you had?"

"This is my first," he answered.

"Do you always bare your soul to Irving in the middle of the night?"

"Only when I need to talk to someone with the power to make me feel really guilty about something that wasn't my fault."

"Oh." She slipped into his lap. "Sounds like Tad is through with his autopsy on Mike's body."

"No." Joshua peered up into her eyes. "I don't need the results of any autopsy. My gut has been screaming ever since they brought that cruiser up from the bottom of the lake. His gun wasn't in his holster. Someone killed him, Cam."

"Maybe when his car went into the lake, he took out his gun to shoot out the window, but drowned before he could do that?" She wrapped her arms around his shoulders and leaned her head against his.

"I'm not buying it." He turned to look at her. Their noses collided.

"His murder isn't your fault," she said. "It's the fault of whoever killed him."

"I should have asked him about the case he was working on," Joshua said. "I was so focused on my own life, my family, my moving, and my career, that I blew him off, Cam. If I hadn't, then maybe—"

"Maybe," she said. "Maybe not."

Even Irving was sitting up on the edge of his seat.

Joshua sighed. "Hunter stopped by."

"You predicted that he would," she said. "Did he have any enlightening information?"

"Seems the Gardner family had a black sheep."

She rested her head on his shoulder. "What kind of black sheep?"

"A prostitute."

"Interesting," she said. "Was she murdered?"

"Hunter doesn't know," Joshua said. "Seems no one in the family will talk to him about it. He's only heard rumors. One of those rumors was that this black sheep was really Mike's mother."

"You mean like a secret adoption?"

"It's not unheard of," Joshua said. "I'm sure Tad would know about it if there were any truth to it." He wrapped his arms around her. "Do you still want that milk and those cookies?" He waited for her to reply.

She didn't.

She had fallen asleep.

CHAPTER FIVE

Cameron couldn't believe it when she woke up to discover that Joshua hadn't set the alarm. When she saw the sun shining into their bedroom from the veranda, she screamed and threw the covers over Irving in her dash for the shower. Seeing the bruise across her forehead and the scrape on her cheek, she tossed aside the idea of heavy makeup and opted only for mascara before running down the stairs and outside and jumping off the porch to find her car missing.

Then she remembered that it was still at the station. Joshua had driven her home from the hospital the day before.

Guess that means I get to drive the Vette!

As much as he claimed he loved her, Joshua had yet to let her drive his black classic 1964 Corvette. He didn't even drive it in the winter months. Grabbing the keys from his desk drawer, she went to the garage tucked into the back corner of the property and opened the door.

When she threw back the tarp that covered up Joshua's baby, an evil giggle escaped from her lips. It was with a sense of exhilaration that she opened the driver's door and slipped in behind the steering wheel. To her surprise, she found an envelope addressed to "My Love" taped to it. It was written in Joshua's brisk and precise handwriting. Her exhilaration was replaced with guilt.

He isn't even here. How does he know?

She opened the envelope and took out the card. The message was brief:

Go back to bed, darling. I'll be home for lunch.

Love, Josh

She tossed the note aside onto the passenger seat.

You're not the boss of me, Joshua Thornton!

She turned the key in the ignition. Nothing happened. Silence.

Ha ha ha. Think you can stop me by disconnecting the distributor cap, huh? I'll show you.

She got out of the car and with a sense of triumph threw open the rear compartment to find the distributor cap attached. Instead, there was an empty hole in the area reserved for the battery. *No, Joshua didn't put a stop to her with something that could be easily fixed by hooking up the caps. He had removed the whole car battery.*

Cameron was still cursing him when her cell phone vibrated on her utility belt. Seeing his name in the caller ID, she answered, "You ..." and then she sputtered out three nasty names at once.

"I see you discovered that I brought my car battery to work with me," Joshua said with an evil tone in his laugh.

"How am I supposed to get to work?"

"You aren't supposed to get to work," he replied. "Do you remember yesterday? Your lieutenant said you're on sick leave for two weeks. You aren't cleared to work until the doctor approves you. So go back to bed."

She slammed down the rear compartment to the Vette. "I hate lying around doing nothing."

"Be gentle with my car," he ordered. "Do something to keep yourself occupied. Take Irving for a walk. Cook lunch for when I come home."

The memory of their conversation in front of the fireplace in the middle of the night came to her mind. She had forgotten all about Joshua drinking a brandy before the fire while telling her about—*Damn! Mike—what was his name? The deputy who had landed in the lake.*

"Did you call Tad yet about the black sheep hooker?" she asked.

"No," he replied. "I'm in court today. I'm hoping to talk to him this afternoon."

"Didn't you say that friend of yours—what was his name?"

"Mike Gardner," he said.

"He was adopted …" The memory came back.

"We don't know that for sure," Joshua said. "This is why you need to take some time off. Your brain is still quaking inside your skull."

"Who came over last night?" she asked. "Why didn't you bring me my cookies and milk?"

"You know where they are," he said. "If you want milk and cookies …"

"I hate this," she said. "I'm calling Tad to find out about Mike's autopsy, and you can't stop me."

Joshua laughed. "If looking into Mike Gardner's murder will keep you home and happy and quiet, then go for it, baby."

By the time she hiked up from the garage to go through the back door into the country kitchen, Cameron's head felt like it was going to explode. The pain was so bad that she broke down and took one of the pain pills prescribed by the emergency room doctor. With Irving and Admiral following at her heels, she went into the study to plop down at Joshua's desk.

Catching her image in the mirror that hung on the wall above the sofa, she started and moved in closer. *Is that me?* Her forehead was puffy and black and blue. The welt across her cheek had swollen up to her eye so that it was almost shut. She dabbed at her tender wounds.

People are going to think Josh is a wife beater. Thinking of her own reputation of being a woman in control, she reconsidered with a smile. *They should see the other guy who's in jail where he belongs.*

Pleased with the satisfaction of her arrest the day before, Cameron dismissed the brutal image in the mirror. Calling her bruises and black eye badges of honor, she plopped down behind Joshua's desk and switched on her laptop.

With some effort, she remembered the name of the missing, and assumed dead, deputy. Michael Gardner.

Maybe this whole concussion thing is worse than I thought.

Using her official log in, Cameron made her way to the police records for the missing persons report for the case file in the database.

Michael Gardner disappeared while on duty on Friday, September 13, 1996.

Friday the thirteenth? I guess it was an unlucky day for him.

When he had failed to make his regular report into the station at two o'clock, his fellow officers went out looking for him. According to the case file, the last person to see Gardner alive was Joshua Thornton and the server at Allison's Restaurant on Carolina Avenue in downtown Chester, where Gardner had gone to pick up his lunch for takeout.

The report indicated that nine months after Gardner had gone missing, Joshua Thornton had contacted the sheriff's department to report that Gardner had told him that he was going out to Tomlinson Run Park to meet an informant about a case he was working on involving the murder of a prostitute, which was news to his fellow deputies and the sheriff at the time. The sheriff's department had no record of what case the deputy could have been investigating, and at no point in their investigation into his disappearance had there been any witness who indicated that Mike Gardner was working on a criminal case during his own time.

A search of the park did not turn up anything.

Guess they didn't drag the lake.

In the same case file was the report that the sheriff had provided the county court on June 11, 2001, which restated basically the same information. The sheriff had no clues and no suspects. Everyone loved Michael Gardner, and they believed he wouldn't simply take off. There were no transactions on his credits cards or any type of activity to indicate that he was alive.

On June 17, 2001, Michael Gardner was declared dead.

A front-page article appeared in *The Review*, for which Jan Martin MacMillan was the editor. The article included a picture of Mike Gardner in his police portrait. Ruggedly handsome would be the right description. Red curly hair and blue eyes. A broad chin and shoulders. Cameron was struck with how much he resembled Hunter.

That must be why I thought Hunter looked familiar last night. ... No, it can't be. I hadn't seen any pictures of Mike Gardner until now. But Hunter looked ... With a sigh, she pushed the idea from her mind. *Hunter and Mike must just look like someone I used to know. But who? It's going to bug me until I can put my finger on it. Who else do they remind me of?* Her head pounding, Cameron gently rubbed her bruised forehead. *You're losing it, Cam.*

Squinting against her headache, she continued to read the various statements in the online file.

Mike had never actually been on the force long enough to make enemies, nor did he have enough experience in investigation to be a threat. No wonder he asked for Joshua's help.

Cameron went onto the Internet to do a search of Michael Gardner's name and a further background check, only to find the background of the average boy next-door. He was born in the hospital in East Liverpool, Ohio—the same one where Joshua had been born. She noted that their birthdates were one week apart.

Suddenly remembering that Hunter had mentioned adoption, Cameron tried to dig further for the names of the parents on Gardner's birth records and found nothing. Striking out, she looked in the search engine for anything, but only came up with the marriage announcement for Belle Gardner, widow of Michael Gardner, to Royce Fontaine. The announcement said that the couple met while both were working at Remington Pharmaceuticals in Pittsburgh, where Belle was an office manager and Royce was a vice president in charge of research.

With a sigh that came from intense thought and exhaustion, Cameron got up from the desk and moved over to the sofa to stretch out with the laptop perched on her bent knees. Welcoming the move that made his mistress more accessible, Irving perched behind her head on the arm of the sofa.

Cameron went on to dig deeper into cold case murders in the surrounding area of Hancock County that involved possible prostitutes that Mike Gardner could have been investigating.

Irving's purr bounced in the back of her head and then to the front. She felt like it was bouncing off the back of her eyeballs. She closed her eyes and felt herself drifting off to sleep on the melody of her cat's purr.

With broad shoulders and curly red hair, he was a ruggedly handsome man.

While Cameron studied the picture, his mother was recounting the same story that she had been telling every detective who had inherited the case over the last forty years. "My son did not commit suicide."

Cameron put down the photograph and looked at the police report from 1966. There wasn't much. Douglas O'Reilly was a student at West Point. He had graduated from high school the year before and was on summer break when his car was found in Raccoon Creek. At first, it had been assumed that he had missed a turn and driven off the road, rolling end over end down the steep, rocky embankment before landing upside down in the lake. However, investigation showed that there were no skid marks. They also discovered that his sixteen-year-old girlfriend, Ava Tucker, had broken the news to him that very day that she was pregnant.

The unwanted pregnancy would kill his academic career at West Point. He would be expected to quit school and marry her. He chose instead to take his own life. The investigators closed the case as a suicide.

"I'm sorry, Mrs. O'Reilly," Cameron said.

"Can't you at least take another look at it?" the elderly woman asked with tears filling her eyes.

Her heart breaking, Cameron tried to think of something, anything, to give the old woman some comfort.

Ring!

Cameron grabbed her phone and yelled into it. "I'm asleep!"

In one movement, Irving flew over the coffee table and out of the room.

"Sorry, Cam," Jan Martin-MacMillan responded. "I didn't mean to wake you. Josh asked me to check in on you to see how you were feeling."

Cameron sat up on the sofa. "I've been better. Hey, has Tad finished the autopsy on Michael Gardner?"

"Josh will find that out before I do."

"Men!"

"Tell me about it," Jan replied. "He did tell me off the record that the dental records were a match. It is Mike."

Cameron was now fully awake. "You knew Mike."

"Grew up with him just like Josh," Jan said. "We all grew up here within a few blocks of each other."

"Did you hear anything about him being adopted?"

Jan was silent.

"Are you still there?" Cameron asked.

"I don't know how much truth there is to it," Jan said. "You know how small towns are. There's always speculation and rumors, especially when something like this happens—or when something like Mike disappearing on duty happens."

"What did you hear?"

"Mike's aunt was Ava Tucker."

Ava Tucker! My dream! Or was it a dream? No, memory. There was an old woman—back when I was first promoted to homicide and—

"Cameron, are you okay?" Jan Martin was calling to her through the phone line. "Are you still there?"

Blinking, Cameron rubbed her aching head. "What did you say, Jan? Something about Ava Tucker."

"Well, we were all little kids—Mike, Josh, and me," Jan said. "I do remember her though. She had quite a reputation. I heard that a man actually killed himself because she had broken his heart. Gorgeous. I used to look at her with her perfect figure and she wore the shortest mini-skirts and high heels. Red hair. She reminded me of Ann Margaret. She dropped out of high school. Never graduated. Went away. Then, she came back into town, and I do remember hearing rumors that she was Mike's birth mother—but I never saw or heard anything that proved it."

"What happened to Ava Tucker?" Cameron asked.

"I …" Jan's voice trailed off. "I don't really know. I can search through the archives at the newspaper to find out. Why? Do you think it's a clue?"

"Maybe," Cameron replied.

Before she could hang up, Jan stopped her. "I almost forgot why I was calling," she said. "Want to go to lunch?"

"Is there ice cream involved?"

"Yes, Cricksters," Jan said. "Every other Monday, the ladies in our neighborhood get together for lunch. Some stay-at-home mothers and a few elderly ladies who don't get out much. There's about a dozen of us. Since none of them had a chance to meet you, and Josh asked me to keep an eye on you, I thought I'd invite you to come along. I'll drive."

"Buy me ice cream and I'll follow you anywhere."

CHAPTER SIX

The official medical examiner's office was down the river in Weirton. However, Dr. Tad MacMillan usually performed his autopsies in the morgue located in the basement of the hospital in East Liverpool, Ohio, directly across the river from his home, and where he was a doctor on staff.

Not a popular place to visit, the morgue was eerily quiet—silent enough for Tad MacMillan to be catching a nap when Joshua stopped in for a briefing on his findings during Mike Gardner's autopsy.

Upon stepping through the swinging doors, Joshua discovered his cousin sound asleep on the cold steel examination table with his arms folded across his chest. Unable to resist, Joshua crept forward and bent down to bring his lips to Tad's ear before shouting in a voice mocking a small child, "Daddy! Wake up!"

With a gasp, Tad jumped so hard and fast that he almost rolled off the table. Seeing Joshua doubled over with laughter, he eased his feet down to the floor. "Very funny," he said with sarcasm. "I'm glad my sleep deprivation is such a source of enjoyment for you."

"I told you that you'd get yours," Joshua said. "I had to wait twenty years, but you know what they say about revenge—its best served cold."

"Revenge?"

"Twenty years ago?" Joshua said. "We came back home to visit. Grandmomma and Valerie had gone to a church meeting and the twins were taking a nap … so was I when a certain little devil came in and drew a mustache and beard on me with permanent marker."

Recalling the incident, a slow grin came to Tad's lips.

"I had to go to the doctor to have it removed," Joshua told him.

"But you looked so cute." Cocking his head at him, Tad noted, "I thought you had court today."

"The defense copped a plea," Joshua said. "Another B and E guy is going behind bars and I got off early to come wake you up from your late morning nap."

"Why don't you go home and spend some time with your bride?"

"Because she's on her way to Cricksters with yours," Joshua said.

"Oh yeah, today is the hen party." Stifling a yawn, Tad went over to his desk and picked up a clipboard with a report attached to it. "How well do you think Cameron is going to fit in with the neighborhood hens?"

"As long as they don't get between her and her ice cream sundae, they'll be fine." Joshua turned to follow him. "Is the ID positive?"

"Dental records were a match for Mike Gardner." After handing the report to him, Tad plopped down into his chair. "C.O.D. is gunshot to the face."

Joshua cringed. "Was it from his gun? Did they find his service weapon?"

Shaking his head, Tad shrugged. "Last I heard, Sawyer sent a crew back to the park to search the bottom of the lake. It wasn't in the car. However, they did find a slug inside the car that's a match for Mike's gun. It's a nine millimeter. That matches the size of the hole in his face."

"Then it appears that the killer disarmed Mike and then shot him in the face with his own gun?"

Tad got up and went to the drawer where Mike's remains were resting. He pulled out the drawer and lifted the sheet to reveal the skeleton. "I suspect Mike was already down and out when the killer finished him off." Lifting the skull from the drawer, Tad showed Joshua a crack along the side of what had once been his friend's head. "There's a long hairline fracture along the left side of his head. It looks like it could have come from a blunt instrument, like a ball bat or something that could have knocked him down and incapacitated him, maybe even knocked him out so that the killer could disarm him and then shoot him in the face with his own gun."

"And then put him in the car and dump it in the lake," Joshua said. "I doubt if they're going to find any evidence in that car after it's been sitting in the bottom of the lake for almost two decades."

"Makes you think that instead of meeting a confidential informant for the case he was working on," Tad said, "he met the murderer he was looking for."

"I guess the best place to start now is to find out the identity of that prostitute."

"Are you really a homicide detective?" The tiny lady's eyes sparkled like those of a star-struck teenybopper meeting her heartthrob.

With a grin, Cameron glanced across the back seat to the elderly woman who, in the year since she had met Joshua, she had never formally met.

Dolly Houseman lived alone in the red brick house across the street from the Thorntons and the MacMillans. Joshua and the MacMillans made it their duty to look out for the lady who had no family. Joshua would take her garbage out to the curb and take the can back into her garage. Tad would mow her lawn and do yard work for her. If she needed any home repairs, one of them would make sure it was done either by himself or an honest repair person. Sitting with her in the back seat of Jan's SUV, Cameron was the closest to Dolly that she had ever been.

Not over five feet tall, Dolly didn't appear to be even an ounce over one hundred pounds. Her hair was blue-gray. Her face was so wrinkled that it resembled a road map. Yet even at her advanced age, she sat with dignity in her blue suit with matching pumps and handbag.

"Do you carry a gun?" Dolly asked Cameron.

"Always," she replied.

"Have you ever shot anyone?"

Cameron answered, "Yes, I have."

She was surprised to see the little old lady clap her hands with glee. "Oh, this is so exciting."

"I think it's terrible," Lorraine said from the front passenger seat. "There's too much violence in the world. Women strapping on guns and shooting people. If they outlawed guns, then people wouldn't be shooting at each other."

"If they outlawed guns, then only the crooks would have them and innocent, law-abiding people would have no way of defending themselves." Cameron would have said more but caught a warning look from Jan in the rear view mirror that ordered her to let it go.

Another exceedingly elderly woman, Lorraine Winter lived up the street from Rock Springs Boulevard. Much to Cameron's displeasure, Jan had stopped to pick up the most unpleasant woman in the neighborhood to give her a ride to the restaurant. Tad Junior was being cared for by a babysitter to allow Jan a break.

Donny joked that even the snakes avoided Lorraine Winter's house and backyard. Within minutes of Lorraine climbing into the front seat across from Jan, Cameron saw that Donny might not have been joking. Tall and broad shouldered even without shoulder pads, her appearance was intimidating. With her long gray hair in a bun tightly secured to the back of her head, she was frightful in presence as well as in attitude. Armed with an opinion about everything, Lorraine Winter was a woman who was itching for a fight.

"Two wrongs don't make a right," Lorraine said with a shake of her head.

"How is my defending myself as a police detective wrong?"

Turning in her seat, Lorraine shook her finger at Cameron. "Did you ever think that maybe those suspected criminals who you shoot at have been wrongly accused and that they are defending themselves from unfair prosecution and that is why they are shooting at you?"

"Are you for real, lady?" Cameron managed to get out before Jan announced that the weather was perfect for their luncheon. Once again, she caught Jan's warning look in the rearview mirror.

Cameron wondered if the ice cream sundae was worth spending a couple of hours with Lorraine, who then launched into a declaration that the last good president the country had had was Dwight D. Eisenhower. Abruptly, Cameron became aware of Dolly's hand on hers.

The little old woman was smiling at her. "How good of a detective are you?" Dolly asked in a whisper.

"I like to think I'm pretty good."

"Have you ever caught a killer?"

Cameron pointed to her black eye. "Got this arresting one yesterday."

Again, Dolly clapped her hands. "Splendid. I'm looking for a detective."

"Really?" Cameron asked. "For what? Have you got a case?"

"Oh, yes," Dolly said. "Someone murdered one of my girls. It was a long time ago and no one has ever captured her killer. I'm an old woman and before I die I would so like to see her killer get justice."

"Your girl?" Cameron cocked her head at her. "I didn't know you had any children. Why did I think you've never been married?"

"Oh, I've never been lucky in love," she said, "but I had eight girls." She sighed. "They're all gone now, though. Oh, Ava was the most beautiful one of all. Long hair that was the color of an Irish setter. Sexy green bedroom eyes. Legs up to here and the perkiest breasts you ever laid eyes on."

"Ava?" Certain that her concussion was affecting her hearing, Cameron shook her head to clear her ears.

Dolly continued, "And her tush was nothing to sneeze at either."

Again, Cameron caught Jan's eye. She was slowly shaking her head.

Cricksters was a 1950s retro diner almost directly under the Chester Bridge on Carolina Avenue. It was Cameron and Joshua's favorite place to eat. It served everything from burgers and sandwiches to full dinners. It also had an ice cream bar that served Cameron's favorite dessert, the C & J Lovers' Delight—created especially for the newlyweds.

If her silver fox was there, she would order and share it with him. But since he wasn't, she was forced to settle for a two-scoop hot fudge sundae with everything. But first, down to business, she needed to eat lunch … or did she?

What are they going to do if I skip the meal and head straight for dessert? Shoot me? Lorraine probably would, or worse, she would say something to make me shoot her. Then Josh will have to come visit me in prison and talk to me through bars. If that didn't put a damper on our marriage …

After they parked, Lorraine jumped out of the SUV and scurried inside, which left Jan and Cameron to help Dolly out of the backseat and across the parking lot to the door.

Jan grasped Cameron's arm as soon as they were out of the SUV and quickly gave her the lowdown while they went around to Dolly's side of the car. "You need to be patient with Lorraine."

"No, I don't," Cameron replied.

"She's had a hard life," Jan said. "Her husband died suddenly, leaving her with a son to raise by herself, and then he committed suicide."

"How awful." Cameron couldn't imagine if Donny had taken his own life.

"He was only twenty-four." Jan paused with her hand on the door handle. "They found him hanging from a tree branch out in Raccoon Creek. Obviously, Lorraine never got over it."

"I can see why."

"In case you haven't noticed, Dolly is a little …" Jan cleared her throat. "Senile. She's never been married."

"Last I heard, you don't have to be married to have children."

"Eight daughters?"

"So she's a slut with issues when it comes to birth control."

Jan squeezed Cameron's arm. "There are no daughters, and there's definitely no daughter named Ava who was murdered. Take my advice. Humor her, but don't waste your time. It's not a real murder." She threw open the door and reached in to take the old lady's arm to help her out.

Inside Cricksters, Cameron ensured that she was sitting next to Dolly and as far away from Lorraine as she could get, which was a difficult maneuver because the diner was busy with the lunch crowd.

Cameron recognized many of the faces of the customers. Most were regulars like her, including one of the men sitting in the booth directly behind the ladies' table in the center of the restaurant. Sheriff Curt Sawyer was having lunch with two men and a woman.

"Cameron," Curt rose up in his seat to shake her hand. "That black eye is a real beauty."

"I'm proud of it."

Curt went on to introduce his guests. He gestured at the older man sitting next to him. "This is Phillip Lipton. He's the head of the state crime scene unit in Weirton."

Cameron shook hands with the baldheaded man with thick glasses.

Curt moved on to the distinguished looking couple sitting across from him. The woman looked very familiar to Cameron. An older woman who wore her silver hair in a straight cut down to her shoulders. The silver in her pantsuit matched the tone of her hair, along with her blouse and silver jewels. Her tall, slender—even regal bearing—made her age difficult to pin, though Cameron estimated that she was in her sixties. She had a tall, slender bearing.

The man sitting next to her wore a dark suit and had black hair with a touch of gray at the temples. His hard-looking face had a square jaw.

Curt introduced the couple. "Congresswoman Hilliard and superintendent of the West Virginia State Police, Colonel Henry MacRae, have flown in from Charleston for a briefing on Deputy Gardner's murder. I invited Phillip to meet with us to go over what his people have put together from Gardner's cruiser."

"Boy, you people sure got here fast," Cameron said. "All the way from Charleston?"

"Deputy Michael Gardner was a police officer," the congresswoman said in a firm tone. "That gives this case the highest priority in my book. We need to send a firm message to the public that people don't go taking out law enforcement officers, even if they are from the smallest of small towns. No matter how long ago the crime occurred, we will hunt down the perpetrators of these crimes—"

"I'm not a resident of West Virginia," Cameron cut her off. "So you can save your campaign speech for someone else. I'm still voting in Pennsylvania."

For the first time, the congresswoman turned to meet Cameron's gaze. The smirk on the homicide detective's lips served to set fire to the politician's cold, pale blue eyes.

Sitting on the outside of the booth, Colonel Henry MacRae, who was between Cameron and the congress-woman, broke off the stare down. "Actually, we came up here because this case is personal to me. I taught Mike Gardner at the police academy. I was sort of his mentor. I'm very interested in finding his killer."

"So is my husband," Cameron said, "which makes me want to find him."

"Cameron is a homicide detective with the Pennsylvania state police," Curt said.

"Hey," Phillip said, "I'm from Pennsylvania." He told Cameron, "I started out with the state police."

"How did you end up in West Virginia?" Cameron asked.

"I was offered the position of *heading* the crime lab," he said. "Granted, we aren't as big as the Pennsylvania crime lab, but there's something to be said about being in charge." The geeky-looking man grinned. "I guess I'm just a power hungry kind of guy."

"Well, Mr. Crime Lab, have your people found anything to tell us who killed Mike Gardner?"

"We can't find Gardner's gun," Curt said. "He was shot in the head, and they recovered the slug, which is a match with his weapon, but the gun itself is missing."

"I think we need to find out what case Gardner was working on," Cameron said.

"Good luck with that," Curt said.

Congresswoman Hilliard said, "I suggest that you not go jumping to conclusions. This deputy was only on the force for six months. He was a patrolman. Have you ever given any consideration to the possibility that it was a random hit by someone who had a thing against police officers, or maybe someone who had a personal grudge against him?"

Cameron felt like reaching across the table to slap the congresswoman. *What is she doing coming all the way up from Charleston to stick her nose into our murder case? Why doesn't she go to Washington with the rest of the troublemakers and screw things up there?* As much as Cameron wanted to announce that Mike was on his way to the park to meet with a confidential informant, she held her tongue. That information wasn't for public knowledge. If the sheriff chose to share it with the congresswoman, he could, but Cameron wasn't going to do it.

"Hey, Cameron, are you with us or not?" Lorraine called out in a harsh voice.

"I believe the congresswoman has a good point," the police superintendent said. "I took the liberty of looking into cases in the Ohio Valley similar to Deputy Gardner's murder. I found one in two thousand and two where a Pennsylvania

State Trooper was run down right outside Pittsburgh while giving a ticket to someone he had pulled over for a broken taillight. A suspect was never arrested, but there has been speculation that the hit was deliberate. Now maybe—"

Cameron didn't hear the rest. It was drowned out by the roar in her ears from the blood rushing to her head due to the rapid beating of her heart brought on by fury.

Sheriff Curt Sawyer slid out of his seat to step between Cameron and MacRae. "That case is in no way connected to Deputy Gardner's disappearance," he insisted.

"How can you be so certain?" MacRae asked.

"Trooper Gates was killed in a hit and run by a drunk driver," the sheriff said.

"You're just assuming he was drunk," MacRae said. "No suspects were ever apprehended. The case was never closed. As long as it is open, an argument could be made that—"

"That was my husband, you idiot," Cameron sputtered out while Sheriff Sawyer ushered her back.

"I think you should go sit down, Cameron," Curt Sawyer said in a low soothing voice. "I'll handle this."

"But—"

"This isn't your case," Curt said in a low voice. "Go order a sundae for yourself. Make it a double. I'll handle these morons."

"Cameron, do you want some lunch or not?" Lorraine raised her voice a notch louder to catch everyone's attention.

Curt grinned at the glare that crossed her face at Lorraine's chastising tone. "Go join the hen party."

Set off by one of the women suggesting that they make sure to say grace before eating, Lorraine was ranting about how God was no more than a myth and she refused to be a part of an ancient ritual when Cameron sat down next to Dolly.

"If you don't want to say grace, Lorraine," Dolly replied, "then no one is making you." Her lips curled up into a smile. Her wrinkled little face was almost childlike when she continued in a sickeningly sweet tone. "While we're giving thanks to God for our blessings, you can go home and pack for warm weather. Believe me, you're going to be needing it where you're going after you bite the big one."

"Dolly!" Jan gasped.

"You'll get there before me." Lorraine's eyes were blazing.

"Lorraine!" Jan turned to gasp at the old woman on the other side of the table.

The expressions on the faces of the other women around the table were a mixture of shock and amusement.

"I'm sorry," Dolly asked, "did I say something wrong? I must have had another one of those mini-strokes that I've been known to have on occasion."

"Funny how you only seem to have them when Lorraine is around," one of the women noted with a smile.

With a wicked giggle, Dolly grasped Cameron's hand, leaned over, and whispered into her ear, "Growing old does have its advantages."

"What's that?" she asked to take her mind off of the conversation at the other end of the table. Lorraine was still sputtering about Dolly's low blow.

"Everyone thinks old people have bad memories," Dolly's voice rose. "In some ways, they are right. Sometimes I do forget what I had for breakfast, but things that happened years ago—people I have met, things that were said, plans that were made, treacherous things that people did, especially horrific things to good people, the evil that some people will do to others and get away with, I remember those things with the clarity of an engraving on my brain."

A hush had fallen around them while Dolly spoke. The little old lady's eyes bore into Cameron's face. The corners of her lips curled into what resembled a devilish smile.

"Do you know who did it?" Cameron asked. "Do you know who the killer is?"

"Oh, yes," Dolly said with a grin. "I know who and I know why."

Cameron glanced across the table at Jan, whose face was white. *She's got quite a lot of details for someone who supposedly imagined this.* "When did this happen? How long ago?"

"Friday the thirteenth," Dolly said.

Cameron was still staring at Dolly in shock when there was a commotion behind them.

Sheriff Curt Sawyer jumped out of his seat when a full glass of water landed in his lap.

"Oh, I am so sorry." Phillip Lipton grabbed a handful of paper napkins and tried to mop up the spill as best he could. But the glass of water had been full and had gotten all over. "The glass just slipped out of my hand."

Meanwhile, the front of Curt's uniform looked like he had peed his pants. Cursing, the sheriff stomped off to the men's restroom. The congresswoman and the detective moved out of the booth to allow room for the server, armed with napkins and paper towels, to clean up.

As humiliating as it was, Cameron couldn't help but smile at the crime lab chief's embarrassment. Lipton glanced up in their direction while helping the server mop. Dolly giggled out loud at the scene. Lipton turned red all the way across his face and up across his bald scalp.

Meanwhile, Lorraine shook her head while making "tsk-tsk" noises with her tongue. "Idiot."

"I wouldn't be so quick to judge about who's the idiot," Cameron muttered. "I'll bet he knows how long an eternity in hell is."

Hearing her, Dolly burst into another round of giggles while clapping her hands with delight. "You are such a clever girl." Grasping her hand in her wrinkled paw, she said, "I like you. I have a feeling you're going to be the one to find Ava's killer."

"Thank you."

"You're such a pretty girl."

Cameron blushed.

"Such a shame about your breasts," the old woman said with a shake of her head.

Cameron glanced down at her chest. "What's wrong with them?"

"They aren't perky enough."

CHAPTER SEVEN

It wasn't until Joshua had pulled up in front of the little white house located one block up the hill from Rock Springs Boulevard that he realized how long it had been since he had visited his childhood friend's home. Mike Gardner had been his best friend. Yet in the decade since he had been back in Chester, Joshua had never stopped by to visit Mike's parents—until this moment.

Stopping by to visit Mike's parents at the same home where Joshua used to hang out with his best bud would confirm that Mike was no longer around. He was missing. Presumed dead.

Now he was truly gone—his body was in Tad's morgue.

There was no denying it any longer.

After sucking in a deep breath, Joshua let it out, unhooked his seatbelt, and climbed out of his SUV to descend the steps down to the two-bedroom house built into the hillside that made up the oldest part of Chester.

Cynthia Gardner, Mike's mother, opened the door before Joshua had the opportunity to ring the doorbell. Her eyes were red rimmed. She clutched a worn tissue in her wrinkled hand. "Josh … it is him, isn't it?"

Joshua nodded his head.

She clutched his arm in both hands and sobbed. "I should be relieved. Now I know, but I guess ... as long as there was no word, then there was a tiny bit of hope. Now ... it's gone."

"I am so sorry." Joshua wrapped his arm around her, eased her across the threshold, and closed the door.

He half-expected to find Lyle Gardner sitting in his easy chair in the living room. Seeing the worn, blue recliner, he recalled that as children, they knew better than to sit in Mike's father's chair. Seeing it empty, he asked, "Where's Mr. Gardner?"

"He's at the club." She wiped her nose with the tissue. "He spends a lot of time there now—ever since ..." Her voice trailed off.

She offered Joshua a seat. Still too intimidated to take the recliner, he chose to sit on the sofa. "I'm hoping that ... with our finding Mike's body ... maybe you can remember more details about the time leading up to his disappearance to help us catch whoever killed him."

Her face went blank. Eying Joshua, she eased down onto the recliner. "So it wasn't an accident?"

Slowly, he shook his head. "I'm sorry. No, he was murdered."

She stared at him in silence. Her face was devoid of expression. Her eyes were searching as if she didn't know what to say.

The only sound in the room was the ticking of the big cuckoo clock on the wall.

Finally, Joshua spoke. "Mrs. Gardner, I need to ask you a question."

"I don't know who would have wanted to hurt Mike," she said with a shake of her head.

"I was the last one to see Mike alive except for his killer," he reminded her. "He told me that he was investigating the murder of a prostitute—"

A flash of anger lurked beneath the surface when she said, "You told me that already and I told you long ago that I have no idea what he could have been talking about. Have you talked to Belle?"

"Yes, she doesn't—"

"She was married to Mike. If anyone knew what types of cases he was investigating on his own and had gotten into, she does." Cynthia's tone was bitter. "If she was a loyal wife," she added under her breath, "she would have kept on top of that type of stuff."

Joshua pounced on her anger directed toward her daughter-in-law. "Was Belle less than loyal?"

"She only waited the minimum amount of time before having Mike declared dead so that she could marry her boss and move to that big house," Cynthia said in a low tone. "She's done everything that she could to cut us out of her life. For years after she remarried, I tried to maintain a relationship with her. I'd call the house and she wouldn't even speak to me. Royce told me that she said it was too painful talking to me because I reminded her of Mike." She blinked away the tears of anger in her eyes. "Hunter is all we have left of Mike."

"Royce keeps a firm rein on his family, huh?" Joshua recalled how persistent he had been when they had visited Mike's widow the night before.

"He considered Mike beneath him," Cynthia said. "He was just a lowly police officer. Royce is a highly regarded scientist and executive. He wasn't one bit pleased when Hunter got accepted to the police academy." A hint of pride and pleasure came to her face. "He's starting this fall."

"So I heard," he said before gently taking her back to the reason for his visit. "Mrs. Gardner, someone murdered your son. If someone killed my son, I would reveal every family secret we had if it meant finding who was responsible."

She sat up tall with her shoulders back. Her chin jutted out when she asked, "What are you talking about, Joshua?"

His tone was equally firm. "Was Mike adopted?"

"How dare—"

"I have it from a reliable source that he was," Joshua replied. "I also did a background check and found that you had a sister whose employment was listed as a dancer. Ava Tucker. In nineteen seventy-six, she was murdered at a boarding house in Newell where she was living. Now this area does not have a big dancing community. There are a few clubs around that employ women who would call themselves dancers. Was that her real profession?"

Tears were streaming down her face when she stood up and turned away. Joshua heard her sobbing with her back to him.

Hating himself for what he had to do, he stood up. "I'm sorry, Mrs. Gardner, but you do have to make a decision. Would you rather protect your family's reputation or find Mike's killer?"

She kept her back to him. "Do you know what it's like to be responsible for someone's death?"

"Yes."

She whirled around to face him.

"I was an officer in the navy," Joshua said. "I served in Desert Storm. It's the hardest thing anyone can do, make a decision that you know could result in people, good people, being killed. But someone has to make the hard decisions. I can only pray that the decisions I make are the best ones overall."

"I'm talking about a kid making a foolish, purely selfish decision that cost a good man his life."

"What decision was that, Mrs. Gardner?"

"Ava was a fool." Her face was hard. "A selfish fool. Her boyfriend, Douglas O'Reilly, got appointed to West Point. He went away. She was scared to death that she was going to lose him, so the next summer, when he came home, she got herself pregnant."

"Got herself ..."

"She seduced him with the intention of getting pregnant and then forcing him to marry her," Mrs. Gardner said. "She was sixteen years old and so wrapped up in herself that she thought that he would take her back to West Point as his wife."

"Wives can't live on campus—"

"This was nineteen sixty-six," she said. "You couldn't be a cadet at West Point and be married. In order to marry her, Doug would have had to drop out of West Point. Or, to stay in school, he would have had to abandon her. He was nineteen. Back then, if he had done that, he could have been charged with statutory rape, which would have gotten him kicked out." She dropped her head. "The morning after she told him, he was found in his Mustang at the bottom of Raccoon Creek. Everyone knew that Ava drove him to kill himself. I was already married to Lyle. After she had the baby, we moved here, hoping that people wouldn't know about it. Ava blamed herself ... I guess. She was completely lost. Next thing I knew, she was one of Dolly's girls."

"Dolly's girls?" Joshua asked.

"Private club out by the race track in Newell," she said. "Dolly's. The girls would dance for the customers and then, if they wanted something extra ..."

"My father dealt in libations."

"Libations?" Cameron fought the tug at the corners of her mouth at the old-fashioned term Dolly used to describe her father's business.

The inside of Dolly Houseman's red brick colonial home was exactly as the detective had imagined. It was neat, tidy, and old. Cameron guessed that the décor was like a flashback to the 1940s, or maybe even to the 1930s.

Jan had unsuccessfully tried to give her an out. "You look tired," she noted when Cameron climbed out of the SUV along with Dolly. "The doctor said you shouldn't exert yourself. You really should rest."

"I'll go home and rest after visiting with Dolly," Cameron said with a slam of the door before taking the elderly woman's arm to help her up the sidewalk to her porch.

Lorraine, who appeared to still be stewing about Dolly's comment at lunch, had climbed out of her seat in the front of the SUV and closed the door.

"Lorraine," Jan objected, "I'll drive you home."

"No need to," Lorraine replied over her shoulder while storming up the hill to her home, which was on the street behind Dolly's house. "I'll walk."

"But I was plan—"

"I'm old, not crippled," Lorraine shot back.

With a sigh, Jan climbed into the driver's seat of the SUV, put it in gear, and pulled it into her driveway across the street and next door to the Thornton's three-story stone home.

After Cameron took a seat on the Queen Anne style sofa, Dolly placed a photograph album in her guest's lap.

"Is Ava's picture in here?" Cameron opened the cover to look at the first picture.

"If she isn't in this album, she's definitely in another one." Dolly tottered over to the bookcase against the wall and peered at the album covers. "I have pictures of all my girls."

Cameron let out a gasp and instinctively reached for her gun, which she forgot she didn't have strapped to her hip, when there was an abrupt movement next to the sofa. A black and white body leapt from the floor to land on the arm of the sofa. With a sigh of relief, she realized it was Irving who had tucked his head under her hand to demand a petting.

"Oh, it's only you," she said before realizing her cat was in someone else's house and she didn't bring him. "Irving, what are you doing here?"

"Most likely he let himself in through the cat door," Dolly replied while studying the dates on the spines of the photo albums lined up along her bookcase. "That's how he lets himself in."

"Lets himself in?" Cameron gave Irving a chastising look. "How long has he been doing that?"

"Oh, I don't know," the elderly woman said. "The days have all blended together for this old mind. He just showed up one day while I was eating my Cheerios and demanded the milk at the bottom of my bowl. I gave it to him and he's been coming over ever since. He's here every morning for breakfast. He loves Cheerios."

Irving flicked his ears with their tuffs sticking out at his mistress. He seemed to smirk at her while plopping down on the arm of the sofa to wash his paws.

"You naughty boy," she said before turning her attention back to the photo album.

"Most boys are." Dolly patted Irving on the head. "Naughty, I mean."

Cameron gasped when she saw a familiar face in one of the pictures. The heavy-set man was sitting in a wing-backed chair with a small girl with curls in his lap. "Is this—"

Dolly squinted her eyes to study the picture that Cameron was pointing at. "Oh, that's me with Uncle Al," the elderly woman said in a matter-of-fact tone before turning back to the bookcase to resume her search. "Ava can't be in that album. That was at least two decades before she was born."

"Uncle Al," Cameron said with a stutter. "Do you mean Al as in Al Capone?"

"Yes, that was his name." Dolly pulled a heavy album from off the shelf and handed it to Cameron.

"You called Al Capone 'Uncle Al?'"

"He was really a very nice man," Dolly said. "He was one of my father's biggest customers."

"Libations?" Cameron said. "Was your father a bootlegger?"

The elderly lady lowered herself into a wing-backed chair across from the detective. Irving leapt off the arm of the sofa to jump into Dolly's lap. His face filled with content, he curled up and purred while she petted him with both hands down the length of his body. Cameron recognized the chair Dolly was sitting in as the same chair in the picture.

"Bootlegger is such a derogatory term for what my father did," she said. "He was one of the best libation makers of his time. Why, orders for his moonshine came from all over the eastern half of the country. Uncle Al used to say that Daddy had the Da Vinci touch. He was an artist, and his booze was the best there ever was."

"How did you end up in Chester, West Virginia?" Cameron asked.

"Prohibition ended, and suddenly everyone was making booze. It wasn't such a specialized profession anymore," Dolly said with a frown. "By the nineteen fifties, Daddy was looking for another line of work. The race track was bringing in a lot of people looking for entertainment—especially men. So he bought a big old farmhouse outside of Newell and opened up a club. But it was a very private club. Extremely exclusive. The only way people could get in was by knowing a member who would vouch for them."

"But alcohol was legal," Cameron said. "What made this club so exclusive and private that—" She gasped. *Eight girls when she was never married.*

"Daddy named it Dolly after me," the elderly woman said with pride.

"Your girls!" Cameron said. "They weren't your daughters."

"I never said they were my daughters," Dolly said, "but they were like daughters to me. I cared very much about every one of my girls. Why, after Daddy passed away and I inherited Dolly's—"

"You were a madam," Cameron said.

"And a very good one." With a scoff, she waved her hand. "But Dolly's wasn't like any run-of- the-mill bordello. We were special."

"How?"

"It wasn't just sex that brought the men to Dolly's," the elderly woman said. "Oh, if a man wanted sex, he could go to an alley across the river in East Liverpool or the East End and get it for a fraction of what we charged for an evening with one of my girls." She shook her head. "At Dolly's, men were paying for an experience that you could get no place else. My girls were the most beautiful ladies in the Ohio Valley. They were dancers and entertainers. Every evening, each one would give a performance on the stage in the lounge. Then, if she had a client, she would take him up to her room. The lounge served only the best in spirits. Some club members would come only to drink and sit by the fire in the drawing room." She leaned over to whisper, "You would not believe some of the deals that got made and broken right there in my parlor." Her giggle took on a naughty tone. "Even a few murder conspiracies."

Cameron didn't know whether to believe her or not. "Murder conspiracies? Really? Is that why one of your girls was murdered?"

Dolly turned serious. "I don't know. No one has looked into her murder to confirm that."

"Why not?"

"Because she was a dead hooker," Dolly said, "and no one cares about a dead hooker."

"Except maybe a young deputy?" Cameron asked in a voice barely above a whisper.

"Yes, there was a deputy who came to visit me one day," Dolly said. "He had heard about Ava and had a lot of questions about her. He left here swearing that he would find out what happened to her." She added in a solemn tone, "I never saw him again. He had a young son."

"Mike Gardner," Cameron said. "His son's name was Hunter."

"I guess he got too close to the truth," Dolly said. "There are people who prefer that the past stays right there—in the past—especially when revelations of the truth about their dirty little secrets threaten their power grip."

"What kind of secrets?" Cameron asked. "Whose power grip?"

Dolly patted the top of a stack of photo albums resting on the table in front of her. "It's all there. Take it. I'm an old woman. My time here on earth is about to end. Then I will need to be answering for keeping the devil's secrets. Maybe God will grant me mercy if I make things right for those I have hurt by doing so."

"Was your girl killed because of the devil's secrets?" Cameron asked.

"Do you know the Nulls?"

"No," Cameron said.

"Russell Null runs the family business now," Dolly said. "The landscaping business just outside of Newell. He's on the board of county commissioners. Ava was with his younger brother, Virgil, when some maniac suffocated them with duct tape across their faces."

"When did this happen? How long ago?"

"February thirteen, nineteen seventy-six," Dolly said. "Friday the thirteenth. The police never really cared to investigate it. Ava was such a nice girl, and no one had a bad thing to say about Virgil. Sweet, sweet boy. It was his first date with Ava."

Cameron dug her notepad out of her purse. "Ava. February thirteen, nineteen seventy-six. What was her last name?"

"Tucker. Her name was Ava Tucker."

CHAPTER EIGHT

"Close your mouth, Josh. You're attracting flies," Cameron said after breaking the news to her husband about the kindly blue-haired lady across the street.

Staring out the living room window through the hedges that blocked his view of Dolly's home, Joshua cleared his throat in search of his voice. As if seeing Dolly would make sense of it all, he leaned up closer to the window to peer at the red brick colonial. "I don't believe it." He turned back to his wife. "You heard her wrong."

Cameron picked up the photo album resting on top of a tall stack that Dolly had given her, opened it, and showed him one of the pictures. "Al Capone was her Uncle Al," she said. "She was born in Chicago in nineteen twenty-five."

"That woman used to babysit me." Joshua pointed out the window.

"Gee, did your grandmother know what she did before her retirement?" Cameron asked with a smile.

"I wonder if Tad knows." Joshua answered his own question. "Tad knows everyone and everything. He has to have known."

"If he did, then he would have known about Ava being a hooker, which would have explained the murder Mike was investigating. If that was the case, wouldn't he have mentioned something about it by now? Did you know about Dolly's?"

Scratching his head, Joshua plopped down into a chair. "I had heard about it."

"She said it closed right after the murder in seventy-six," Cameron said, "You would have been just a kid."

"I had heard of a private club down by the race track where they had dancing girls who were practically naked," he said. "I was told that it was like something you would see in the gangster movies with rich men in fancy suits flashing a lot of money and beautiful women. I thought it was made-up stuff of pubescent boys … until today."

"What happened to change your mind?"

"I finally got Mike's mother to admit that he was adopted," Joshua said.

"And his birth mother was Ava Tucker," she finished.

"Who told you that?"

"No one told me," she said. "Have you forgotten that I'm a detective?" With a shake of her head, Cameron folded her arms under her breasts. "From what you and I have found out, Ava Tucker wasn't a dancer, she was a prostitute—"

"And Mike Gardner's mother."

"And she was murdered."

"That had to be the case Mike was looking into when he was killed. Ava Tucker's murder at Dolly's." Still not believing it, Joshua turned to look over his shoulder at the house across the street. "We need to get that case file and have a talk with Dolly, the sweet little madam next door."

"Dolly was insistent that there's something in one of these albums that will help." Cameron resumed leafing through the books. "I finally met the infamous Lorraine Winter today," she added in a matter-of-fact tone.

"That woman scares the dickens out of me," Joshua continued staring out the window.

"She reminds me of an aunt I had who didn't like children," she said, "especially me because I would let her know how much I didn't like her back. The sound of Lorraine's voice makes the hair on the back of my neck stand up on end the same way it did when I heard Aunt Vivian's voice."

"One of my earliest childhood memories is of that witch," Joshua said. "My grandmother about tossed her off our front porch—literally."

"What did she do?" Cameron set down the album and went over to ask him.

"I was maybe about six years old," he recalled. "Lorraine had come over to the house to meet with Grandmomma to go over something for some church committee they were on—"

"Lorraine went to church?" Cameron asked. "She made it very clear at lunch today that she was an atheist."

"That happened after her son Toby killed himself," he muttered, "probably to get away from her. Lorraine is a nutcase. She was here meeting with Grandmomma and Toby came over after school. He was a teenager then. Well, when I went to tell her that he was here, she almost knocked me over running out. She was mad as a wet hen over something. Grabbed him by the ear and dragged him bodily out onto the porch and slapped him." He paused. "That was the first time that I had ever seen anyone hit anyone. I must have screamed, or maybe it was Lorraine's screaming at Toby that brought Grandmomma out onto the porch just in time to see Lorraine backhand him a second time. Well, Grandmomma weighed in like a giant momma bear, grabbed Lorraine by the bun that she always wore her hair in, and gave her what for."

"Lorraine really knows how to make friends, huh?"

"She's a very unhappy woman," Joshua said with a shrug of his shoulders. "She's been playing the victim card since I've known her. Though as a child, I only knew that she scared the dickens out of me. But then, I got to know her story. Her husband died of a massive heart attack when he was in his thirties—leaving her with a toddler to raise alone. Then, she got mad at Grandmomma about the fight and resigned from every charity board that Grandmomma was on. Then, more fights and arguments with more people in town. She got mad at the priest over something and left the Catholic Church. When Toby killed himself, she decided there was no God and that all of us was fools for believing there was a God who would let all of that happen to her."

"Sounds more like she's angry with God," Cameron said, "not so much that she doesn't believe in Him."

"Didn't you get angry with God when Nick was killed?" He watched her from over his shoulder while she paused to come up with the words to answer him.

"I don't think I was so much mad at God as I was angry at whoever it was that took Nick from me and the lack of closure due to Nick's killer never being caught. That's the difference. Lorraine's husband died of a heart attack. There's no one to point to and blame. Toby killed himself ... why did he kill himself?"

"He was in his early twenties," Joshua said. "Imagine being told for twenty years that you're a loser and you're never going to amount to anything. After a while, you start to ask yourself why you bother."

"Is that what Lorraine did?"

"Heard it myself." He went back to peering out the window.

"Why did he kill himself at Raccoon Creek? People usually go someplace that has some significance to them to kill themselves. What was significant about Raccoon?"

"What wasn't?" Joshua asked. "Kids around here either hang out at Tomlinson Run Park or Raccoon. Maybe that was where he had spent some happy times with his friends. He did have friends. I remember he was pretty tight with Virgil Null."

Cameron grabbed his wrist. "Virgil Null? The same—"

"Just a minute, hon!" Seeing Tad drive past, Joshua rushed outside. Cameron was directly behind him when he jogged to the end of the driveway and up Rock Spring's cobblestone street to the house next door to intercept Tad climbing out of his SUV.

In Chester, when neighbors refer to the next street up, they are speaking literally. From the shore of the Ohio River, the small town was built into the side of the mountain. Each road that crossed the face of the mountain rose up above the street beneath it. One of the oldest streets was Rock Springs Boulevard, which crossed the width of the mountain before wrapping uphill. Side streets that contained tiny homes, including the Gardner house, shot off of Rock Springs like tiny tree branches.

"What's with the welcoming committee?" the doctor asked when he saw Joshua and Cameron jogging up the sidewalk to meet him in his driveway. "Should I be scared?"

"You've known Dolly Houseman your whole life, right?" Joshua asked.

A perplexed expression crossed his face when Tad nodded his head.

Folding his arms across his chest, Joshua asked, "Did you know she owned Dolly's?"

"Dolly's what?"

"The private bordello out by the race track," Cameron said.

"*That* Dolly's?" Tad asked with a gasp.

"*That* Dolly's." Joshua nodded his head.

Tad looked beyond them to the quiet red brick house across the road. "Are you telling me that our sweet little Dolly is the same Dolly who—"

"That's what she told Cameron." Joshua jerked his thumb in the direction of his wife.

"She was a madam," Cameron said. "And a good one, too."

"Whoever would have thought?" Tad replied in a low voice.

"Dolly's was real?" Joshua asked. "Why didn't you tell me? I thought it was an urban legend in these parts."

"I didn't tell you because that club closed back in the seventies," Tad replied. "The prostitution was only a small part of what Dolly's was known for. By the time you were old enough to know or care about it, Josh, it was only a distant legend that most people thought had been blown way out of proportion." He shrugged. "You know, it grows and grows until it's almost impossible to know what's real and what's concocted."

"Well, one thing that is true is that one of Dolly's girls was murdered," Joshua said, "and that girl was a prostitute."

Tad let out a breath. "Was that the murder Mike Gardner was investigating?"

"We think so," Joshua said.

"On record, that girl would have been a dancer," Tad said.

"But the *police* knew she was a call girl," Cameron said.

"More than likely the sheriff and prosecutor were afraid of what would come out if they asked too many questions," Tad said. "Some real movers and shakers from the tri-state area were regulars at Dolly's, and they met there for more than the girls. I heard that if you wanted to have the most secret of secret meetings, then Dolly's parlor was the place to go. Politicians would meet syndicate types and be all buddy-buddy there and then call each other nasty names as soon as their limos turned out onto route two-oh-eight."

Cameron nodded her head. "Sounds like the perfect backdrop for a murder. Maybe Ava overheard something she shouldn't have while serving the wrong mover and shaker."

"Do you think you could get your hands on the autopsy reports for Ava Tucker's murder?" Joshua asked Tad.

"Wasn't her john killed, too?" Tad asked.

"Yes," Cameron said.

Tad looked her up and down. "I guess you have no intention of spending your medical leave resting."

"You're going to feed me, right?" Donny asked from the back seat of Joshua's SUV. "I mean, that's the only reason I'm coming."

"You're big enough," Cameron shot back from the front passenger seat. "You can catch your own."

Laughing, Joshua told Donny that they intended to stop for dinner on the way back from the sheriff's office in New Cumberland.

"But I need to tag along with you and Cameron and wait while you talk to Sawyer about that murder case," Donny said. "I wish you would have let me stay home."

"So that you could microwave hot dogs for your dinner again," Joshua said.

"Hot dogs aren't bad for you."

"They are if you eat them for every meal."

Leaning forward, Donny grasped the back of Joshua's seat. "How about pizza then? You can drop me off at Roma's and I can hang out with my friends while you're meeting with Sheriff Sawyer. Call me on your cell when you leave and I'll order our dinner. By the time you get there, it'll be waiting."

"Now that sounds like a plan," Cameron said.

"Anything that gets you out of cooking dinner sounds like a plan." Joshua turned onto Route Eight to take them out to New Cumberland. They would be passing Roma's Pizzeria a few miles up the road. Without a yea or nay from his father, Donny waited in apprehension for the answer, which came when Joshua turned left into Roma's parking lot.

"Don't run up a huge root beer tab," Joshua ordered while the teenager leapt out of the back seat. "Do you have your cell phone?"

Pausing, Donny tapped his back pocket. "Right here."

With a reminder that they would call him upon leaving New Cumberland, Joshua backed out of the parking lot to resume the drive to the other end of the county.

Once they were back on the road, Cameron asked, "Have you ever heard of Douglas O'Reilly?"

"Actually, I have," Joshua said. "Today, as a matter of fact."

Cameron squinted at him. "You're kidding."

"He was the boy who got Ava Tucker pregnant," Joshua said. "Her sister told me that she got pregnant on purpose because she was afraid of losing him after he went to West Point. Instead of marrying her, he committed suicide by driving his car off a cliff into Raccoon Creek."

"Did he?" Cameron asked.

"O'Reilly couldn't stay in the academy if he got married," Joshua said, "and if he didn't marry her, then she could claim statutory rape, which would have gotten him kicked out. He was stuck between a rock and a hard place and decided to take the coward's way out."

She said, "Back when I first became a state homicide detective, Doug O'Reilly's mother came in to see me. Every year or two, she would come in and try to get a detective to take another look at her son's case, which was closed as a suicide. She swore that he wouldn't have killed himself." She looked down at her hands in her lap. "In light of how Mike's cruiser ended up in the bottom of Tomlinson Run's lake, don't you find it interesting that his father's Mustang was found at the bottom of Raccoon Creek?"

Joshua turned to look at her. In the moment that he took his eyes off the road, he swerved.

"Look out!" Cameron yelled.

Regaining control of the car, Joshua hit the brake to slow down on the winding country road. "Are you thinking it's not a coincidence?"

"Think about it, Josh," she said. "What are the odds?"

"It was suicide."

"Was it?" Cameron asked. "Mike Gardner was murdered. Someone killed his birth mother. Isn't it possible that Mike's father, whose car was also found at the bottom of a lake, was murdered, too?"

"When you put it that way …" Joshua said. "Makes me wonder if it was a murder conspiracy or a family curse."

CHAPTER NINE

"We're still waiting for forensics to finish examining the cruiser," Sheriff Sawyer told Joshua and Cameron when they arrived at his office next to the county courthouse in New Cumberland.

"There's no reason why we can't proceed where things were left off when Mike disappeared," Joshua said while Cameron took a seat in the sheriff's small office. "He told me he was going to meet with a CI. A good place to start would be to find out where he was in his investigation and the identity of this informant."

Noticing two dusty white folder boxes, one stacked on top of the other, on the chair across from the sheriff's desk, Cameron asked, "Are these the cold case files Josh requested you dig up?" Without waiting for an answer, she swung the top box around to read the label on the end. In black marker, it read:

Null, Virgil R.
02/13/1976

"They are," Curt said. "Take a gander at the check-out roster."

While Cameron peered inside the folder box, Joshua opened the flap of the envelope taped to the top of the lid. Inside the envelope was a roster on which officers and other law enforcement officials were to write their names, badge numbers, and the date and time they checked out the evidence box. There was an identical roster in the file room. If a detective or officer went looking for a case box, the roster would show who had it. Both rosters needed to be signed, even if the officer didn't remove the box, as Curt had done.

While Joshua read the second to last name on the roster, Cameron gazed up at him. She could see the recognition in his eyes.

"I think you're on to something," Curt said.

"Mike Gardner checked out this evidence box ten days before he disappeared," Joshua told her. "On September third, nineteen ninety-six. He checked it back in on Friday, September sixth. Then, a couple of months later, the files were checked out on Monday, November fourth, by Philip Lipton."

"That name sounds familiar," Cameron said.

"He's the head of the state forensics lab in Weirton," Curt said. "Been there around twenty years. I checked when I saw his name on the roster there. That check out date is less than a month after he took the position. He's the clumsy bum who spilt his drink in my lap at lunch today."

"What would prompt the head of the forensics unit to check out *these* files for two cold cases as soon as he came on board?" Cameron asked. "If your forensics unit is like ours, they don't go digging into old case files unless something or someone, usually the investigating officer, asks for something."

"Like a deputy," Curt said.

"Which would have meant that Lipton would have known what case Mike was digging into," Joshua said. "When I contacted the sheriff after Mike's disappearance, I was told that no one had any idea what I was talking about." He showed Sawyer the roster. "This right here proves that Mike was looking into Ava Tucker's and Virgil Null's murders. His disappearance was all over the news. At least Philip Lipton should have noticed the missing deputy's name on this roster and the check-out date being less than a month before he went missing. Why didn't Lipton say anything?"

"Being new on the job at the time," Cameron said, "it would have been to Lipton's advantage in discovering a possible clue to Mike's disappearance. Why did he keep his mouth shut all these years?"

"Don't ask me," Curt said. "Ask him. And I want to be there when you do."

"Virgil Null." Cameron read the name on the end of the box. "That's the john who got murdered along with Ava Tucker." She reminded Joshua. "He was tight with Lorraine Winter's son who committed suicide."

"There was never any question that Toby Winter committed suicide," Joshua said. "He left a note."

"What did the note say?" Cameron asked.

"Ask his mother," Joshua said. "She'll tell you it's none of your bee's wax."

"Lorraine Winter is one nasty scary old lady," Curt said in agreement. "She could make the Hulk pee his pants."

The label on the box underneath Null's read "Tucker, Ava" and contained the same date.

"How do you know about Virgil Null being Ava's john?" Curt asked.

"Dolly told me." She removed the police case file from the box.

"Dolly?" Curt turned to Joshua, who was digging through the top box as well. "The name of the gentlemen's club where they were murdered was called Dolly's. Are you saying there really is a Dolly?"

"Why else would they call it Dolly's?" Cameron asked him.

"Because it was the place to go to meet dolls," Curt said. "Remember, back when people were politically incorrect. Women were called chicks, broads, and …" He gestured with a shrug of his shoulders. "—dolls? That's where I assumed the name Dolly came from."

"No, there is a real Dolly," Cameron said. "She's in her eighties now. I had lunch with her today."

"Are you talking about one of those little old ladies you were at Cricksters with this afternoon?" Curt leaned forward in his seat. "Which one?"

"The sweet little old lady sitting next to me."

Curt gasped. "That darling little blue-haired lady? Are you serious? She was a …"

"Madam," Cameron said with a giggle. "And she used to babysit Josh."

"Seriously?" Curt looked up at Joshua. "Your grandmother used to let a madam babysit you?"

"I don't think she knew," Joshua said.

"Still," Curt said. "Did she ever give you any advice about …" He waved one of his hands in a circle. "You know … secrets about how to …"

"Secrets of the trade?" Cameron asked.

"No." The pink that came to Joshua's cheeks stood out against his thick silver hair, which brought a grin to Cameron's face.

On the other side of his desk, Sheriff Sawyer shot her a wink at Joshua's embarrassment. After clearing his throat, he settled back to business. "Well, it's not surprising that no one knew what you were talking about back when you called in after Gardner's disappearance. On record in these case files,

Ava Tucker is listed as a dancer at a gentlemen's club. There's about a half dozen of those clubs around the track. Generally, the women who work there are considered dancers or bartenders, not prostitutes. If they hook, it's on their own time, and I don't think they list that profession on their resume. Did this sweet little blue-haired madam tell you why Gardner put his life on the line to look into this murder that had happened like twenty years before he became a cop?"

Cameron waited to let Joshua answer.

Deciding that it was best to keep their sheriff in the loop, Joshua replied, "Because Ava Tucker was his birth mother. It's a family secret. Mike Gardner was raised by Ava's sister and her husband. I only got Mike's mother, or rather, aunt, to confirm that today. So we need to be discrete."

Understanding, Curt nodded his head.

"Both victims were suffocated to death," Cameron noted. "The killer tied them up and then covered their faces, noses, and mouths with duct tape. They died of asphyxiation. What a way to go."

Joshua took note of a comment in Virgil Null's autopsy. "It may not have been so bad for Virgil. He had a fractured skull. He may have been knocked out before being suffocated."

Cameron continued to leaf through the case file. "The roll of duct tape wasn't found on the scene. The killer had to have taken it with him." She scanned reports in search of the witness statements. "They were killed in Ava's room. Wouldn't someone have noticed her taking two men up to her room? Or was the killer hiding in her room when she walked in with this Null guy?"

Joshua reached into the box for the police report on Virgil Null's murder. "Did the police at the time investigate to see if Null was the intended victim? This was the seventies. Maybe he was into drugs as well as women. Ava could have been collateral damage?" He scanned through the reports in the file.

"That's a good question." She closed the folder and held it in her lap. "Think about it. How long would Virgil Null have been in her room?"

When she turned to Curt, he shook his head while waving his hands. "Don't look at me. I have no need to visit hookers."

"Cameron's point is," Joshua said, "why kill both of them? If Ava was the intended victim, why didn't the killer wait for Virgil to go home? It certainly would have been less difficult to control one victim instead of two."

"And if Virgil was the intended victim," Cameron asked, "why kill him in Ava's room? According to this case report, there were possible multiple witnesses in the rooms on either side of hers. It was a Friday night—"

"Better for the killer to get lost in a crowd," the sheriff said.

"Speaking of crowds …" Joshua folded the case file inside out to read through a section in a witness statement. "What type of person stands out in the crowd in a bordello?"

Both Cameron and the sheriff had to think before they could answer.

"An ugly woman?" Curt finally responded.

"Give the man a cigar." Joshua held up the case file. "We have a statement from the bouncer that the bartender reported walking in on a middle-aged woman in the kitchen who ran out the backdoor into the night as soon as he spotted her."

"What time did that happen?" Cameron asked.

"Close to one o'clock," Joshua said. "They assumed that it was a suspicious wife checking on her husband."

"Any name on her?" Curt asked.

Joshua paused to read through the statement before shaking his head. He flipped to the statement from the bartender and shook his head again. "None. They had never seen her before."

"It could just be a coincidence," Cameron said. "At those types of places, it would not be unusual for a wife to sneak in to check on her husband. But even if she's not the killer, she may have seen something upstairs while looking for hm."

"The bouncer's name is Bart Walker," Joshua said. "I know his family. He died more than ten years ago. Maybe the bartender is still around. He's the one who saw her. He might be able to give us a description."

"Listen to this." Standing up, Cameron read from a statement in the case file for Ava Tucker's murder. "One of the girls at the club, who had the room next to Ava's, swore that she thought she saw someone on the verandah off her bedroom. She tried to check it out, but her client had other things on his mind and wouldn't let her. She said that was about midnight. The murders were discovered shortly after one o'clock." She closed the file. "Verandah? Could that be like the verandah off our bedroom, Josh? It wouldn't be that hard to climb up. The killer could have gotten into her room from the outside and escaped the same way without anyone seeing him."

"It was late at night," Curt said. "Dolly's was way out in the country. Secluded. The killer would have had no problem escaping into the night."

"I think the killer has gotten away with these murders due to luck, not skill," Cameron said. "How did he control both Ava and Null without them running for help from the people in the rooms around her bedroom?"

"Maybe he had a gun," Joshua said. "He just decided to use the duct tape because the shots would have attracted too much attention."

"I'm hearing a lot of speculation and no proof of anything," Curt said.

Cameron resumed scanning the reports. "Did Null and Tucker have any connection before that night?"

Joshua turned to the sheriff who shook his head while shrugging his shoulders. "These are two cold cases. I haven't had a chance to read the reports yet."

"Can I take them home to examine them more closely?" Cameron asked.

"No," the sheriff replied. "Did that concussion make you forget that you don't work in this state, let alone this county?"

With a chuckle, Joshua asked, "Can I check out these case files to go over them?"

"Yes, you may, Mr. County Prosecutor."

While Joshua went about signing the roster to check out the case files, Cameron asked, "How many people would Virgil have told that he was going to a whore house? Do men advertise that type of stuff?"

"Dolly's was a prestigious and very private club," Curt told her.

"Null was only twenty-four years old," Joshua noted from the file.

"His brother is a county commissioner," she told him. "Dolly told me that."

"According to a statement here from the bouncer," Joshua said, "it was Null's first time there, and he was very nervous." He leafed through the other statements in the file. "The other witnesses all say the same thing. It was Null's first time there. One witness noted in her statement that he looked scared to death."

Curt said, "Maybe it was his first time in more ways than one."

Ignoring the chuckle in the sheriff's voice, Joshua asked, "If this club was so prestigious and private, how did this twenty-four year old guy get in there?"

"Dolly said that perspective members had to be vouched for by current members," Cameron said.

"We're talking about people who have both power and money." Joshua leafed back to the first page of the police report. "Virgil's occupation is listed as a gardener in his father's landscaping business."

"He certainly didn't have the money to pay for any club membership," Cameron said.

"Unless he got the money from his daddy," Curt said.

"Brandon Null was the type to belong to those types of places," Joshua said in agreement. "Virgil's father is retired now. His son Russell is running the business and on the board of county commissioners. I think I'm going to go have a talk to him."

Cameron said, "Meanwhile, I'll poke around to see if I can find the connection between all of these murders."

"I thought you were on medical leave," Curt said.

"Cameron is reopening a cold case that smells funny to her in her own jurisdiction." Joshua winked at her while saying, "Douglas O'Reilly. Mike Gardner's birth father."

Cameron turned to Curt. "What do you think? What are the odds of three members of the same family all being killed separately without there being a connection?"

"Pretty bad," Curt said. "Was Mike Gardner's father murdered?"

"His car was found at the bottom of a lake, just like Mike's," she said. "His death was ruled a suicide. His mother swore that it wasn't. The police have been stonewalling her for years claiming that she was refusing to accept the truth." She gestured at the case files in the boxes. "Now, I'm thinking it would be worth taking a closer look."

Joshua and Curt exchanged glances.

Curt scratched his head. "Now you're making me wonder just how far over his head Mike could have gotten."

"And over what?" Joshua asked.

CHAPTER TEN

"I'm stuffed." Joshua groaned while turning the steering wheel to pull the SUV onto their cobblestone driveway. "Did we really have to order the extra-large platter of Buffalo wings?"

"It isn't like you had to eat the very last one." Donny said with a moan from the back seat. The teenager's stomach was usually a bottomless pit. This evening, though, Cameron suspected they had reached the bottom when they were forced to bring home the last two slices of pizza in a takeout box.

Joshua's SUV came to a halt behind a metallic blue sedan with New York tags resting in front of the porch steps.

"Oh, no." Cameron sucked in a deep breath with the realization of who was the owner of the car. "When did Tracy decide to come home?"

"She told me that she was coming home last night," Joshua reminded her while throwing open the door. "I told you …"

The vague memory was coming back to her when Tracy came running out the front door with Admiral galloping next to her. Irving was close behind them. While Joshua gave his older daughter a bear hug, Irving raced across the yard, through the hedges, and out onto Rock Springs Boulevard.

At twenty-two, Tracy Thornton was every father's dream. The slightly built young woman had a flawless figure, lush auburn hair, and her father's striking blue eyes. With culinary talent, and a compassion for the family that she had taken care of after her mother's sudden death when she was only a teenager, Tracy was every bit Daddy's little girl.

Joshua did have another daughter, Sarah, who was in her first year at the Naval Academy. Strong-willed and independent, Sarah lacked the feminine vulnerability that endeared Tracy to her father's heart. The fact that Tracy strongly resembled her mother, Joshua's first wife, didn't hurt either.

While Cameron waited for what seemed like an hour for Joshua to release Tracy, who was hanging onto him with her arms wrapped around his neck, she felt the pang of hurt that comes from being displaced.

The hug was broken up by Donny, who tapped his sister's shoulder for her to notice him standing there and the fact that he was now a head taller than her. "Hey, short-stuff," he said. "Remember me?"

Tracy released her arms from Joshua's neck to gawk up at Donny. "When are you going to stop growing?" She had to reach up to hug him and give him a kiss on the cheek while he wrapped his arms around her.

Cameron saw Joshua waving his arm for her to step around to the front of the SUV to join them. When she hesitated, he rolled his eyes and cleared his throat. Stepping behind Tracy, who was still hugging Donny, he reached over to grasp her wrist and pull her over to his side. "Tracy, you remember Cameron?"

In whirling around from where she was greeting Donny, Tracy whipped a lock of long hair across Cameron's face. Grimacing, Cameron rubbed her nose to stop the impending sneeze.

"Cameron!" Even though her tone was filled with enthusiasm, Tracy's body language, which caused distance between the two women, betrayed less affection for her father's new wife. "It is so good to see you. Should I be calling you, Mom?"

"No," Cameron said more forcibly than she intended. Swallowing hard, she was aware of Joshua watching the two women with apprehension. It was as if he expected them to break into a catfight. "Call me Cameron. That's what Donny calls me." With a nervous giggle, she added, "I answer to anything."

"I wish I could have made it out to be here when you two decided to get married so quickly," Tracy said.

"It was nothing fancy," Cameron said. "We just went to the church. Tad and Jan stood up for us."

"I was there, too," Donny said. "We went to Cricksters afterwards and they made this giant wedding sundae with a bride and groom on top." He whipped out his cell phone. "I sent you guys the picture. Did you get it?" He held out the phone to show her.

"No." Tracy slapped it away.

"I'll resend it then."

"I mean I don't care to see their wedding sundae," she replied. "Who has wedding sundaes instead of cake anyway?"

"We did." Cameron saw the same smoldering look in Tracy's eyes that Joshua would get when holding back rising fury.

She had seen it only the week before when Irving got even with him for throwing away his latest prize, a dead mouse that he had brought in to show Joshua while he was drinking his first cup of coffee in the morning. Irving's revenge was to pee in Joshua's bedroom slippers.

Tracy's blue eyes turned dark like the sky right before a thunderstorm bursts to take its wrath on anyone unlucky enough to be in the vicinity. "I hope y'all are hungry," she said with a forced smile. "I made dinner."

"Oh, we already ate," Donny said.

Cameron felt Joshua's grip on her arm tighten when Tracy turned her glare to her brother.

"What did you make?" Donny asked.

"Homemade chicken cordon bleu," Tracy replied. "Garlic mashed potatoes. All of Dad's favorites. Plus, I picked up a bottle of pinot grigio for him to have with it." She turned to Cameron. "I got root beer for you since you can't drink."

Cameron ignored the cutting tone in the reminder that she did not drink alcohol. The words between the lines were clear. " … Since you're a drunk." Or rather, recovering drunk. Forget that she hadn't had a drink for several years. It was still a worthy weapon for inflicting a wound—if Cameron allowed it to do so, which she refused to let happen. "Root beer float for dessert," she smiled broadly to show all of her teeth. "My favorite."

"Great! Let's get started." Donny raced inside. Admiral galloped next to him.

"I guess we're having a second dinner," Joshua said.

"If I knew—" Tracy said.

"You didn't tell me what time you'd be here," Joshua said.

"Did you check your voice mails?" she asked.

"Yes," Joshua said while taking his cell phone from its case. His groan told both Cameron and Tracy that he had left his cell phone in airplane mode, which he put it in when he had a court appearance. Since he had not switched it back, Tracy's calls had gone straight to voice mail. He didn't notice it earlier because Cameron had called Donny when they left the sheriff's office. "Sorry, hon." He slipped the cell phone back into its case.

"That's okay, Daddy." Tracy slipped back into his embrace. "I'm just glad to be home again. Let's go inside and have a cocktail and you can tell me all about where you are on the case. Do you know who killed Hunter's dad yet?"

"Cameron and I have made some headway." With his arm around her waist, Joshua led her up the steps.

Tracy turned around to where Cameron had opened up the back of the SUV to take out one of the case boxes. "Cameron and you?"

"Yes," Joshua said. "Cameron and I are working together. We make a good team."

When she carried the box up to the porch, Cameron saw that the smile on Tracy's lips did not reach her eyes.

Tearing her glare from Cameron, Tracy told her father, "That's good. I'm glad you two get along so well." She hurried inside. "I need to check the chicken."

"Is she upset about us eating dinner without her?" Joshua asked Cameron while taking the folder box from her.

"Gee," Cameron replied with sarcasm, "I don't know."

Joshua had started up the steps when she muttered under her breath, "But I do know this. When she gives me that root beer float, I'm not drinking it before she tastes it first."

Hearing her, Joshua turned around so fast that his elbow bumped her nose. "What did you say?"

Holding her aching nose, Cameron blinked away the stars shooting in front of her eyes. "I said I love root beer floats. Can't wait."

Sometimes, Cameron thought there was something wrong with her. Most women, she assumed, fantasized about the day when they would have daughters old enough to talk to like sisters while cooking together in the kitchen.

Cameron had never had that fantasy. As a matter of fact, she never pictured herself with children—period. Being an only child, she had no siblings or nieces or nephews to babysit. When she approached the age of forty, she felt no urgency to beat the biological clock by having a child. That was one reason why she believed Joshua Thornton was perfect for her. His children were grown so that she could relate to them as adults. She spoke to Donny as a friend, and he related to her likewise. They had an understanding.

With Tracy Thornton, it proved to be a different matter altogether.

The huge country kitchen in the Thornton home had been renovated upon Joshua's return to Chester with his children. Then sixteen years old, Tracy had had a hand in renovating the kitchen to bring it up to modern standards.

It was Tracy's kitchen—where she used to cook for her family. It was her territory.

Cameron was the outsider … or so she sensed when she came into the kitchen to find Tracy searching through the drawers. "What are you looking for?"

"The whisk." Tracy extracted the tool from the drawer and slammed it shut. "It belongs in this basket with the frequently used utensils." With the end of the whisk, she tapped the wire container holding spatulas and other kitchen tools next to the stove before proceeding to use it to stir the sauce on the stove.

"I'm sorry," Cameron said, "I guess I don't use the whisk frequently enough to consider it a frequently used utensil."

Tracy shot a quick glance in her direction.

There was definitely a tension present that had not been there when Tracy and her brothers and sister had met Cameron at Christmas. Things had been different then. Cameron had been their dad's girlfriend. While Cameron and Irving spent much of their time in the Thornton home, there was no hint that Cameron and Irving would become a permanent fixture.

But Cameron had not only become a fixture—she was also a full-fledged member of the family.

"Do you know how to use a whisk?" Tracy asked her.

"I believe so," Cameron replied.

Abandoning the whisk and saucepan, Tracy moved on to where she was mashing the potatoes.

Cameron peered into the saucepan at the thick yellowish sauce. It smelled delicious. "What's this?" She picked up the whisk and stirred it.

"Light lemon hollandaise sauce," Tracy replied. "It's for the chicken. Mom taught me how to make it. She was a great cook."

"Your dad told me that," Cameron said. "He says you take after her."

There was a moment of silence. Cameron noticed Tracy pause while mashing the potatoes to stare into the bowl.

"You look like her." Cameron peered over her shoulder at her. "Her picture is still in the study on the bookcase."

"Yours is on his desk now." Tracy abandoned the mashed potatoes to return to the saucepan. "You're doing it wrong." She took the whisk from Cameron's hand. "You don't stir with it. You whip it. Let me show you how to properly use a whisk." Edging Cameron to the side, she proceeded to make quick whipping motions with the whisk in the sauce to thicken it. "It's all in the wrist. Your goal is to incorporate air into the sauce to thicken it and make it creamier." She turned to her. "See?" Holding up the whisk that was covered in the light yellow sauce, she shook it in Cameron's face. "That is how you properly use a whisk."

The two women's eyes met.

Like two gunfighters, they faced each other eye to eye.

"How're my two favorite ladies?" Joshua trotted in from the back staircase and stopped when he saw them. "What's going on?"

Without a word, Cameron grabbed the whisk out of Tracy's hand and turned back to the saucepan.

Tracy scurried back to the mashed potatoes at the other end of the counter.

"Did I miss something?" Apprehension made his question come out in a stutter.

Forcing a smile across her face, Cameron held up the whisk and shook it menacingly in his direction. "I'm learning how to use a whisk properly."

As if he feared that she was going to use the whisk as a weapon against him, Joshua backed up a step.

"Hey, Cam …" Donny came in from the back porch. He was holding Irving's food dish filled with his dinner. "Have you seen Irving?"

"Last I saw him, he was running out the driveway," Cameron said.

"Well, I just saw Mr. Grant drive by," Donny said. "If he was down at the bar tying one on, and he sees Irving, he's going to be calling—"

"I'll go find him." Anxious to get out of the line of fire, Joshua hurried to the door.

"Try Ms. Houseman's house," Cameron suggested.

"Why Ms. Houseman?" Tracy asked.

"It turns out the two of them have become very good friends," Cameron said.

Joshua paused at the door.

Seeing his hesitation, Tracy asked, "What's wrong, Dad?"

"Are you afraid of Dolly?" Cameron asked with a sly grin.

Tracy turned to him. "She's a sweet little old lady. Before I went to New York, she gave me a secret family recipe for a homemade liquor that had been passed down to her from her father. Why are you afraid of her?"

"I'm not afraid of anything." Joshua reached into the cabinet for Irving's can of cat treats. "I'm going to get Irving before Mr. Grant calls the police again." He slammed the door on his way out.

Women! Joshua cursed under his breath while making his way around the house and out the driveway. *Why do women have to make everything so difficult? And don't tell me it isn't a woman thing. Even Cameron says it's women. She actually prefers working with men because when women get involved, things get stupid.*

Joshua was shaking his head by the time he came out of his circular drive to the sidewalk. *What's the big deal over a wedding anyway? Tracy and J. J. have it completely wrong. It isn't like we're twenty-one and getting married for the first time. Big weddings with parties and white gowns and tuxes? Nah! Been there. Done that. It would have taken months to get all of the kids home at the same time, and Cameron and I wanted to be together. What kind of example would it have set for Donny to have her move in and for us to live together without being married? So we did it. We got married in the church and the big guy who counted, God, was there to bless our union. That's what was important. What is the big deal about us not waiting for all of the kids to get here for a big hoopla? Why can't Tracy and J. J. understand?*

"Raw-awl!" Irving cried out from across the street.

"My sentiments exactly," Joshua said in response while peering through the dark to where the black and white cat was perched on the top step of Dolly Houseman's porch. He pointed at him. "You! Get over here!"

Standing up, Irving screeched at him. With his back arched and fur up on end, he jumped down off the porch and ran around the corner of the house to the backyard.

"Get back here!" Joshua gave chase. "I'm not in the mood for this, Irving!" When he rounded the corner of the house to go into Dolly's backyard, he found Irving pacing back and forth on the porch. Having played that game more often than he would have liked, Joshua knew that if he immediately ran after him, Irving would run. Better to entice the feline to come to him. Taking the canister of treats out of his pocket, Joshua casually came from around the corner of the house and shook the treats for Irving to hear. The sound of the treats rattling in the canister never failed to bring Irving running from any corner of the house when they were home.

As soon as he saw Joshua, Irving ran up onto the porch, pried open the screen door with his paw, and slipped into the house.

"No!" Joshua was cursing the embarrassment that would surely come upon knocking on the door and then explaining to Dolly Houseman about how his cat had barged into her home like he owned the place.

Sucking up the nerve to knock on her door, Joshua felt the flush come to his face as he realized that this would be the first time he would face her knowing that she was a retired madam. Surely, she would see the embarrassment on his face when he looked at her and envisioned her running a cathouse.

Maybe that's why Irving has struck up such a friendship with her.

Joshua lifted his fist. Before his knuckles met the wooden door, he saw that it was not latched. It swung open when he rapped on it.

Irving stuck his head out through the crack and looked up at Joshua. He could see sparks of light in the cat's emerald green eyes where they caught the light from the porch lamp. "Rhawl!" the cat meowed before coming back out, rubbing against Joshua's legs, and then trotting back inside.

Joshua pushed the door open to step into the dark kitchen. "Ms. Houseman?" he called out in a loud voice. "It's Josh. I'm sorry to bother you. Your door was open and Irving came in. I'm in your kitchen. Are you home?"

Irving meowed from the middle of the kitchen.

"Irving, come on," Joshua hissed at him. "Come to Daddy." He shook the can of treats again.

Irving spun around and bound out of the kitchen into the dining room.

"You're in big trouble, cat!"

Joshua scurried after him. In the dining room, Irving was waiting on the other side of the table. When Joshua came around the table, he found that the chair at the head of the table was overturned.

What happened here?

Then, he noticed that the centerpiece was knocked over and the plastic flowers were scattered across the table.

Irving hissed before trotting into the next room.

Shoving the can of treats into his pocket, Joshua ran into the living room where Irving was circling a fallen figure in the middle of the floor. In the dark, Joshua was unable to tell for sure who it was, but he had a good guess. He flipped on the wall switch to bathe the living room in light.

At her advanced age, it would have been assumed that Dolly Houseman had collapsed from a heart attack or stroke. But that notion was easily dismissed by the pool of blood forming under her body, which was covered with unmistakable stab wounds.

Blood splatters covered the wall and the furniture.

The room looked like a blood bath.

Irving pawed at the elderly woman's bloody face.

Joshua started to rush to her when he suddenly thought about who had done it. *Are they still here in the house?*

The answer came in an instant when he saw a shadow move on the wall across from him.

Joshua whirled around. The last thing he saw before the lights went out was the bloody knife raised up over his head and coming down toward him.

He threw up his arm to block the blow of the butcher knife that came down on him. At the same time, he threw a fist into the assailant's midsection.

He heard the knife clatter when it hit the floor.

The assailant tackled Joshua and propelled him backwards. They stumbled together over the coffee table, which collapsed under their weight.

Joshua tried to get a look at his assailant's face in the glow of the porch light shining in through the window. All he could see was a shadow from the shade of the black hoodie that he had pulled up to cover his head.

The dark figure scrambled to his feet and turned to run, but Joshua sprung up to tackle him by his legs. Desperate, the assailant kicked Joshua in the face to get him to release his grip on him. Then, he jumped to his feet.

Refusing to give up the chase, Joshua climbed up onto his knees when the bookcase that the assailant pulled down from the wall collapsed on top of him.

As he was losing consciousness, Joshua could hear a man screaming while Irving screeched at an ear shattering pitch.

CHAPTER ELEVEN

"Mr. Thornton, are you okay? Can you hear me, Mr. Thornton?"

It all came back to him in an instant. Irving screeching and running away.

Dolly Houseman lying in the middle of her living room covered in blood. The pool of blood forming under her. The streaks of blood across the walls and furniture.

The knife coming down toward him.

Then, the lights had gone out.

Joshua jumped up onto his elbows. He felt a hand grasp his shoulder to ease him down. "Easy, Mr. Thornton. EMTs are on their way. So is Sheriff Sawyer."

Joshua recognized the voice.

Hunter Gardner.

His vision cleared as he focused in on Hunter kneeling next to him. "Are you okay, Mr. Thornton? Do you remember what happened?"

Joshua looked beyond Hunter to Miss Houseman.

Then, he turned back to Hunter, who was gazing at him. Spotting the dark hoodie that Hunter was clad in, he remembered. The assailant's jacket was identical to the one Hunter was wearing.

"Did you see who did this, Mr. Thornton?" Hunter was asking. "Looks like you're pretty lucky."

"Josh?" Cameron called out while running in through the front door. Carrying his medical bag, Tad was directly behind her. Cameron practically pushed Hunter out of the way to get to him. "What happened, Josh?"

Instead of answering, Joshua could only look at Hunter in his dark hoodie.

"I was coming to see Tracy when I saw some guy come running out of the house into the street," Hunter told her. "Irving was attached to his head. I almost hit the guy with my car. He stopped and grabbed Irving off his head with both hands and hurled him down onto the hood of my car and kept on running. Then, Irving ran back in here. The front door was open so I followed him and found this." He gestured at the dead body. "Then I found Mr. Thornton under the bookcase. I thought he was dead until I heard him moaning."

"Did you get a look at the guy?" Joshua sat up to ask Hunter only to find Tad, who was shining his pen light into his eyes, blocking his view.

"No, the hoodie was pulled up over his head," Hunter said. "After throwing Irving down, he took off down the street and turned onto Fifth toward Indiana."

"No! Why? Who—" Cameron got up and went over to where Dolly Houseman was laying on her stomach and covered with stab wounds. "Who could do this to an old woman? What kind—"

"What's going on here?" Curt Sawyer shouted when he came through the front door. "Is this some sort of party?"

"Dad!" Tracy ran through the door.

Curt Sawyer blocked her way to Joshua. "You need to wait outside, Tracy."

"Tracy!" Hunter got up and went to her. "I was coming to see you when—"

"Tell her outside." Curt ushered Hunter and Tracy out the door. "Don't go anywhere until we get your statements."

Joshua was peering around Tad to where Cameron was checking Dolly Houseman's body for a pulse. When Irving came near her, Cameron scooped up the cat and backed away from the scene. Wordlessly, she shook her head at the sheriff to communicate that Dolly Houseman was dead. She stroked the big cat while they gazed down at the elderly woman.

"Do you hurt anywhere, Josh?" Tad was asking him.

"I'm in better shape than Dolly." When Joshua pushed the pen light away, he noticed blood on his sleeve going all the way up to his shoulder. Then he noticed blotches going up his leg to his rump where he landed when the killer tackled him. "Look at all this blood." He pointed out the spray pattern across the wall. "It was a blood bath."

"She had to have been stabbed in a major artery or vein." Tad put the pen light away and offered his arm. "Judging from the height of the blood spatter, most likely the jugular." He glanced around while helping Joshua to his feet. "Doesn't look like anything was taken that I can see."

"Our guy has to be covered in blood, too," Joshua said. "Between the murder and the fight we got into, he had to have gotten blood on him." With relief, he recalled that Hunter had no blood on his clothes.

"Well if you got into a fight with the killer, there had to be some transference." Tad noted the blood and tears in Joshua's clothes. "That means you're wearing evidence. Take one of the crime scene investigators back across the street with you and get processed so that we can catch this creep."

"Will do, boss." Joshua took Cameron's arm. "Are you okay?" he asked her in a soft voice.

She cast a quick glance into his eyes before turning her attention back to Irving, who was chewing on one of his paws while she held him. "I'm okay." She coughed to cover up the sob in her voice.

"I don't believe in animals being so smart," Joshua stroked the top of Irving's head, "but if he hadn't come running in here ..." He stopped when he noticed Irving shaking his paw before putting it back into his mouth. Something was hanging from his claw that was driving the cat crazy. "What have you got there?" To Joshua's surprise, Irving let him grasp the paw to examine it. Long strands of dark hair had become caught in the cat's claws. "Tad, come here and take a look at this."

"What is it?" Cameron asked while holding Irving still.

"Hunter said that Irving was attached to the man's head when he went running out into the street," Joshua said. "He had the hood up, but I think Irving managed to yank some of the hair out of his head."

Tad was peering closely at the strands of hair caught on the cat's claw. "They're too long to be his own." He glanced at Joshua. "And too dark to be yours or Dolly's." He knelt down next to his medical bag and removed an evidence envelope. With a pair of tweezers, he removed the strands of hair from Irving's claw. As soon as it was gone, Irving shook his paw and uttered a sound that was a mixture between a meow and a growl. Not wanting him to disturb any possible evidence, Cameron tightened her grip on him when he tried to wiggle out of her grasp.

Tad and Joshua examined the hair in the bag. "He managed to get a full lock, follicle and all," Tad said. "It may be optimistic, but I think we might have his DNA." He sealed the envelope and marked it.

"Problem may be in proving that Irving got that hair from the killer and not someone who happened to be walking by," Joshua said.

"It's still a start." With a toss of her head, Cameron gestured for Joshua to step outside of the house to allow the officers to process the scene. "I need to get Irving out of here before he wears out his welcome."

"Looks like it's our lucky day." Tad caught their attention from where he was kneeling near Dolly's head. He snapped a picture of what had caught his attention.

"What did you find?" Joshua turned back to him.

Still clutching Irving, Cameron waited in the background as close as she dared to get.

Tad pointed his finger toward Dolly's hand. A gold chain with a pendant was wrapped around her fingers. "The clasp is broken."

"She yanked it off her killer," Cameron said.

Carefully, Tad removed the chain from the elderly woman's hand and dropped it into an evidence bag. He held it up to the light. "There's hair on it."

"Same color as the hair Irving got?" Cameron asked the two men who were studying the find on the other side of the room.

"No," Tad said, "this hair is silver, like Josh's." He turned to Joshua.

"The killer tackled me before I could get close enough to examine the body."

"I know," Tad said with a grin. "The hair matches you, but not the pendant. This looks too girlish for you."

Joshua took the bag and examined the hair himself. "'It's also three times longer than my hair."

"The hair Irving got off the killer was dark," Cameron said. "But that hair is silver. How many killers were there, Josh?"

"I only got into a fight with one," Joshua said. "And the guy doused the lights so I never saw him. I couldn't tell you what color his hair was."

"Well, you two and Irving need to get out of the crime scene." Snatching the evidence bag out of Joshua's hand, Tad pointed to the door.

As soon as Joshua stepped outside, Tracy raced up to escort him home. Joshua got a forensic officer to go with him and left Cameron to collect as much information as she could from those working the scene. He saw that Hunter was being questioned by Sheriff Curt Sawyer.

Cameron caught up with Tad when he came out of the house after ordering the morgue attendants to prepare Dolly Houseman for transport to his morgue.

"Awful lot of blood on the scene," she said to him.

Tad's face was pale. His eyes met Cameron. "I've known Dolly my whole life," he said with a husky voice.

"I'm sorry, Tad," she said in a low tone. "I've known her less than a day, but we did become friends. I promised her that I would find out who killed one of her girls, and now I'm going to find out who killed her."

"You're out of your jurisdiction, Cameron," Curt said from behind her. "I hate to be territorial, but this is our case."

"Don't you find it to be a pretty big coincidence that on the same day that Josh and I came to talk to you about Ava Tucker's murder, her madam, who asked for my help in finding Ava's killer, gets offed?"

The sheriff planted his hands on his hips. "For the sake of my professional relationship with your husband, I hope you're not suggesting something, Gates."

"Just saying," she replied. "Don't tell me that you don't find the timing interesting. Here's another coincidence. Mike Gardner has been missing for close to twenty years. He told Josh that he was investigating the murder of a prostitute. Dolly confirmed that he was investigating Ava's murder. Now, one day after his body is found, Dolly gets murdered in her own home." She asked the sheriff, "Was there any sign of a break in?"

"Not that we can see."

"That's not such a big clue," Tad said. "I know for a fact that Dolly didn't lock her doors."

"It has to be someone who knew that Dolly had managed to get me interested in the case," Cameron said.

"Not necessarily," Curt said. "She was an old woman who lived alone and didn't lock her doors. That makes her easy pickings for a kid out to rob her."

"She was stabbed multiple times," Tad said. "Clearly it was overkill. That points to a crime of passion. Not your usual type of murder that occurs during a break-in."

"Did you find the murder weapon on the scene?" Cameron asked both of them.

"Yes," Curt said, "it appeared to be a butcher knife from the victim's kitchen. Forensics is still working the scene. If we're lucky, there will be fingerprints on it."

"Weapon of convenience," she said. "Or the killer brought his own weapon but opted for the knife."

"Gates?" Curt asked.

"Yes, Sheriff?"

"Did you hear me say that this is my case?"

"Yes, I heard you," Cameron replied before turning to Tad. "When will you have the autopsy done?"

"I'll get on it first thing in the morning."

"Then I'll be calling you," she said.

"Hey, Chief," one of the deputies trotted up to them. "You're maybe going to want to see this."

Cameron didn't hesitate to follow the sheriff back inside the house. The deputy led them into the living room where Dolly Houseman's body was now covered with a white sheet.

"The morgue guys noticed it when they started to move the body." The deputy knelt down onto all fours and pointed under the sofa. "We didn't touch it. We thought you'd want to see it. She doesn't strike me as one to carry a cell phone."

Cameron knelt down next to the sheriff to peer under the sofa. A smart phone rested on the floor just out of plain sight.

The sheriff cocked his head to ask Cameron, "Is it the victim's?"

Cameron looked up to see Tad standing over them. "Did Dolly have a cell phone?"

Tad shook his head. "Dolly wasn't into all that. Look around. No computers, no e-readers, none of that stuff."

"It's not Josh's." Sitting up, Cameron noticed that the broken coffee table was directly behind her. "It must have fallen out of the killer's pocket while he was fighting with Josh."

Instructing the deputy to bag the cell phone for evidence, the sheriff rose to his feet and offered his hand to help Cameron up. "This may be an easy case after all."

"Unless that phone is a burner," Cameron said. "If so, we might get lucky and be able to trace it by the serial number to where the killer bought it if he used a credit card."

"Gates—" The sheriff once again tried to remind her that it was not her case when he was interrupted by a man's scream from out on the street. "You better take Irving home before Mr. Grant has a stroke."

The scent of chicken cordon bleu and the light hollandaise sauce wafted into the living room from the kitchen to remind Cameron that she hadn't eaten her second dinner yet. The grandfather clock in the living room announced that it was eleven o'clock. Too late for dinner, but certainly a good time for a little snack.

The scent was enough to make Irving wiggle out of her arms. Running, he hit the hardwood floors in the foyer and scurried down the hallway to the kitchen.

Expecting to find Joshua taking advantage of his daughter's cooking, Cameron pressed through the swinging door to find Tracy and Hunter Gardner at the kitchen table in the midst of a lip lock.

Backing out of the kitchen, Cameron cleared her throat loudly before stepping into the room.

Tracy and Hunter parted like they had been hit with a bolt of lightning. In an effort to put distance between them, Tracy rushed around behind the kitchen counter. "I didn't know anyone was up." She yanked open the dishwasher.

"I smelled the chicken and remembered that with all of the excitement none of us ate," Cameron explained while noticing that there was a dirty plate in front of Hunter.

"Uh," Tracy stammered, "some of us did. Dad wasn't hungry, but ... you know Donny. There was only one breast left after Donny was done and I just now gave it to Hunter. I didn't think you'd be hungry."

A hint of fear came to Hunter's eyes while he looked up at Cameron. "Tracy offered. If I had known it was yours—"

"Actually, I'm hungry for milk and cookies," Cameron interrupted him. It was a lie when she uttered it, but once she got the words out of her mouth, she realized that some Oreos dunked in milk did appeal to her.

Tracy hurriedly took a glass out of the cupboard and filled it with milk while Cameron got the package of cookies. When Tracy tried to remove a few cookies to put on the plate, Cameron refused the offer. Tucking the whole package under her arm, she took the glass of milk. When she turned around, she saw that Hunter was sitting straight up in his seat with his back to her. He looked afraid to move. "Have a nice evening," she said with a wicked grin.

"You too," Tracy said.

"Good night, Hunter," Cameron made a point of saying to him.

He refused to look at her. "Good night, Ma'am."

Upstairs, Cameron found Joshua stretched out on the bed with an ice pack pressed against the top of his head. With his eyes shut, she was uncertain if he was asleep or not. While she had been prying information from the sheriff and his deputies across the street, Joshua was being processed by the forensics team. They had taken his clothes and scoured his body for pieces of physical evidence. They had even clipped his fingernails and run a fine-toothed comb through his hair in search of anything that might have connected them to the killer. It was a long process. After they left, Joshua had showered, put on his bathrobe, and laid down on the bed to relax.

"Cookie?" she whispered to him. Removing one from the package, she stepped over Admiral's sleeping form on the floor next to her side of the bed and crawled into it.

Irving jumped up onto the bed. Seeing Joshua, he paused as if surprised before creeping up to take a closer look at him.

"No, thanks." Joshua opened his eyes, lifted the ice pack from his head, and sat up.

Taking that as an invitation, Irving pressed his body up against Joshua's side and stretched out against him.

"If we don't look like an old couple." Sitting cross-legged next to him, she dunked the cookie into her glass of milk. "The two of us with our concussions." Her attempt at a smile was weak.

"I don't have a concussion. Just a bruise." Placing the ice pack on the nightstand, Joshua offered her an equally weak smile. He even felt sorry for Irving, who was curled up against him and resting his head on his thigh. "I didn't know you knew Miss Houseman that well."

"I only officially met her today." She pulled out the cookie to check on how soft it was from the milk. Deciding that it was ripe, she popped the soggy goodie into her mouth.

Joshua took the glass from her and set it on the nightstand next to his side of the bed. He then reached across to her and eased her down next to him. Welcoming his touch when he brushed her hair across her forehead, she rested her head on his shoulder.

Not enjoying being wedged between them, Irving scurried to the foot of the bed and jumped up onto the dresser. He shook out his fur as if to express his displeasure.

"She was a feisty old bird," Cameron told Joshua, "Just like I aspire to be when I'm her age. It had to be Ava and Mike's killer."

"It's quite a big jump to assume that the same person who murdered Ava killed her son, Mike."

"Who else could it be?" Cameron lifted her head to peer up at him.

"Why kill Dolly now?" Joshua asked. "Mike was killed eighteen years ago."

"But his patrol car was found yesterday," she reminded him. "Theoretically, that woke up the beast from the bottom of the lake. Did Sawyer tell you that the superintendent from the West Virginia State Police, Henry MacRae, came all the way up from Charleston to check on the case?"

"I know Hank MacRae," Joshua said. "He's very big."

"He's an idiot," Cameron said.

"Because he brought up Nick's murder?"

She looked up at him. "Sawyer told you."

"Jan told me." He brushed her hair out of her eyes. "I don't think MacRae knew Nick Gates was your husband."

"Nick was killed by a drunk driver."

"Who left the scene and was never caught," Joshua said.
"Do you—"

"No," he said firmly, "there's no connection between Nick and Mike. Mike was shot."

"Which proves MacRae is an idiot," she said. "If he was so brilliant, why did he jump on trying to tie Mike's murder here to Nick's in Pittsburgh?"

"Because he is exploring various possibilities to come up with a solution," he said. "Just like you. Don't you think it's a big jump from Mike's murder to Dolly Houseman?" he said.

"Dolly told me that Mike had met with her to discuss Ava's murder and told her that he was investigating it."

"Did she know that Mike was Ava's son?" Joshua asked.

"That, she didn't mention." She sat up. "Maybe Ava told her." She bent over him where he was propped up on the pillows at the head of the bed.

Joshua shrugged his shoulders. "Maybe ... but would Ava have told Dolly if it was a family secret?" He reached up toward her throat to where her shirt was buttoned up.

"Jan said Dolly has been talking about her girl's murder for years, trying to get justice for her."

"True." He unbuttoned the top two buttons of her shirt. "She kept saying 'her girl.' I thought she was senile."

"If Dolly knew Mike was Ava's son, don't you think it's possible that she initiated his investigation into the murders—especially when she found out that he was a deputy?" She glanced down to where Joshua had unbuttoned her shirt down below her bra.

A smile crossed Joshua's face.

With a wicked grin, she threw her leg over his midsection and straddled him. "Maybe it was Dolly who told him the truth about being adopted and Ava being his mother. Then, because he was a police officer, he went after his mother's killer and that was what got him killed?"

"Anything is possible." Joshua reached up to slip her shirt down off her shoulders. "However, with both Dolly and Ava dead, and Mike, how can we know if that is the link in all three murders?"

"Let me think about that." She looked down at her open shirt and where he was eyeing her. The corners of her lips curled in anticipation. "What are you doing?"

"Proving that I'm being truthful to you," he said while directing his gaze at her breasts. He grasped her by the back of her neck and pulled her down to kiss her passionately on the lips.

"Oh, I love a man who's not afraid of facing the truth." She reached up to turn off the light.

CHAPTER TWELVE

The answer to their question about a potential connection between Dolly Houseman and Mike Gardner came by noon the next day when Sheriff Curt Sawyer stopped by to deliver the latest development in their murder investigation.

As he usually did when he knew Tracy Thornton was in town, the sheriff managed to move the meeting into the kitchen where she served him the last of a breakfast casserole that she had prepared for brunch.

"There was no sign of a break in," the sheriff said. "Miss Houseman wasn't one to make many phone calls. Yet, in the last five weeks, there was a change in her call pattern."

"What change?" Cameron asked.

"She made a handful of calls to East Liverpool City Hospital," Sawyer said. "Tad is checking to see who she spoke to there. Could have been a friend who was in the hospital. We don't know. Then, they stopped. Then, a call to a Weirton phone number, which is registered to a bar featuring exotic dancers. After that, her call pattern returned to normal."

"She called a strip joint?" Joshua asked. "What was that about? Before yesterday, I would have said that that doesn't sound anything like the Dolly I thought I knew."

"That's not the only peculiar thing. You'll never guess who she made the sole beneficiary of her will," he said to Joshua while Tracy poured him a mug of hot coffee.

"She had no family," Joshua said. "Charity? Maybe the best little whorehouse in Texas." He flashed a grin at Cameron who saw the humor in his quip.

"No." Curt chuckled before dropping his bomb. "Hunter Gardner." Smiling at the silence that dropped over the kitchen, the sheriff took the first bite of his breakfast casserole.

Cameron noticed the pink that came to Tracy's cheeks while she quickly glanced away to hide her blush. Tracy had to be wondering if she had told Joshua about walking in on her and Hunter the night before. Truthfully, it had slipped Cameron's mind.

Tracy found her voice first. "Hunter barely knew Ms. Houseman."

"Are you sure about that?" the sheriff asked.

"Even if Hunter did know Dolly, he didn't do it," Joshua said. "He has red hair. The hair Irving yanked out of the killer's head was dark brown."

"You know when we catch the guy, his slimy lawyer is going to claim that his hair fell out someplace else in the neighborhood and Irving picked it up." Remembering that Joshua was a lawyer, the sheriff added in his direction, "No offense, Josh."

"None taken."

"We can't ignore the fact that now Hunter has motive for killing Dolly," Cameron said.

Tracy stepped in her direction with the force of an enraged bear. "Hunter would never—"

"Forensics already cleared Hunter of the murder," Curt said. "The blood on his shoes and clothes are consistent with his statement that he came onto the scene after the murder had been committed and got blood on his clothes while checking on Miss Houseman and your father."

"Then why is Cameron saying Hunter has a motive?" Tracy asked.

"Because he does," she replied. "It could have been a murder for hire. He wouldn't have had to have been on the scene."

With his arm out to separate them, Joshua stepped into the line of fire. "No one is trying to pin Ms. Houseman's murder on anyone. But we would be negligent to ignore him benefiting from her death."

"Oh, yeah," Tracy said, "I can see Hunter killing a sweet elderly lady like Ms. Houseman for her drafty old house and a couple hundred dollars she has stashed in her cookie jar."

"Actually," Curt said over the rim of his coffee mug, "it's a drafty old house, ten point two million dollars in trust, and a couple thousand dollars cash stashed in a cookie jar." He shoved a fork full of the scrambled egg casserole mixed with cheese and hash browns into his mouth and uttered a moan of pleasure.

"Ten point two million?" Joshua gasped. "How?"

Tracy clutched her throat.

"That whorehouse was a very popular place," Curt said.

"What whorehouse?" Tracy asked. "Was Ms. Houseman running a whorehouse across the street?"

"Not across the street," Cameron answered.

"Did Hunter inherit a whorehouse?" Tracy asked. "I thought those were illegal. Is that—"

"Later," Joshua said in a firm tone.

"According to Ms. Houseman's lawyer," Curt said, "Dolly had inherited a bundle from her father. Plus, her business brought in a ton of money. The house that she lives in has been without a mortgage for the last forty years or so."

"She's lived very frugally," Joshua noted. "She doesn't even have a car. She walked into town for her groceries."

"However, she did have a regular income," Curt said. "Her social security was direct deposit, which she never touched. Also, according to the bank, she made monthly deposits into her account, always in cash, like clockwork on the first of the month. Ten thousand dollars. Not a dollar more. Not a dollar less."

"Ten thousand dollars in cash?" Cameron asked.

"Does Hunter know about the inheritance?" Tracy asked.

"Dolly's lawyer called him first thing this morning while I was meeting with him," Curt said. "It's standard operating procedure to find out who stood to gain from her death. Gardner was absolutely clueless about being in Houseman's will. The lawyer will tell him in person when he meets with him later today. He has no idea what's coming his way."

"I can vouch for that," Tracy said in a firm tone. "We both thought Ms. Houseman was a poor little old lady."

"I know Hunter is no killer," Curt said before turning to Joshua. "Our department is sponsoring him at the police academy. We did a full background check on him, including psych tests. He's completely clean. If the academy even suspects Hunter of being a person of interest in this murder case, he'll be kicked out of there so fast—" He snapped his fingers.

"So we need to keep this hush-hush," Joshua said with a nod of his head.

"How do you keep a multi-million dollar inheritance hush-hush?" Cameron said. "This is big news." With a sweep of her arm, she gestured at the modest red brick house across the street. "No one knew Dolly Houseman was the grand madam of the best little whorehouse in the valley."

"Are you serious?" Tracy gasped. "That sweet little old lady was a madam?"

"And used to be your father's babysitter," the sheriff added.

"Seriously?" Tracy stepped back and looked her father up and down.

"See?" Cameron pointed out. "The news media is going to eat this up."

"I know," Joshua said. "That's why we aren't going to let the news media know about it." He turned in his seat to the sheriff who was scraping the bottom of the casserole pan with his fork in hopes of getting some last remnants of breakfast. "When is Gardner meeting with the lawyer?"

"Later on this afternoon," Curt said. "Do you think we should be there?"

"Yes," Joshua said. "I want to see his reaction to the news that he's a multi-millionaire."

As much as Cameron wanted to stay in on the conversation between Joshua and Sheriff Sawyer, she had other matters to contend with. When Tracy ran up the stairs to her room, Cameron was close behind.

She counted to ten before throwing open the bedroom door and catching Tracy on her cell phone. "It's not a good idea to give Hunter a heads up about what he's coming into."

Tracy almost dropped her phone. "This murder is not your case."

"Do you really want to put your father in the position of prosecuting your boyfriend?" Cameron cocked her head at her. "Does even know about Hunter and you?"

"Not really." She dropped the phone onto the bed. "In case you haven't noticed, Dad is real protective of us, especially me."

"Daddy's little girl." Cameron closed the door.

"Sarah is different," Tracy said. "She refused to put up with it, but me …" She shrugged her shoulders. "I kind of like having my daddy watching over me, but then I didn't want him scaring Hunter away. Then there was the matter of Hunter always wanting to take his dad's place in the sheriff's department. He didn't want to get in because he was dating Joshua Thornton's daughter."

"So you two kept it a secret."

"It wasn't difficult," Tracy said. "Hunter was in the Marines and did two tours in Iraq. I was up in New York going to college. We rarely saw each other, which was great. We knew that, with being apart the way we were, if we managed to feel the same way we did back when we first fell in love, we were meant to be together."

Cameron placed her hands on her hips. "How long has this been going on between you two?"

Tracy cleared her throat. "Senior prom." Her cheeks turned pink. She shrugged. "Hunter's girlfriend broke up with him right before prom because she was cheating on him with my boyfriend. They suggested that we swap dates. It was no big deal because both Hunter and I kind of suspected that they were cheating on us anyway. We went as friends, but by the end of the evening … and we were both going away. Talk about timing."

With a sigh, Cameron sat on the edge of the bed next to her. "Yeah, talk about timing. Your boyfriend is in a terrible position. He has the most to gain from Dolly Houseman's murder."

"He had no idea," Tracy said. "Why would she leave it all to him? And where did all that money come from? What's this about a whorehouse?"

"I'll explain it all to you." Cameron stood up. "In the meantime, my car is at the police station in Pennsylvania. Can you give me a ride? We can talk on the way."

Tracy stood up. "Are you going to tell Dad about me and Hunter?"

"You mean tell your dad that his little princess is dating a murder suspect? That will go over real well."

"He wasn't a murder suspect when we started dating," Tracy said.

"I don't keep secrets from your dad," Cameron said, "but I will give you a chance to tell him yourself."

She picked up the phone. "I need to call Hunter."

Cameron snatched the phone out of her hand. "After he meets with the lawyer. You'll be hurting his chances of clearing himself if you tell him about the money. Then he won't be surprised, and Sawyer and your dad will think that he knew about it before the murder, which would give him motive. The best way to help Hunter is to keep mum and drive me to Hookstown."

"You're supposed to be on medical leave," Lieutenant Miles Dugan yelled across the squad room to Cameron from his office door when he saw her introducing Tracy to the desk sergeant.

"Good to see you, too, Chief," Cameron called back to him while crossing the office to greet him. "I'd like you to meet my step-daughter, Tracy."

Tracy clasped his hand in a firm grip. "Nice to meet you, Lieutenant."

"Is this the step-daughter who's in the CIA?" the lieutenant asked with a grin.

"Yes, I am." Tracy returned the grin. "My specialty is international cuisine. You won't believe all the secrets they taught me at the Culinary Institute of America. They don't call themselves the CIA for nothing."

"Maybe you can teach Gates here a thing or two," he said.

"I doubt it," Cameron said.

With a laugh, he told Tracy, "As you can see, she's too hard headed to learn anything. She's got two weeks sick leave after jumping off a two-story building, and where is she? Here nagging me about something." He asked Cameron, "Why aren't you home playing house?"

"Because I have a murder to investigate."

"Figures," he replied. "Whose?"

"Douglas O'Reilly," she replied.

"Who's Douglas O'Reilly?" Tracy asked.

"Cold case," Cameron said.

"Suicide," the lieutenant countered. "Every newbie detective we get in here gets a visit from O'Reilly's mother claiming that her son was murdered. Haven't seen her lately. She's probably passed away. She has to be in her nineties if she's still alive."

"Has anyone bothered taking a look at the case?" Cameron asked, "or do they do like I did, just dismiss her as a poor old lady unable to accept reality?"

"If wasting your time investigating this non-murder will keep you out of my hair, Gates," the lieutenant said, "knock yourself out."

"I already did that," Cameron said. "That's why I'm on two weeks medical leave. Now give me the case file and we'll be on our way."

"Who is Douglas O'Reilly?" Tracy asked again once they were back in her car.

Cameron immediately opened up the file box and took out the case file to read while Tracy drove them toward the West Virginia state line.

"Your boyfriend's grandfather." Cameron flipped through the reports in the file in search of the medical examiner's report.

"Huh?"

"Hunter has a very interesting family legacy," Cameron said. "Did he tell you that his grandmother was a prostitute?"

"No," Tracy gasped. "Seriously?"

Finding the report, Cameron scanned the contents while trying to explain to Tracy. "Ava Tucker was a desperate sixteen-year-old girl. Her boyfriend went off to West Point. She decided to get herself knocked up when he came home for a visit. Only things backfired. His future shot in the foot, he ended up dead. His car was found at the bottom of Raccoon Creek … with him in it."

"Just like Hunter's dad."

"Police closed the case as a suicide. His mother said it was murder, but no one would listen. Ava had the baby and gave him to her sister and her husband to raise as their own. That baby was Hunter's dad. Ava went on to become a call girl at Dolly's Gentleman's Club. A few years later, she was murdered."

"Hunter's dad was investigating the murder of a prostitute when he disappeared," Tracy said. "Do you think all of this is connected?"

"Maybe," Cameron said. "I certainly think it warrants looking into. Your father will have a cow if you marry a man who comes from a long line of murder victims."

"I said nothing about us getting married," Tracy said.

"Yeah, right." Cameron laughed. "Take me to the morgue in East Liverpool. I want Tad to read this autopsy report."

"Do you see anything interesting in there?"

"Yeah," Cameron said. "I need Tad to confirm it, but I think Mrs. O'Reilly's maternal instincts were right."

Attorney Vince Rudolph's assistant had been directed to request that Joshua Thornton and Sheriff Curt Sawyer wait in the reception area of his small office while he met with Hunter Gardner.

In contrast to the type of lawyer that a multi-millionaire would go to, Vince Rudolph had a tiny office in an old three-story office building in downtown New Cumberland. The walls were thin and the windows were leaky enough for a breeze to feel like it was blowing through the dusty walls.

His office reminded Joshua of something out of a film noir.

"What would you do?" Curt asked in a low voice.

"About what?" Joshua asked before realizing Curt's question. "You mean if I found out that I was a inheriting a ton of money from someone I barely knew?"

"Yeah."

A slow smile came to Joshua's face. "I have a friend who that happened to. Mac Faraday. He lives in Deep Creek Lake. After twenty years of marriage, his wife left him. She didn't like being married to an underpaid detective and decided to trade up. On the day their divorce became final, Mac inherited two hundred and seventy million dollars from his birth mother—"

"Yeah, that was big news a few years ago," Curt said. "Turns out his mother was Robin Spencer—world famous author. She wrote those Mickey Forsythe movies."

"Books," Joshua corrected him. "The movies were made from the books."

"You know Mickey Forsythe?"

"Mac Faraday."

"But Mickey Forsythe was a homicide detective who came into a huge inheritance," Curt said.

143

"I know," Joshua said. "But Mickey Forsythe is a fictional character. Mac Faraday is a real guy who was a homicide detective who came into a huge inheritance." Seeing the confusion on the sheriff's face, he sighed. "It's complicated. Point is, do you want to know what Mac Faraday does now that he's rich and famous?"

"Living large I suppose?"

"He's a detective with the police department in Spencer, Maryland." Joshua shrugged his shoulders. "He doesn't like golf, and he's bad at tennis. He's perfectly happy investigating murders. It's who he is."

"What would you do?"

"Pay for all of my kids' colleges," Joshua said, "and continue putting slimy killers behind bars. It's who I am."

"Is this some sort of sick joke?" They heard Hunter shout from inside the office.

"I think he just found out," Curt said.

"I don't understand," Hunter yelled. "I don't think I even met—you have to have the wrong guy. She must have left it to someone else. Why me? People don't … how much?"

A sound of what appeared to be a scuffle came from inside the office before the door flew open and the attorney came out at a run. "Mary, can you get Mr. Gardner a glass of water please?" He rushed back inside.

Joshua and Curt followed him into the office to find Hunter sitting in a chair with his head between his knees.

"I think he's in shock," the lawyer whispered to them.

"This is a nightmare," Hunter muttered.

"I think you misunderstood me," Vince said. "It's a good thing. Did you hear me say how many millions—"

Mary, the assistant, hurried in with a glass of water, which she handed to Hunter.

"You don't understand," Hunter said while taking the glass of water. "I found the body."

"Actually, Josh found the body," Curt said.

"But the murder victim is leaving everything to me," Hunter said. "Do you know what that makes me? A person of interest. And Mr. Thornton is the county prosecutor. Like he's going to let me marry his daughter when I'm a prime suspect in a murder." He clutched his stomach. "Oh, this is terrible. This is a nightmare—an absolute nightmare."

Joshua's head was spinning. The last thing he had heard Hunter say was "marry his daughter." After that, everything was jumbled. What?

"Wait a minute," Curt said. "You're dating Tracy?"

"How long have you been—" Joshua couldn't even get the words out of his mouth. His throat felt tight.

Hunter shrugged. "A few years."

"Years!"

"I'm going to be sick."

"Now everyone stay calm," Vince said. "Hunter, once you get over the shock—"

"No, I'm going to be sick." Hunter jumped to his feet and ran for the bathroom. He slammed the door behind him.

"So am I." Joshua sank down into a chair. "Where's your other bathroom?"

"At least no one's shooting at anyone," Curt said.

"I would prefer that," Vince said while watching Joshua put his head between his knees. "I only have one bathroom." He took a handkerchief out of his pocket and wiped the sweat from the top of his bald head.

"Think of it this way, Josh," Curt said with a chuckle, "you're not losing a daughter, you're gaining a rich son."

Joshua lifted his head. Slowly, he turned to Vince. "Are you absolutely certain Hunter had no idea?"

Vince pointed to the bathroom door. "My reaction was the same as his when Dolly came in here last month and said she wanted Hunter Gardner to get it all. I was like, 'What's a Hunter Gardner?'"

"That was just last month?" Joshua asked.

Vince nodded his head. "She didn't have a will up until then. I had been bugging her for years to get one, but she said the state could take it because she didn't have any family. Then suddenly, out of the blue, she came in and wanted a will, wanted it all to go to Hunter, and wanted the will done ASAP."

Perplexed, Joshua shook his head.

"How is it that Dolly Houseman made so much money?" Curt Sawyer asked. "Ten thousand dollars a month is an awful lot of dough for an old woman who doesn't appear to have any means of employment."

"If she wasn't a little old lady, we'd be assuming that it was money gained illegally," Joshua said while directing his gaze at Vince.

Holding up his hands, Vince shook his head. "I have no idea where she got it and I didn't want to know."

"You had to suspect," Curt said.

"Of course, I suspected," Vince said. "My mother didn't raise any dummies."

"She had to have told you—" Joshua started to say.

"All she told me was that the money was a return from investments she and her father had made throughout the years."

"Investments throughout the years." Joshua looked up at Curt. "Tad told me that Dolly's was known as a place for movers and shakers in business and politics to have secret meetings."

"Sounds like the makings for extortion to me," Curt said.

"Dolly gave Cameron a bunch of stuff from the cathouse. I bet we can find something in there." Joshua stood up as Hunter came out of the bathroom.

"Mr. Thornton," Hunter said, "I guess you want to talk to me."

"Not right now, kid," Joshua said. "Congratulations on your inheritance." He stopped at the door and turned back to him. "Oh, and you're paying for the wedding."

Cameron and Tracy found Tad MacMillan asleep at his desk in the morgue.

"Is business slow?" Cameron tapped him on the shoulder on one side while standing on his other side.

When Tad woke up, he smiled as he saw Tracy. "How's my girl?"

"I thought Jan was your girl." Tracy greeted him with a hug.

"One of many."

"I thought you gave that up." She flashed him a naughty grin.

Casting a glance in Cameron's direction, Tad asked, "I hope you aren't letting her get you into trouble."

"The doctor told Josh that I shouldn't drive for a few more days," Cameron said. "So that leaves us playing Thelma and Louise."

"That's not good," Tad said.

"Tell me about it," Cameron said.

"If you're here to coerce the details of Ms. Houseman's autopsy from me," Tad said, "I'm not giving them to you."

"That's okay," she replied while opening the case file she had under her arm. "Josh will tell me. I want your opinion about something."

"What?" Tad glanced at Tracy, who responded with a shrug of her shoulders.

Cameron placed the case file in his hands. "Read the details of this autopsy report and tell me what you think happened to the victim."

"Who is it?" Tad sat down at his desk.

"Just read the injuries and cause of death and tell me what you think."

Tracy and Cameron exchanged glances while Tad read through the pages of the report. Even though he was aware of them looking at each other and then down at him while he read, he took his time leafing through the pages.

"Cause of death was massive internal injuries and hemorrhaging," Tad said. "Broken back, ribs, legs, and pelvis. Consistent with being hit by a car."

"Not drowning?" Cameron asked.

"No water in the lungs," Tad said with a shake of his head. "He didn't drown."

"But he was found in a car at the bottom of Raccoon Creek," Cameron said.

"Well if he was found in the bottom of the lake, he was dead before he hit the water," Tad said. "Was he supposed to be driving?"

"Yep."

"But most of the injuries are on the right side of the body," Tad said. "If he was driving when he hit the lake, then he would have had injuries to the left side where he hit the door or got thrown from the car ... supposedly. Who is this?" He went to the front of the report to read the name. "Douglas O'Reilly. I remember him. Everyone said he drove his car into Raccoon Creek to commit suicide after his girlfriend got pregnant."

"That was the legend." Cameron took the report back. "As you can see, not all legends are true."

CHAPTER THIRTEEN

It was almost dark when Tracy slowly drove her blue sedan up the long rut-filled driveway to the old farmhouse tucked back in the rural Pennsylvania woods. Before she could come to a stop, three large dogs darted out from around the corner of the house and made straight for the car. Their snarling barks announced the visitors' arrival.

Afraid to open her door, Tracy peered out at the mud-covered dogs jumping on the side of her car. "Maybe we should have called first," she told Cameron.

"This is not something that I want to discuss over the phone." Seeing a woman with long salt and pepper colored hair dressed in worn jeans and a plaid shirt trotting toward them from the barn located further up the road, Cameron nodded her head. "She'll take care of them."

"If you're selling cosmetics, I don't need any," the woman called out to them above the barking while grabbing for dog collars. Based on the woman's weathered face and lack of attempt to pretty herself up, the reference to cosmetics appeared to be made in humor.

Stretching her arm across in front of Tracy, Cameron held up her police badge for the woman to see. "I'm Detective

Cameron Gates. I've come to talk to Mrs. O'Reilly about the death of Douglas O'Reilly."

At first, shock filled the woman's face. Then, anger seeped in. "Now? *Now* you want to investigate my brother's murder? Where have you people been for the last fifty years?"

"We got held up in traffic," Cameron said while flashing a smile that was begging for forgiveness.

"Better late than never," the woman grumbled while dragging the largest of the three dogs away from the car. "Come inside."

Seeing that the visitors were friends and not foes, the dogs allowed the two women to climb out of the car, but not without sniffing their clothes.

"Mother's inside," the woman said over her shoulder while leading the way around the corner of the house to where a wooden porch stretched across the length of the two-story farmhouse. She kept hold of the huge shaggy dog's collar. Up on the porch, she yanked open the screen door and held it for Cameron and Tracy to step inside to a big old country kitchen that appeared as worn as the farm woman. Once inside, she released the dog after closing the door.

"Mother, we have visitors," she hollered.

The dog galloped out of the room and up the flight of stairs to the second floor.

Cameron introduced herself and Tracy to their host. "And you are ..." She offered her hand.

"Flo," she gave Cameron's hand a firm shake. "Flo O'Reilly. Doug was my big brother. My mother is Eleanor." Her tough demeanor lifted for an instant. "We were all very proud of him—getting into West Point and all. He was going to see the world, and ..." She looked around at the worn-out kitchen and her surroundings. "He was going to make our family proud and take care of us. After he died, I tried to pick up where he left off. I became an army nurse and ended up in Vietnam. Eventually, I came back here to take care of my folks. Pa died twenty years ago. He never got over …" She stopped to swallow. "Since Mother's stroke a couple of years ago, I've been taking care of the farm all by myself."

She led them up the staircase to a bedroom on the second floor. At the end of the hallway, she opened the door to a spacious bedroom. Sitting in a wheelchair by the window, a tiny elderly woman was gazing at the farmland and countryside.

"She used to love sitting out on the porch and admiring her rose garden," Flo said.

"Why not anymore?" Tracy asked.

"I can't carry her downstairs," Flo said in a low voice. "It was all we could do to get one wheelchair. So she has to stay up here."

Cameron tapped Tracy's arm to point out the dinner dishes on the bed tray that rested on the table by the window.

"Mom, we have visitors." Flo ushered them across the room. "She can hear okay and understand, but it's hard for her to talk since her stroke."

The elderly woman peered up at Cameron, who pulled up a chair to sit close to her.

The detective clutched the case file in her lap "Mrs. O'Reilly, I don't know if you remember me. I'm Detective Cameron Gates with the Pennsylvania State Police. You came to see me several years ago about the death of your son, Douglas."

Cameron saw hope come to the elderly woman's eyes. "I remember," she said in a low voice. She nodded her head to show Cameron that she understood.

"I decided to take a good look at your son's file," Cameron said, "and I believe you were right. He did not commit suicide."

"Someone did murder him?" Flo asked in an anxious tone.

Cameron didn't want to give away too much of her findings. "I took the autopsy report to another medical examiner, and he believes the injuries are consistent with Douglas being struck by a car. When I looked at the inventory of what was inside the car that they pulled up from the bottom of the lake, the Mustang had a new tire on the front driver's side, but there was no spare in the trunk. Also, the jack was missing." She turned her attention to the old woman. "Mrs. O'Reilly, I believe your son got a flat tire that evening. He was changing it on the side of the road. It was a Friday night. Dark. Someone hit him with their car."

"They were probably drunk," Flo said with anger.

"Could be," Cameron said with a nod of her head, "or they just plain panicked. Whatever happened, they decided to cover it up by dumping Douglas and his car in the lake. They probably intended for it to look like an accident. But when the police found out about Douglas' circumstances, they assumed he had committed suicide." She touched the elderly woman's hand. "I'm so sorry, Mrs. O'Reilly. Someone should have taken the time to read the file before. I'm sorry I didn't. But I'm going to do everything I can to find out who did this."

"You think it was an accident?" Flo asked. "What about Ava? Couldn't she have killed him when he dumped her after she got herself pregnant?"

"Do you know for a fact that Douglas was going to dump her?"

"We don't," Eleanor O'Reilly said. "Douglas refused … to tell us what … he was going to do."

"She swore she didn't see him," Flo said. "I always thought she was lying."

"Do you know where she is?" Tracy asked. "Now that we know he didn't commit suicide, we should certainly question her. If he dumped her, then she had motive to kill him."

"She's dead," Flo said before Cameron had a chance to respond.

Playing dumb, Cameron asked, "How long ago did she die?"

Flo shrugged. "Decades ago. I don't know the details. People talk. Someone—I don't even remember who—told me that Ava had given the baby up for adoption and then started turning tricks. One of her johns throttled her to death. She probably deserved it. Her last name was Tucker. Ava Tucker. I'm sure your people should be able to find out what happened." She sighed. "Doug's baby would be grown up by now. In his late forties. Wish I knew how he turned out." She went to the end table next to the bed and took a tissue from the box to blow her nose.

"We'll find out what happened to Ava as we dig deeper into this case," Cameron said. "I'll see to it personally. Can you think about anything that happened about that time? Strange phone calls or letters. Very often, in a circumstance like this—"

"Like money?" Flo asked.

"What about money?"

Flo rubbed her face with a hand that was filthy from her work in the barn. "A long time ago. It started years after Douglas died. For a while, by the third or fourth of the month, we would get an envelope with cash in it. A couple of hundred dollars. This went on for years."

"No," the elderly woman mumbled in a slurred voice. "Blood money. You shouldn't …"

"We needed it, Mother," Flo said.

"Was there a letter with it?" Cameron asked Flo.

"There was always a card saying that they were very sorry," Flo said. "Nothing else. No signature. Just cash inside."

"I don't suppose you kept the envelopes and cards," Tracy asked.

"Those are long gone," Flo said. "We kind of figured that it was from whoever had killed Doug. We thought that if the police weren't going to investigate that we should go ahead and make him pay this way."

"Are you still getting that money?" Cameron asked.

"It only went on for a few years," Flo said. "Just as suddenly as it started, it stopped coming."

"Do you remember when it started?" Cameron asked.

"Not exactly."

"Blood money." The elderly woman banged her wrinkled hand on the arm of her wheelchair.

"Let me see." Flo rubbed her fingers through her long gray hair. "I was fifteen—just started the ninth grade when Doug was killed that September second. He was nineteen. It was right after I graduated from high school that we got the first envelope," she said with a grin at being able to remember. "Then, it stopped in the spring before the bicentennial. Nineteen seventy-six."

"How do you remember that?" Tracy was impressed.

"Because that winter the roof caved in on the barn," Flo said, "after a major snow storm. So Dad and I counted on the money the next month to make the deposit for the contractor to rebuild it, but the money never came. Dad and I ended up building that roof ourselves—the two of us. We were working on it during the bicentennial Fourth of July. So I know exactly when it stopped coming. After the blizzard in nineteen seventy-six. No more money came after that."

"So something happened to make the person stop sending it, which we can assume he was doing out of guilt for killing Doug," Cameron said.

"That's a big assumption," Tracy said.

"It's all we've got right now." Cameron patted Eleanor's hand. "But it's enough to get started. You take care of yourself, Eleanor. I'll be back, and we're going to have answers for you."

Tracy waited for them to climb into the car before she asked Cameron. "How can you possibly get answers for them? They have no copies of the envelopes. I doubt if the car is still around after fifty years."

"We have pictures of Doug O'Reilly's body and his car," Cameron said. "Plus, I have a hunch about why the money stopped coming."

"Why?"

"Doug's killer got murdered."

CHAPTER FOURTEEN

"Looks like we have a full house," Cameron said when Tracy turned her car into the driveway to find it filled with vehicles. In addition to Joshua's SUV and Donny's truck, the sheriff's cruiser and Hunter's red Mustang were lined up around the cobblestone circle. Tracy had to park at the end of the line near the street.

"I hope you have enough food to feed everyone," Cameron said.

"Sheriff Sawyer's stomach is a bottomless pit." Tracy grinned. "It will be a contest between him, Donny, and Hunter as to who can eat the most."

"It's not their stomachs," Cameron said. "It's your cooking."

"You know what they say," she replied while stepping out of the car, "the way to a man's heart is through his stomach."

"Is that really true?"

"It was my chicken marsala that won Hunter's heart for me."

The albums that Dolly had given to Cameron the day before were spread out across Joshua's study. Donny was laying on his stomach on the floor with Admiral stretched out in front of him. Donny used the dog's midsection for an easel on which to prop up the album he was examining. Stretched out along the length of Donny's back, Irving appeared to be reading the album from over his broad shoulders. Curt was sitting on the sofa with several albums opened up. Joshua was behind his desk with Hunter sitting at the corner. The two of them had their heads next to each other while they studied each page in one of the albums.

"I take it Hunter has been cleared of suspicion since you have included him in the investigation," Cameron said with her hands on her hips.

All four of them were startled.

Hunter turned toward Tracy, and then, thinking better of it, stopped and glanced over his shoulder back at Joshua.

"Go ahead and kiss her," Joshua said with a sigh.

With a wide grin, Hunter hurried across the room to take Tracy into his arms and kiss her on the mouth.

"You told him?" Tracy asked Hunter.

"Kind of."

"You're okay with this?" Tracy asked Joshua.

"Do I have a choice?" Joshua replied. "As long as Hunter pays for the wedding and doesn't break your heart …"

Reminded of his inheritance, Hunter grasped Tracy by the shoulders. "Did you know that Dolly Houseman was a multi-millionaire?"

"I did hear—"

"She left me all of it," Hunter said. "Do you know what that means? We can start that catering business you've always dreamed about."

"But she didn't leave it to me—"

"It will be ours when we get married." Hunter grasped her hands in both of his. "That's what we talked about. After I graduate from the academy and you finish with the CIA, then we'll come back here. Ms. Houseman left me the house, too. While we're finishing with school, we'll renovate it and put in a commercial kitchen and get you a catering van. I'll be a deputy and you'll be the biggest caterer in the Ohio Valley and I'll get fat eating your food but you won't mind because we love each other."

"Sounds like a plan," Curt said.

Cameron grabbed Joshua's arm. "Are they moving in across the street?" The specks in her eyes turned into flashing green sparks.

"Did Hunter just ask Tracy to marry him?" Donny asked Joshua. "Shouldn't he take her out on a date first to see what she's really like?"

"What do you say, Tracy?" Hunter asked her. "We'll have a big wedding next summer after you graduate."

Tracy squealed and jumped into his arms. Laughing, Hunter whirled her around in a circle.

"Great," Donny said, "with Tracy across the street, I'll never go hungry again."

Joshua felt Cameron's elbow stab him in the ribs. "I'm on it," he muttered before casually crossing the study to the couple enthralled in loving bliss. "Excuse me."

Suddenly aware of the others in the room, Hunter and Tracy parted.

Seeing tears of joy in his daughter's eyes, Joshua's heart skipped a beat. He swallowed before saying in a raspy voice, "I'm thrilled for you two."

"Oh, Daddy," she blubbered before throwing her arms around his neck, "I'm so happy you approve."

"So I can see," he said while hugging her back and kissing her on the cheek. He cleared his throat. "I hate to be a spoiled sport by bringing in the voice of reason here, but ..." He eased her arms from around his neck and took her hands into his. "About Dolly's house ..."

"What about it?" Tracy asked.

"You know Tad and I have been helping Dolly out," he said. "So I am familiar with that house. It's over seventy-five years old. It seems like once a week, Tad or I or both of us have to go over there to fix something. The plumbing needs to be replaced …"

"So we'll renovate it," Hunter said.

"The kitchen is very small," Cameron said. "If you're going to run a catering business, you'll need a lot more room for a commercial kitchen with big modern appliances."

"Plus, the house only has one bathroom and two bedrooms," Joshua said. "Nowadays, a young couple needs more room for a growing family." He draped his arms around both of their shoulders. "For what it's worth, here's what I suggest. Tracy," he kissed her on top of her head, "you have one more year of school in New York. Hunter, you're going away to the police academy. While you're both gone, sell this house across the street as-is to a realtor looking for a property to fix up and flip and invest in some acreage out in the country."

"Yeah, out in the country," Cameron said, "away from town."

"Build your own dream house," Joshua said. "With a big yard, garage, state-of-the-art–commercial-grade kitchen, plenty of bedrooms, and modern appliances."

"You could even build a loading dock with the driveway going right up to the back deck off the commercial kitchen," Curt said.

"And you have the beauty of the time," Joshua said, "plus the funds, so you can build the perfect home and have it ready to move right inside as soon as you come back from your honeymoon."

"I like that idea," Hunter said. "I've always wanted to live in the country. We could get a couple of horses."

"And build my own custom kitchen," Tracy gushed through tears of happiness. "That would be a dream come true." She threw her arms around Joshua's neck again. "Thank you, Dad. You always were so smart."

"That's what I'm here for." He smiled at the thumbs up that Cameron shot in his direction.

While Tracy and Hunter hurried away to the kitchen to make plans, Curt and Donny laughed at Joshua's brilliant maneuvering.

"Damn, you're good," Cameron said with awe in her tone.

Joshua chuckled. "I aced manipulation one-oh-one in law school."

"Why don't you want Tracy living across the street?" Donny asked. "I could start eating my meals over there."

"If they get a place out toward New Cumberland, I'll be able to drop in for lunch," Curt said. "Maybe Tracy will hire me to be a taste tester."

"I'm her brother," Donny said. "Only right she should give that job to me." He turned back to Joshua. "Don't you like Hunter, Dad?"

"Nothing against Hunter or Tracy," Joshua said. "But the place for grown children is out of the nest where they can keep their personal business and fights private. I can see it now. Every time she has a fight with her new husband, which she will because all newlyweds fight—"

"You and Cameron don't fight," Donny said.

"You haven't been paying attention," Joshua said.

"I prefer to call them marital moments," Cameron said. "If Tracy and Hunter lived across the street, one of them would be over here crying every time they had one of those moments." She shook her head. "Too close. They need a place all their own—out in the country—away from Daddy's nest."

"I wasn't just manipulating them." Joshua went back to the albums. "I was telling them the truth. That house is a wreck. For what it would cost to get it to pass inspection they could build a new one twice as big with a huge front and backyard."

"Is this the Ava we were looking for?" Cameron pointed to an eight-by-ten glossy picture at the front of the album on top. The photograph was of a red-haired young woman clad in a rose colored teddy, posed provocatively on a bed filled with pillows. Her long hair was thick and wavy and fell down past her shoulders with locks tickling her abundant breasts. The name written in calligraphy under the photo read "Ava."

"The only Ava in the albums." Joshua turned several pages back to show her pages of news clippings about the double murder at the private club in Newell, West Virginia. "These articles confirm that she was the Ava in question. They say she was a hostess at a private gentleman's club."

"Considering who the sheriff was at the time, her real profession was kept hush hush." Curt held up his hand and rubbed his fingers together to signify a payoff from Dolly's to the late sheriff had kept them in business. "Over the years as those in the know passed away, her real profession was completely forgotten … at least until Mike Gardner picked up on the case."

Uttering a sigh filled with remorse, Cameron closed the album. "He was trying to find out who killed his mother."

"And got killed himself looking into it," Donny said. "He must have gotten too close."

"I wish we had his notes," Joshua said. "If his notebook was in the cruiser, it would have become fish food more than a decade ago."

"And you're certain that his widow had no idea?" Curt asked.

Joshua shook his head. "Every time I have talked to Belle she claimed she didn't. All Hunter knows is from eavesdropping on grownups when he was a kid."

"That's the best way to find out family secrets," Donny said with a grin. "You'd be surprised what I've overheard."

"Maybe now that Mike's mother has admitted to the family secret," Cameron said, "Belle may be more open about what she knew and didn't know and when she knew it." She set the album aside and opened the one underneath it, which had a similar photograph on the first page.

The name on that album was Bianca. Like Ava, she was a redhead. Her look was more sophisticated, and she wore a royal blue teddy and thigh-high stockings with garters.

Working her way through the albums, Cameron read the name of each one of Dolly's girls and flipped through a few pages of the pictures before moving on to the next album. After Bianca, there was a Bambi, who had doe-like eyes. Morgan was a petite buxom brunette. There were also Farrah, Sabrina, and Jaclyn.

The bottom album was devoted to a hard-looking woman with long straight silver hair down to her shoulders. Her light blue eyes were penetrating. She was clad in a black leather and lace teddy. Her expression, lacking sensuality, was hard and intimidating.

Where's the whip? Narrowing her eyes, Cameron cocked her head to look more closely at the face.

The name underneath was Rachel.

Where have I seen her before?

Just as she was about to mentally put her finger on what was familiar about the woman in the picture, Curt's phone rang. He checked the caller ID. "It's the forensics lab." He pressed the phone to his ear and hurried out into the hallway.

"Not your common used-up hookers, huh?" Joshua whispered into her ear.

Cameron glanced at him from over her shoulder. Looking at the picture of the scantily clad silver-haired vixen, a smile tugged at the corner of his lips. Her stomach lurched.

She never thought of Joshua as the type to go for gorgeous women with "perky" breasts, as Dolly had referred to them. "All boys are naughty," the elderly madam had said.

Just how naughty? Certainly not my Josh.

"See something?" Joshua's question broke through her thoughts.

"Not sure." Slipping her fingers in between the pages of the album to look further, she turned her attention back to the album.

"There's over a dozen of these," Joshua told her. "A few seem to be memorabilia of the club and the girls who worked there throughout the years. Then, she has eight albums dedicated to specific girls. They even have news clippings about them. Some have marriage announcements. I guess these albums are for girls she considered special."

"Like daughters to her." Cameron was about to turn the page when Admiral's low pitch bark interrupted them. They could hear the huge dog galloping from the living room and into the foyer. She slapped the album shut.

"Hey, buddy, how are you doing?" they heard Tad greet the dog before coming into the study where he stopped in the doorway to admire the albums strewn across the floor. "What's this?"

"It's called a murder investigation," Donny said.

In response to Tad's questioning expression, Joshua explained, "We have concluded that our retired madam changed careers to extortion. She was making regular deposits of ten thousand dollars in cash to her bank account every month. So we're searching these books that she gave to Cam to see if we can find evidence of who she was blackmailing and over what. Ten thousand dollars a month in blackmail is a big motive."

"When I was talking to Dolly, she insinuated that a lot of different secret meetings took place at Dolly's," Cameron said. "So we could have more than one blackmail victim. That ten thousand didn't necessarily all come from the same source."

"That's true." Joshua turned to Tad, who was practically being pinned down in his chair by Admiral, who had climbed up for a petting. "Admiral, down! Donny, help Tad."

Donny jumped to his feet to pull Admiral off Tad.

"Were there any surprises in Dolly's autopsy?" Joshua asked him.

"Yes and no. She was stabbed in the neck and bled out." Tad straightened his clothes, now covered in dog hair and drool. "Whoever did it was very angry. It was a crime of passion. I counted forty-five stab wounds. Three in the neck. Some in the chest, and then in the back. Her jugular was practically cut all the way through. Massive blood loss was the cause of death."

"Certainly not a suicide," Donny said.

"We got lucky, though," Tad said. "Your killer got cut."

"Dolly fought back?" Donny asked.

"Not necessarily," Tad said. "You see, usually in these types of attacks, where this is so much blood, the knife will get slippery and the killer's hand will slip down onto the blade, causing him to cut himself. Forensics told me that they picked up a second blood type at the scene and that they think they have enough for a DNA comparison. The crime lab is working it up and will be calling you. If you're really lucky, they'll have someone in the national database to match it to."

"So we have a crime of passion," Joshua said. "The killer has to be someone Dolly knew."

Tad agreed. "Usually when you see that much overkill, it's someone who was furious about something—someone the victim is familiar with."

"Someone she made angry," Joshua said, "like by bleeding them dry."

"Dolly said something very cryptic when she gave these albums to me," Cameron said. "Something about how maybe she could be forgiven if she made things right before she died … " She paused to remember Dolly's exact words, but her memory failed.

"Doesn't surprise me." Tad scooped up Irving from where he was rubbing against his leg. Displeased about being picked up when he didn't want to be, Irving squirmed out of his hands, jumped over the arm of the chair, and scurried out of the room. "I found out who she was seeing at the hospital last month. It was Dr. Meyers. She had been having health issues. Dr. Meyers diagnosed it as cancer and tried to send her to an oncologist in Pittsburgh. She refused to go, and he never saw or heard from her again."

"At her age, she probably didn't think it was worth the heartache," Cameron said.

"Probably not," Tad agreed. "Based on her autopsy, she was much too far advanced. She would have been dead in four months."

"So that explains the call record." Curt came back into the room to overhear. "Dolly made those calls to the hospital to find out she was dying. Then, the next call that was out of ordinary for her calling pattern was to that dance joint down the river."

"If I knew I was dying, I would put my affairs in order," Joshua said, "not call a dance place."

"She did get her affairs in order," Curt said. "She had that will made up in the last month."

"Who did she call at the bar?" Joshua asked.

"The call was made to the main number listed in the directory," Curt said. "But I've got a suspicion about who she could have talked to. The owner's name is Larry Van Patton. Guess where he worked up until nineteen seventy-six."

"Dolly's?" Cameron asked.

Curt placed one finger on his nose and pointed another in her direction. "Dolly's closed up a few weeks after Ava Tucker's murder. Then Larry bought his own bar in Weirton. The question of the day is why did Dolly call her old bartender when she found out she was dying?"

"To put pressure on him," Joshua suggested. "Maybe he's a blackmail victim."

Curt shrugged his shoulders. "Background check says Larry had a boatload of cash to buy that bar."

"Maybe Dolly lent him the money to start his own business," Tad suggested. "Maybe the money that Dolly was collecting every month was payoff on loans that she had made while Dolly's was in operation—not blackmail."

"It's more fun to think Dolly bought Larry the bar as payment for a hit," Donny said.

"Speaking of paid hits," Curt said with a grin. "Forensics got a match in the federal database, CODIS, for the DNA they got off the hair that Irving ripped from our suspect's head. Anthony Tanner."

Sitting up straight in his seat, Tad exchanged glances with Joshua.

"Do you know him?" Cameron asked them.

"He got put away back in the nineties for second-degree murder," Tad said. "He beat a woman to death in New Cumberland. The thing is, the police were convinced that the victim's husband paid him to do it. There were all kinds of rumors to support it. But there was no clear evidence and Tanner refused to turn. He was offered manslaughter if he testified. He took second-degree murder and got fifteen years. The victim's husband took the life insurance and went out west. Someone told me that he was found dead in a seedy motel—in equally suspicious circumstances."

"Tanner was released six years ago," Curt said.

"Maybe he's back in business," Tad said.

"Where was Tanner when Mike disappeared?" Joshua asked.

"I checked already," Curt said. "Tanner was already doing time. He went to jail in ninety three. I put a BOLO out on him."

"If he's smart, he's laying low, if not out of the area," Cameron said. "Were his prints on the knife?"

"No usable prints on the knife," Curt said. "Killer most likely wore gloves."

"What about the medallion and the hair that Dolly had clutched in her hand?" Cameron asked.

"No hit in CODIS on the DNA for the hair, which they say came from a woman. "

"Woman?" Joshua asked. "But I only saw one perp in the house."

"Maybe there were two," Cameron said. "The female suspect escaped without you seeing her?"

"Forensics did get a partial fingerprint off the medallion," Curt told them, "which matches fingerprints on the cell phone. So we can assume that they belong to the same person. Forensics doesn't have a hit in the database yet. They're still running it."

Joshua said, "Even so, we do have the name of Anthony Tanner. That's a very good start. Now all we have to do is locate him."

"Well, I do know where one of our suspects can be found," Curt said. "Larry Van Patton, the sleazy bar owner who Dolly called when she found out she was dying. What do you say we find out what was so important for her to tell him that she reached out to him after all these years."

CHAPTER FIFTEEN

Late in the evening was the Blue Moon's busy time, and the sheriff, Joshua, and Cameron headed down Route Eight to Weirton, located on the other side of New Cumberland. The club that featured exotic dancers was owned by Dolly's former bartender, Larry Van Patton.

Thinking about the slightly naughty grin that she had seen on Joshua's face while he was looking over her shoulder at the silver-haired Rachel and Dolly's comment, "All boys are naughty," Cameron stared at the back of her husband's head in the front seat of Sheriff Sawyer's cruiser.

"Too bad your breasts aren't perkier." Rachel certainly had perky breasts. Joshua isn't into that type of stuff. If he was, I'd have seen it by now. Nudie magazines. Trolling porno sites on his laptop.

Then, her thoughts turned to a murder case she had investigated years before. A husband and father of three was found murdered in a park. The murderer ended up being his young male lover who had killed him in a rage because the victim refused to come out of the closet about their relationship. The wife had been married to him for over twenty-five years and they had grown children. She never suspected his real sexual tendency.

How well does anyone know anyone? I've known Joshua for only a year. Maybe …

"Here we are?" Joshua sang out in an upbeat tone from the front passenger seat. "Wake up, Cam. You look like you've fallen asleep back there."

As expected, the establishment had no windows. But in keeping with the name of Blue Moon, the club's exterior, including the door, was painted blue. The parking lot was completely filled with every type of vehicle possible.

The sheriff parked his cruiser and unsnapped his seatbelt. "Are we ready to go check out some flesh?" Through the rear-view mirror, he flashed Cameron a smile.

While the sheriff trotted to the main entrance, Joshua opened the cruiser's rear door for her to climb out.

"Josh …" she started to ask, and then thought better of it.

"What?" Joshua squeezed her hand. "What's wrong?" He took her face in his hands. "You don't look well. Maybe you've been exerting yourself too much. You were in the emergency room with a concussion only the day before yesterday."

"Josh," she asked, "do you think my breasts aren't perky enough?"

"Hey, you two," the sheriff called to them from the door. "You insisted on coming. Are we going in?"

Joshua gazed into her eyes while replying to him, "We're coming. Go on in, Curt. We'll be right with you."

With a shrug of his shoulders, Curt yanked open the door and went inside.

"What's this about?" Joshua asked her.

"You didn't answer my question about my breasts."

"You aren't thinking about getting surgery, are you?" Joshua said with genuine concern in his tone.

"No," she said with a squawk, "but the way you were looking at Rachel's pic—"

"Who's Rachel?"

"One of Dolly's girls," Cameron said. "The one with the leather teddy and perky breasts. You were looking at her—"

"I was looking at all of those call girls' pictures trying to find out which one Dolly was blackmailing and who would want to kill her." He pointed out, "If this had to do with male strippers, then I'd be expecting you to look at pictures of half-naked men, and it wouldn't bother me in the least."

"Even if someone told you that your breasts were less than perky?"

"Who told you that," Joshua replied, "and why is someone other than me examining their perk level anyway?"

The conversation was getting out of hand. Cameron gazed up at him while he peered down at her with concern filling his face. "Do you think I'm pretty?"

"You're the prettiest woman I know," he replied quickly. "Why are you even asking me that?"

"Even if my breasts are less than perky?"

"Cameron." He took her face into his hands and pressed his forehead against hers. "Every one of those women in those albums was in her early twenties. I'd be lying if I told you that your forty-year-old breasts are just as perky as theirs. But I can also tell you that when I look at you, any part of you, *my* whole body instantly becomes very perky. Looking at you, even thinking about you when you aren't around, every part of my body perks up." He kissed her on the lips. As they parted, he brushed his lips across her cheek and pulled her in close to whisper into her ear. "Most especially my heart—and that's a whole lot more stimulating than perky breasts."

Wrapping her arms around him, she leaned her head against his shoulder. She could feel his heart beating. He held her close. She breathed in his musky scent. The urban sounds of the busy rusty downtown noise dissolved into the background while she took in the warmth of his arms.

"Are we good?" His voice sounded miles away.

"Uh-huh," she sighed.

"Curt is waiting inside for us." He took her hand. "Let's go."

"No." She pulled him back when he started to lead the way inside. "I'm not going in." She brought his hand to her lips. "You go without me." She kissed his knuckles and then his wedding band on his ring finger. "I trust you."

"I know you trust me."

"Then we have nothing to worry about," she said. "Go. I'll wait here."

He hesitated.

"Go before I change my mind."

As he backed away, he held onto her hand even as the distance between them grew until their fingers slid away. "Wait for me," he said.

"I'll wait for you right here until you come back," she said.

"Behave yourself," he ordered in a half-serious tone.

Inside the Blue Moon Club, Joshua paused at the door to allow his eyes to adjust to the dim lighting. He also had to allow time for his ears to adjust to the pounding, eardrum-blasting music that came from all corners.

There were three mini-stages with poles from the stage floor to the ceiling. Tables surrounded the stages where young women dressed in little more than a thong bikini erotically danced around the poles for patrons. The lounge was packed with drooling men being served by scantily clad women.

If I ever caught one of my children—

"Thornton!" Sheriff Sawyer yelled above the music.

Joshua found the sheriff waving to him from a table in the far corner. Tearing his eyes from the women at the poles, Joshua elbowed his way across the lounge to join Sheriff Sawyer and a tall, slim elderly man with long thin grey hair tied back into a ponytail that fell down to the middle of his back. His face was dominated by a giant nose under which he wore a bushy gray mustache.

"Larry Van Patton," Sheriff Sawyer introduced him before ordering the bar owner, "Tell Thornton what you just told me."

"Yeah," the elderly man said in a nasal voice, "Dolly Houseman called me. She was returning my call."

"You called her?" Joshua asked. "When? Have you kept in touch all these years?"

"Not really," Larry said. "I mean, we were friends." He gestured at the bar. "She gave me the money to start up this bar on account that she felt guilty about my losing my job after she closed Dolly's. She gave it to me. No loan. So I had no beef with her. That's why I called her—to warn her."

"About what?" Joshua said.

"Some guy came in here looking for someone to do a whack job for a friend of his," Larry said. "Every once in a great while, guys will come in wanting to hire someone to do something illegal. I usually look the other way. But the more this dude talked about the target—an old woman who lived alone, so it was an easy job, a woman who used to own a private club with women—I realized that the target was Dolly. So I called and left a message for her to call me. So she called and I warned her. End of story."

"What about this guy that was in here?" Joshua asked. "What did you tell him?"

"Nothing," Larry said. "I told him I knew no one and sent him on his way. I didn't get the name of the person he was looking to have this done for."

"Can you give us his description?" Curt asked.

"Better than that," Larry said with a chuckle. "I can tell you his name. I'd seen him before when I worked at Dolly's. I guess he didn't remember me, but I recognized him all right."

"Who was he?" Joshua asked.

"A cop—now the biggest of the big cops." Larry smirked. "Hank MacRae, head of the state police from down in Charleston."

Joshua's eyes met with Sheriff Sawyer's. After blinking away the shock, he asked, "Why would Colonel MacRae want to hit an old retired madam?"

Larry laughed. "Because he's Congresswoman Rachel Hilliard's lapdog. I have no doubt that she wanted Dolly hit—and that she had it done, too. Just because I sent MacRae on his way doesn't mean that he didn't find someone to do the job. That's why I warned Dolly."

"What was Dolly's reaction when you told her?"

"She said for Rachel to bring it on," Larry laughed. "That's Dolly for you."

"Why would a big influential Congresswoman hire a hitman to knock off a retired madam?" Sheriff Sawyer asked Larry at the same time that Joshua grabbed his arm.

"Rachel!" Joshua gasped out. "The hooker with the leather teddy. I thought she looked familiar."

Larry was nodding his head. "That was our Rachel. She was into black leather and handcuffs and whips and that type of stuff. Her husband had no idea that he had married a prostitute, and Rachel paid Dolly heavily to keep it a secret after she left the club to become a congressman's wife, which she used as a stepping stone for launching her own political career after her hubby's sudden death."

"Why kill Dolly *now?*" the sheriff asked.

"Because the congresswoman has her eyes on the governor's mansion. MacRae didn't say anything about any of that. But after he left, knowing how tight he and Rachel were back in the day, I did some digging on the Internet and found that Rachel's been making noises that sound like she wanted to run. The way the media is, she'd be a fool to not be afraid of one of those vultures getting their hands on Dolly and uncovering what she really is. So she's tying up loose ends."

"With murder?" the sheriff asked.

The door flew open and a couple of customers came running in. "Call the police! There's some psycho with a gun out in the parking lot!"

The sound of gunshots from outside added its own beat to the music in the club.

Alone in the parking lot, Cameron felt empowered by Joshua's words of love for her. Suddenly, she felt silly for her insecurity. *Were my breasts ever perky?*

She went back to Curt's cruiser to lean against the fender while waiting. *I was never one of those girly girls anyway, and Josh knew that from the start. What's wrong with me? What's gotten into me? Must have been the bump on my head that led to that marital moment.*

The slam of a car door directly behind her startled her out of her thoughts. She turned around in time to see a slender middle-aged man wearing baggy dark pants and a long dark jacket over a t-shirt crossing the parking lot in her direction. His dark hair was in stark contrast to his pale complexion, which served to make the deep scratches on both sides of his face stand out—scratches like those from a cat—a big one—maybe one that resembles a skunk.

He saw her at the same time that she saw him.

Cameron assumed that it was the look on her face that scared him. Rather, it was the Hancock County sheriff's cruiser that she was leaning against. "Anthony? Anthony Tanner?"

Immediately, he turned and ran back through the lot the same way that he had come—darting and dodging around the parked cars.

"Stop! Police!" Yanking her gun from where she wore it in her hip holster, Cameron gave chase.

While Anthony rounded a corner at the end of a row of parked cars, she took a shortcut by jumping up onto a trunk of a Cadillac and rolling over to drop down onto the ground and cut him off. When he rounded the corner, he found her crouching on the ground with her gun aimed at him. "Stop or I'll shoot!"

Anthony answered by whipping his arm out from behind his back and firing two shots from the gun he had torn out of his jacket pocket during his attempted escape. Cameron ducked and returned fire. She heard patrons in the parking lot scream and run in every direction.

One young dancer dressed in a form fitting, low cut dress made the bad decision to dart directly in front of Anthony Tanner, who reached out and grabbed her. Pressing his gun against her head, he yelled at Cameron, "I'll shoot her. I swear!"

"That's really not necessary, Anthony," Cameron said while easing up to her feet. She kept her gun trained on him. "I only want to talk to you."

"That's bull and you know it!"

While she inched her way forward, he backed up. Whimpering, the young woman fought to stay upright in her stiletto heels.

"Gates!" Sheriff Sawyer shouted while coming around the side of a van. With his gun drawn, he was searching to locate the source of the threat.

"Get back!" Tanner ordered.

Seeing the man with the hostage, Curt dropped back behind the van.

Out of the corner of her eye, Cameron saw Joshua, who had not come into Anthony's line of sight yet, dart back behind the van and go around.

Sheriff Sawyer pressed the button on his shoulder mike. "Dispatch, we have a hostage situation at the Blue Moon Club."

Cameron held up her gun to show Anthony that she didn't have her finger on the trigger. "Anthony, let's take a deep breath and calm down. All we want is to get your side of the story. So just let her—" She asked the young woman, "What's your name, honey?"

"Tiffany," she blubbered.

"Tiffany," Cameron said. "Anthony, why don't you let Tiffany go and we'll talk about who scratched you—"

"It wasn't my fault!" Anthony said. "I was attacked by a rabid skunk."

"A skunk?" Cameron fought the grin that wanted to come to her lips. *Of course, he'd think Irving was a skunk.*

"Yeah!" Anthony yelled. "I was walking down the street, minding my own business, and this giant skunk, screeching like a bat out of hell, jumped out of the bushes and landed on my head and started scratching the daylights out of me."

Cameron spotted Joshua several feet behind Anthony, who was backing up toward an old truck. Jostling to stay directly behind Anthony and out of his sight, Joshua kept low between the truck and the van parked next to it.

Keep your eyes on Anthony. Don't give away that there's someone behind him.

"If he was a skunk he would have sprayed you," Cameron said.

"He was crazy, I tell you." Anthony glanced over his shoulder toward the old truck.

176

Joshua ducked down. He caught Sheriff Sawyer's eye. With hand motions, he communicated his plan. Then, he held up three fingers.

"Where did this skunk attack happen?" Cameron asked.

Joshua held up two fingers for the sheriff to see.

"We can't let a rabid skunk go running lose."

One finger.

"He may attack other innocent people."

Springing forward, Joshua sprinted toward Anthony's back. Simultaneously, the sheriff charged. Joshua grabbed the arm holding the gun and twisted it away from Tiffany while delivering a kick to the back of Anthony's knee. Throwing his arms around the dancer, Sheriff Sawyer yanked her out of Anthony's grasp, spun around, and plunged her to the ground. He then threw his body on top of her to protect her from any possible gunshots.

In a matter of seconds, Joshua had Anthony Tanner pinned to the ground with his knee on his shoulder.

"Nice moves." Cameron handed Joshua a pair of handcuffs to secure their suspect.

"I hope I didn't hurt you, ma'am," Sheriff Sawyer said to Tiffany while helping her up. He adverted his eyes while she adjusted her dress, which had come up to her hips to reveal a butterfly tattoo on her buttock.

"I've never been so scared in my life." Tiffany's voice shook. Once her dress was pulled down and straightened, she threw both of her arms around Sheriff Sawyer. "I'm still shaking."

Holding her tight, the sheriff picked up the sweet scent of citrus in her hair. "It's okay, ma'am. We've got everything under control now."

"Tiffany," she said into his chest. She took in a deep breath. "Call me Tiffany."

"I think you've finally stopped trembling," Sawyer said.

She squeezed his muscular biceps. "You're so big and strong." She pushed herself back into his arms. "Hold me please. I'm still scared."

"Cameron," Joshua said in a low voice, "we should go put Tanner in the cruiser and take him back to the sheriff's department."

"Did Sawyer just giggle?" she asked Joshua while they ushered the gunman to the car.

"Yeah, he did," Anthony answered from where he was between the two of them.

"I wasn't talking to you," Cameron said.

"I thought I told you to behave yourself," Joshua said.

"I was until this crazy woman tried to arrest me," Anthony said.

"I wasn't talking to you, Tanner," Joshua said. "I was talking to her." He pointed at Cameron. "What was the last thing I told you before going into the bar?"

"He started it," Cameron pointed at their suspect.

Sighing, Joshua turned around in time to see Tiffany passing her business card with her phone number to Sheriff Sawyer, who was grinning like a teenage boy getting a date with the prom queen.

CHAPTER SIXTEEN

"Well, his DNA places him in Dolly's house," Sheriff Sawyer said while conferring with Joshua in the observation room. On the other side of the two-way mirror, Anthony Tanner was sitting handcuffed to a chair at the conference table.

"Is it a match for the second blood-type found on the knife and at the scene?"

"Forensics is still working on that," Curt said. "But we can place him in the house."

"Not necessarily." Joshua turned his back on the interrogation room.

Cameron told them, "Tanner claims Irving attacked him outside while he was walking down the street ... while he was minding his own business."

"Since I was knocked out under the bookcase, I can't refute that," Joshua said. "I didn't get a look at the killer. I didn't see Tanner kill Dolly. So without real evidence connecting Tanner to the murder, a case could be made for Irving picking up his DNA outside where he was an innocent bystander."

"I hate lawyers," Curt grumbled.

"We haven't lost yet," Joshua said. "I found a burner phone in his pocket. Do any of the numbers in the call log connect him to the phone you found under the sofa at Dolly's house?"

"Several," Curt said. "The last call on the phone at the scene was made to the phone in Tanner's pocket. It was placed less than two hours before you found her body."

"Forensics get a match on the fingerprints on the phone and medallion yet?" Cameron turned around to ask.

"Not yet," Curt answered before asking Joshua, "Do you want to take this or me?"

"You do it," Joshua said. "Pretend we have more than we do. I'm convinced Tanner's a gun for hire. I want the guy who hired him."

Curt chuckled. "Do you really want to go up against the Ice Queen?"

"Ice Queen?" Cameron asked.

"That's the name those in the government arena use for Congresswoman Rachel Hilliard," Joshua said.

"Rachel," she gasped. "From Dolly's album. Is that the same Rachel?"

"According to our source inside the Blue Moon," Curt said. "Her lackey, Colonel MacRae, was looking for someone to off Dolly for them to clear Hilliard's way to the governor's mansion."

"But something isn't sitting right with me about that," Joshua said.

"What's that?"

"You saw the Blue Moon," Joshua said. "You saw the clientele. Colonel MacRae is a polished professional. His face is known in Charleston and the Ohio Valley. I can't see someone as smart as he is walking into an exotic dance club and asking for someone to do a hit for him. That's so sloppy."

"I can't see that either," Cameron said.

"You think they're being set up?" Curt asked.

"I definitely want to get Tanner to talk," Joshua said.

"Well, he didn't talk before when he was arrested for murder," Curt said. "What makes you think he'll flip on who hired him this time?"

"Let's hope he didn't like jail enough to want to take the fall again."

Cameron waited for Curt to step out into the hall before she said, "Dolly's closed back in the seventies. Apparently, she's been collecting blackmail money for at least that long. Why would the congresswoman suddenly want her dead now?"

"Maybe Mike's body being uncovered made her nervous," Joshua squinted at her. "You know, if I were to investigate Ava Tucker's murder, the first thing that I would do is contact every one of Dolly's girls to find out what was going on in that cat house in the days or weeks leading up to the murder."

"Which means Mike would have contacted Congresswoman Hilliard," Cameron said, "who probably wouldn't have been very happy about that connection." She grinned. "Sounds like a motive for killing him to me. Dolly was with me when I ran into them at Cricksters. Wouldn't be a very big jump for her to delete that connection to her past."

Joshua pointed into the interrogation room. "Curt's getting started."

Anthony continued to slouch in his seat when Sheriff Sawyer, carrying a folder under his arm, came in. Placing the closed folder on the table between them, the sheriff sat in the chair across from him. "Anthony, looks like you've been up to your old tricks again."

"You can't prove I had anything to do with it."

"Do with what?" Sheriff Sawyer asked.

The two men regarded each other.

181

"You're looking for a scapegoat and since I've got a record, you figured you'd come after me, that's all," Anthony said. "Well, this isn't gonna be like the last time. This time, I'm not taking the fall for anyone, especially when they set me up. I didn't do it, and since I didn't do it, you can't prove it."

The sheriff shook his head. "Nah, I think we can because we got evidence to prove you were there. For one, we have a witness."

Anthony sat up in his seat. "It was too dark for that guy to see my face!"

Wordlessly, Curt looked across the table at him. A grin slowly crossed his face.

Realizing his blunder, Anthony's face screwed up into a deep frown. "I didn't do it," he said with a pout. "I didn't kill that old woman."

"If you didn't kill her, what were you doing there?"

"I went there to kill her," Anthony said, "but someone else did it before I got there. I told you, I was set up!"

"That doesn't make sense," Cameron muttered to Joshua. He shushed her.

"You expect me to believe that you went there to kill her, but someone beat you to it?" Curt asked with a laugh. "Who?"

"I think it was the woman who hired me." Anthony pounded the table with his fists. "Here's what happened. A couple of weeks ago, I got a call on my burner phone from this woman, she was an old woman. She dropped the name of a friend who vouched for her that she was clean. So I thought she was on the up and up. She had a job for me—to whack this other old woman."

"Why did she want her killed?"

"She said it was none of my business and told me not to ask her again." Anthony shrugged his shoulders. "She offered me ten thousand to do the job and I told her that I needed half up front. So I gave her a drop point, she made the drop."

"Did you see her?"

"No," Anthony said. "I don't want to see my clients. That way I can't rat out any of them."

"Nor can you help in your own defense when you get caught," Curt said.

"I would have been out clean if I wasn't set up and that skunk didn't go ape on me."

"Get on with your story."

"She didn't want it done right away," Anthony said. "I had to be on alert for when it was time to do the job."

"Why did she want you to wait?"

"I don't know," Anthony shrugged. "Probably because she needed time to set me up! She told me to stand by and that she would call when the time was right and the old woman was alone. So, a couple of days ago, in the middle of the afternoon, she calls my burner phone and says that it was the day. To go to the house at the address she had given me and to come in the back door, that it would be unlock—oh!" Jabbing his finger in the air, he sat up. "Another thing! She wanted it done a particular way."

"What particular way?"

"I was to bean her in the back of the head and knock her out," Anthony said, "And then I was to wrap duct tape around her head to cover her mouth and nose so that she would suffocate." He pointed to the two-way mirror. "I still have the duct tape that I brought to do it."

In the observation room, Cameron grabbed Joshua's elbow. "That's the same way Ava Tucker and Virgil Null were killed."

"Can't be an accident that whoever hired Tanner wanted Dolly killed in precisely the same way one of her hookers was killed," Joshua said.

183

His brows furrowed, Curt folded his arms on top of the table when he asked Tanner, "Did your client tell you why she wanted Houseman killed that way?"

"Hey!" Anthony held up both of his hands as best he could with them handcuffed and shook his head. "Like I said, she refused to give me any details."

"Which is bad for you since you're looking for a deal," the sheriff said. "Go on. So your client wanted the old lady killed in a specific way. She wanted her knocked out, tied up, and suffocated with duct tape. Tell me what happened next."

"I go to the place like the lady on the phone told me to do," Anthony said. "It was dark. The back door was unlocked, like she said it would be. I went in, like she told me to do. I crept into the dining room and found furniture overturned and went into the living room, expecting to find the old lady reading or watching TV or napping or whatever it is old women do at night. I had the numb chuck to knock her out like I was supposed to, but when I went in to the living room I found the old lady on the floor with blood all over the place—not at all the way the lady on the phone told me. So then, I'm thinking, 'This is not good,' and that was when the skunk and that man came in and everything went to hell."

"Sounds like it did," Curt said.

"You're telling me." Anthony nodded his head. "So I grabbed the knife from the floor in case I needed to defend myself. I mean, I knew then that I had been set up. Next thing I know, I'm wearing a skunk cap." He pointed at the scratches on his face.

"Do you have the clothes and shoes that you were wearing last night?"

"Why? So you can prove I was there by the skunk hair and—"

"The pattern of the blood on the clothes—"

"There was blood all over and that guy went after me," Anthony objected.

"The blood splatter pattern could prove that you walked in after she was dead, or that you were there when she was killed. The clothes you were wearing can prove if you are telling the truth or not."

Anthony's face fell.

"What did you do with your clothes, Tanner?"

Hanging his head, he muttered his reply.

"What did you say?"

"Burned them," Anthony said. "I burned them in the trash."

"You're an idiot, you know that, Tanner?" Curt said. "You do know where you made your first mistake, don't you?"

"Sure do," Anthony replied. "I never should have trusted that old woman."

"Do you believe that?" Cameron turned to Joshua to ask.

Before he could answer, one of the sheriff's deputies came in with a report in his hand. "Where's Sawyer?" he asked Joshua, who motioned to the interrogation room next door. "He's going to want to see this." The deputy handed the report to Joshua. "I guess you will, too."

Joshua's brow furrowed while reading the printed notice.

"What is it?" Cameron asked.

"Forensics got a hit on the fingerprints from the cell phone and medallion."

"That's good."

"No, it's not," Joshua said. "They were a match for Congresswoman Rachel Hilliard." He slapped the report against his thigh. "Tanner says someone hired him to hit Dolly Houseman. The owner of the Blue Moon says that a few weeks ago Colonel MacRae was in there looking for someone to do a hit for someone, who he assumed to be Dolly. Tanner takes the job, but before he gets there," a question came to his tone, "she kills Dolly herself?"

"To get Dolly out of the way while pinning the blame on someone else," Cameron said.

"Congresswoman Hilliard did not get where she is by being stupid," Joshua said. "I'm thinking this is a set up all right, with Hilliard being the fall guy, or rather woman."

"She was in town at the time of the murder," Cameron said. "She stands to lose a whole lot if Dolly revealed that she was a hooker."

"Really?" Joshua shook his head. "Maybe thirty years ago, but look at Washington now. Look at the media. In to-day's society, she could spin this around to make herself a role model."

"Then maybe Dolly had something bigger on the congresswoman," Cameron said. "We need to find out who Dolly was blackmailing and over what."

CHAPTER SEVENTEEN

"Do I smell coffee?" Joshua awoke with a start and sat up onto his elbows to find Cameron studying pictures from a case file through a magnifying glass while propped up against the headboard.

Without saying a word, she pointed across him to where she had placed a mug on the nightstand on his side of the bed.

"You think of everything." He reached over to kiss her before grabbing his coffee mug, laying back against the pillows, and taking the first sip of his morning coffee. While kissing her again, his eyes fell to the pictures that she was reviewing. The photos were of a mangled and muddy red car. "What are you looking at?"

"Douglas O'Reilly's car," she said. "Since the investigators closed the case as a suicide, the car was destroyed decades ago. All we've got left are the reports and police photos. I'm hoping to find something in these pictures to help find out who killed him."

"You're convinced someone killed him." He wiped the sleep out of his eyes.

"There was no water in his lungs," Cameron said. "Tad says the injuries are consistent with him being hit by a car. I think someone dumped him and his car in the lake to cover up an accident."

He took the picture on top of the pile in the folder. "Let's see what you have."

The corners of her lips curled to form a devilish grin. "You know Douglas O'Reilly was Hunter's grandfather, which will make him Tracy's—"

"Don't say it."

"You probably also don't want me to point out the irony that Douglas O'Reilly drove a red Mustang, and so does his grandson."

"Coincidence."

"Spooky."

Joshua examined the picture of the car, which showed a deep dent on the top of the front fender. "That big dent is kind of high up, like above the wheel well."

"There was a spanking new tire on the front driver's side," she said. "I think he was changing a flat tire when he was killed."

"Can you find a close up of that dent?" Joshua took the pile of pictures.

Without searching, she handed the folder to him and reached for the mug of coffee she had on her side of the bed. "Help yourself."

"I don't think he was hit by a car," Joshua said. "I think he was hit by a truck. If it was a car, the dent would be lower." Finding the picture, he examined it through the magnifying glass. "Look at what we have."

"What have you got?" She took the picture and magnifying glass.

"Paint transfer," he said. "Green. You're looking for a green truck. When did this happen?"

"September second, nineteen sixty-six," she said.

"What do you think are the odds of that truck still being around?"

"I'm not looking for the truck," she said, "I'm looking for the driver who killed O'Reilly and then dumped his body in the lake to make everyone think he had killed himself."

She searched through the stack of pictures in his lap until she found one of the front driver's side tire. Holding the magnifying glass over the picture, she told him, "Look at this. Don't these dark marks on the hubcap look like tire impressions to you—like someone ran over the hubcap—like maybe when it was lying along the side of the road while Douglas was changing the tire? Then, his killer put the hubcap back on the wheel while cleaning up his mess."

"Very good theory." Joshua agreed with a frown. "But without any tires to compare them to, it's going to be impossible to make a case against O'Reilly's killer."

"Douglas' family needs closure, Josh."

"And I have no doubt but that you'll find some way of giving it to them. Even if you can't get a conviction in court, at least you'll get answers for them. That's the important thing." Joshua grasped her by the back of the neck and kissed her. "Thank you for the coffee, my love."

"Thank you for finding the paint transfer, my darling." Tossing the folder onto the floor, she wrapped her arms around his neck and kissed him again. Before she could slip under the covers, there was a knock at the bedroom door. With a groan, she dropped back onto the bed.

"Who is it?" Joshua called out.

"Dad," Tracy replied, "there's a delivery man downstairs with a package for you and he needs your signature."

"I'll be right down." He shrugged his shoulders when Cameron slipped away from him to the other side of the bed.

"What's that about?" As if she feared Tracy listening outside the door, Cameron asked him in a whisper while he put on his bathrobe and slipped his feet into his slippers.

"Probably something from the courthouse," he muttered. "Don't go anywhere. I'll be right back." He reached across the bed to grab one last kiss from her.

"You've got five minutes and then I'm starting without you." Giggling, she pulled the covers up under her chin.

Downstairs, Joshua opened the front door to find the deliveryman on the porch. Clutching an oversized tan envelope and tablet to his chest, he stood motionless while staring wide-eyed in the direction of the steps leading down to his truck in the driveway.

"I'm Joshua Thornton. I understand you have a package that needs my signature."

The deliveryman nodded his head very slightly while saying in a hoarse whisper, "Quiet."

"Why?" Joshua asked.

With a jerk of his head, he motioned toward the porch steps. With a deep sigh, Joshua stepped out to see what had the man so terror-stricken. Squatting down with his front paws tucked up under him, Irving was enjoying the morning sun in a spot directly between the deliveryman and his truck.

"It's a skunk," the deliveryman whispered. "And he's a big one. Biggest one I've ever seen. Be very quiet. Whatever you do, don't move. Don't move a muscle."

With a shake of his head, Joshua snatched the package out of his arms and waved it in Irving's direction. "Irving, stop scaring people and go catch a mouse or something."

In contrast to the volume of Joshua's firm order, Irving took his time standing up and arching his back in a long leisurely stretch. He then sauntered in the direction of the open door. The deliveryman leapt back to the other end of the porch while the cat casually strolled inside. As if to taunt the deliveryman, he jerked up his tail once his rear was facing him, an action that prompted a scream. The deliveryman covered his face with his arm. With a dreamy expression on his face, Irving took his time rubbing the length of his body along the doorway until he was inside.

"He actually lives here?" he asked while Joshua signed the tablet.

"His name is Irving, but if he likes you, he lets you call him Irv." Joshua closed the door. Spotting Irving sitting up tall in the foyer, he shook his finger at him. "You are a bad cat. I think you enjoy looking like a skunk and scaring people."

Irving stood up, turned around, and hitched his tail in Joshua's direction before sauntering down the hallway to the kitchen. It was his feline version of an obscene gesture.

"Same to you."

While climbing the stairs, Joshua read the return address: Dolly Houseman, Rock Springs Boulevard, Chester, West Virginia. The postmark was from the day before—the day after her murder.

He was so enthralled by the envelope and so anxious to open it up that he had to remind himself to watch the steps going back upstairs to the bedroom.

"What is it?" Cameron asked when he came inside and kicked the door behind him while studying the delivery.

"A package from Dolly."

"Dolly?"

"Mailed yesterday," he said.

"She was dead yesterday."

"I know that," he said. "I found her body. Remember?"

"Of course I do."

"Obviously, someone mailed this for her," he said. "I'll bet it was her lawyer. She must have left this with instructions to mail to me upon her death."

Cameron threw back the covers and crawled to the foot of the bed where Joshua sat down. "Open it." Wrapping her arms around his shoulders, she rested her head against the side of his to peer at the package.

He slipped his finger under the seal and tore open the oversized envelope, which contained four thick brown envelopes. A handwritten letter was taped to the top one.

Joshua only had to glance at the handwriting before saying, "This is from Dolly all right."

"What does it say?" Cameron attempted to reach for the letter.

"She sent it to me." Joshua playfully jerked it out of her reach.

Unable to get the letter, she took one of the envelopes. In a shaky hand, the name of Commissioner Russell Null was written across the front of it. Beneath it, she had written, "Newell, West Virginia."

Joshua grasped her hand to prevent her from slipping her finger under the seal and ripping open the envelope. "Wait. Let me read the letter to see what this says," he said. "We may need to open this in front of Sheriff Sawyer so that we have witnesses to confirm that we aren't tampering with or planting evidence."

"Spoken like a lawyer," she sighed.

"Do you want Dolly's killer to get away when we find him?"

"No." Mocking a snit, she slipped out of the bed and put on her bathrobe. "Just for that, I'm going to drink your coffee."

"It has no cream or sugar in it," he said with a grin. She only drank coffee with two sugars and two creams.

She picked up the mug that he had left on the end table. "I'll suffer to make you suffer." Instead, she handed the mug to him.

While taking a sip, he finished reading the letter. "Okay, do you want to know what Dolly tells me in this letter?"

"She tells us who killed her … from the grave?"

"Something like that." Getting up, he placed the mug on the end table. "Dolly says that there were many secret meetings in the parlor at the club over the decades and that the albums that she has—had—"

"Gave to me," Cameron said.

Joshua nodded his head. "If you look through them they have a lot of history of very important betrayals and even conspiracies that were organized at Dolly's."

"Dolly said something to me about a murder conspiracy or two."

"Very possibly," Joshua said. "She says that her father had set up a hidden compartment in the parlor where these meetings would take place and that he had a recorder set up to tape the meetings—that was something that he learned from her Uncle Al."

"Al Capone," she said.

"She says these meetings were recorded for their own protection—just in case someone decided to shut Dolly's down or maybe cause some sort of trouble. But after Ava's and Virgil's murders, and after the club was shut down, Dolly decided to take advantage of the last couple of recordings for some retirement income. One of these people, Dolly says, killed Ava and Virgil. She has her suspicions but she never had any evidence to prove it, which was why she never turned this over to the police."

"So these are recordings," Cameron felt the padded envelope and could make out the shape of a cassette tape. "The people on these recordings were the blackmail victims. That's where the ten-thousand dollars that she deposited every month came from."

"Along with transcripts that Dolly had written out to document who said what during these dirty dealings."

Cameron read the names on the envelopes. Commissioner Russell Null, Dr. Philip Lipton, Mr. Henry MacRae, and Congresswoman Rachel Hilliard. "Four divided by ten-thousand. I'll bet she got twenty-five hundred dollars from each one of them."

"When you calculate how much that comes to annually," Joshua said, "it adds up to a pretty expensive motive for murder."

"Three of these four were meeting with Sawyer at Cricksters when we came in with Dolly...on the same day that she was murdered." With a gasp, she recalled, "and she said something very weird—right about the time that Philip Lipton dumped his drink in Sawyer's lap."

"What did she say?"

Cameron paused to think. "Have you forgotten that I have a concussion?"

"How convenient."

"She said that even though she was old and she had trouble remembering what she ate for breakfast, she could recall what happened years ago, and who did it, and—and then Lipton dumped his drink in Sawyer's lap."

"And Lipton checked out those case files for Ava's and Virgil's murders right after Mike disappeared," Joshua said.

"We need to talk to Lipton," she said.

"But first," Joshua said, "we call Sawyer and have him come over to witness us opening these envelopes and have him listen to these tapes with us."

CHAPTER EIGHTEEN

After showering and dressing, Cameron went downstairs in hopes of finding one of Tracy's delectable breakfasts waiting. Instead, she found Donny eating a plate of toaster waffles slathered in maple syrup. While refilling her coffee mug, she noticed an over-packed document box set at one end of the kitchen table. With notepads and folders overflowing beyond the rim, the lid rested sloppily on top.

"That's some heavy-duty homework, isn't it?" she asked in a good-natured tone.

"I'm on summer break now," Donny said before explaining the box. "Hunter brought it over. His mom gave it to him last night. It was his dad's stuff that she had packed up from his desk. Hunter wants Dad to go through it with him to see if they can find something to help him find his killer."

"Is Hunter here?"

"He took Tracy out for breakfast and then they're going to look at engagement rings," he said between bites of waffles. "They're moving kind of fast, aren't they? Kind of reminds me of you and Dad."

"Actually, they're not." Her hopes for a gourmet breakfast dashed, she opened the refrigerator door and peered

195

inside to see if any meal ideas struck her. "They've been quote-unquote-dating for years."

"Why'd they keep it a secret?"

"Maybe they didn't." She wondered if she wanted scrambled eggs badly enough to clean up the mess it would create cooking them. "Maybe y'all just weren't paying enough attention to notice." The answer was no, she did not want scrambled eggs that much.

Donny was silent while she continued to stare into the refrigerator and pray for inspiration. Eventually, with a thought-filled drawl, he said, "She did go out with him every time they were both in town, but I thought they were going out as friends. I mean, they've never been kissy face like you and Dad."

"Your dad and I are not kissy face."

"I never caught the two of them naked down in the family room."

"There's more to a committed relationship than sex," she said.

"I know," Donny said with a sad sigh. "So far, I haven't experienced either."

"That's good."

She was still staring into the refrigerator when Joshua came in. Grasping her shoulders with both hands from behind, he kissed her on the cheek. When she didn't respond, he looked at her and then into the open refrigerator to see what she was staring at before reaching inside and taking a grapefruit from the fruit drawer. "Grapefruit is easy," he said.

"But I really want some carbs."

"Then eat some."

"Then I'd have to clean up the kitchen."

"Sounds like a personal problem to me," he said with a cock of his head and an arched eyebrow. He took a dish out of the cupboard. "I'll give you half."

With a resigned sigh and shrug of her shoulders, she took juice out of the fridge and poured two glasses.

A knock at the front door prompted Admiral to jump up from where he was lying under the table and bump his head. With a screech, Irving leapt from where he was sunning himself on a windowsill and followed Admiral in the direction of the foyer.

Joshua checked the clock on the wall. "That can't be Curt. I only spoke to him ten minutes ago."

"There's only one way to find out who it is. Answer the door." Donny pushed back his chair and rose from the table.

As if to urge his master to hurry up, Admiral raced back into the doorway to escort Donny to the foyer. The huge mongrel uttered his loud, deep barks along the way. Irving accompanied his barking with high-pitched shrieks.

"No one will ever be able to sneak into this house," Cameron said.

"That's the way I like it." Joshua cut through the grapefruit with a knife and separated the halves into two bowls, which Cameron had set out on plates. After he cut the fruit into sections with a paring knife, she sprinkled it with sugar, carried the plates to the kitchen table, and turned back to hand Donny's dirty plate and juice glass to him.

Joshua was placing the dishes in the sink when Donny returned to the kitchen with Hunter Gardner's stepfather directly behind him. "Dad, Mr. Fontaine wanted to talk to you," Donny explained. "I'm heading out to meet some friends. We're going four wheeling in the park. I'll be back in time for dinner."

Surprised by the visit from Royce Fontaine, a man who had never had reason to come to his home before, Joshua turned around, leaned back against the counter, and took his time drying his hands on the dishtowel.

197

"What are you going to do about lunch?" Cameron asked Donny before he had a chance to gallop up the back stairs to his room to gather his stuff for the outing.

"Pizza or buffalo wings or both at Roma's," he replied. "Most likely both. I'll put it on Dad's tab." With the energy that comes with youth, Donny rushed up the stairs.

Joshua wondered if his son was rushing to go meet his friends or to escape what he suspected was coming. While taking his time drying his hands on the dishtowel, he studied Royce Fontaine's temper simmering beneath the surface. Possibly calculating on how best to proceed, his guest was waiting to launch into the purpose of his visit. "Would you like some coffee, Royce?"

"No, thanks." The visitor stood up as tall as his stooped-over frame would allow him and jutted out his chin.

Sensing that it would be best to get straight to business, Joshua asked, "What can I do for you, Royce?"

"I'm sure you heard the news … about Hunter and your daughter, Tracy."

"Yes, I have."

"Belle is very upset about it," Royce said. "Now, nothing against Tracy. She's a very nice girl. Lovely. But don't you think this timing is the worst? We're still trying to get Mike's body released by the medical examiner—" He pointed his finger at Joshua. "—your cousin Doc MacMillan, I might add."

"You may add that."

"And then for those two kids—they're only kids—Belle thinks they're too young. They hardly know each other—"

"They went all through high school together," Joshua said. "They've kept in touch all through college."

"*You* approve of this?"

Joshua was aware of Cameron's eyes on him. She was waiting for his answer. No one had yet to ask him if he did approve. It took a full moment for him to come to an answer.

"Yes, I give them my blessing," Joshua said. "Hunter's father was my best friend growing up. Hunter has a good head on his shoulders. He's shown nothing but respect for my daughter." He stood up straight. "It would be an honor to have him in my family."

Royce's face twisted with emotion. "You have no idea what you're doing!"

"Yes, I do," Joshua replied. "I'm counting my blessings. Do you know how many jerks there are out there? I see them every day in my job. Just this week Cameron caught a monster who raped and killed his girlfriend in front of her young son. The world is full of monsters, Royce! I pray every night that they don't gobble up any of my children. Yes, ideally, I would have liked Tracy to be a few years older and settled before marrying anyone. Obviously, that wasn't God's plan. But considering that He has chosen a good man like Hunter ... yes, to answer your question, Royce, yes, I know exactly what I'm doing and ..." he pointed at Royce, "if you're smart, you'll give them your blessing, too. You're right, Tracy is a lovely young woman, and you and Belle should be proud to have her for a daughter-in-law."

Royce gritted his teeth. He worked his jaw before responding in a tone that rang of forced calm. "Look at it from *Belle's* point of view."

"If this is so important to her, why isn't she here?" Cameron interjected to ask.

"She's too upset," Royce said quickly. "I—we thought this whole thing with Mike was over. He'd been declared dead."

"He is dead," Cameron said, "because someone killed him."

"And now Hunter has it in his head that he's going to find his father's killer."

"Do you blame him?" Joshua asked.

"Like there's any chance of that happening," Royce said. "Hunter is upsetting his mother, asking her over and over again the same questions about what his father was doing those last few days before he disappeared. What did he say? Who did he call? Who did he talk to? Where did he go? He's putting her into an emotional blender. She's snapping at me. She can't sleep at night. She's been taking sedatives every day since this all came up."

"If you were murdered and your body was dumped in a lake for twenty years, wouldn't you want your family doing everything they could to find your killer?" Cameron asked.

"Not if it was going to drive them crazy," Royce shot back. "Belle had moved on. She's with me." He pounded his chest with his fist. "After years of waiting and hoping—taking chances—doing whatever it took—I finally won the only woman I have ever loved, and she was mine. Everything was perfect!"

"Until Mike's body showed up," Cameron said.

"Yes!"

"And your apple cart has been toppled over," she said.

"We can't not investigate Mike's murder, Royce," Joshua said. "I'm sorry you're upset—"

"Not me. Belle."

Joshua and Cameron exchanged knowing grins.

"Belle," Joshua corrected himself. "But the law dictates that Mike's murder must be investigated, and when we find the killer, I intend to prosecute him to the fullest extent of the law."

"And it goes without saying that since Hunter is now going to be your son-in-law, you're going to work with him on this," Royce said.

"This case was personal to me even before Hunter and Tracy got engaged," Joshua said. "Their engagement only gives me additional personal motivation."

Royce let out a sigh that sounded like a bull snorting before charging. "And now, this woman that we never even knew existed has left Hunter all this money and he's running off and getting married and leaving me with his mother on the brink of a breakdown."

"Maybe if I talk to Belle," Joshua offered.

"No!" Royce shouted.

Neither of them was prepared for his abrupt outburst.

Everyone in the kitchen was still.

Even Irving had stopped grooming himself where he was sprawled out on the floor in a sunbeam.

"Belle just wants to be left alone," Royce said. "I think that's best for now."

Arching an eyebrow, Joshua glanced over at Cameron, who was cocking her head in Royce's direction.

Royce Fontaine was a man with an agenda.

Joshua let out a deep sigh. "Royce … what do you want me to do? I'm not going to split Hunter and Tracy up. I'm unable to put an end to Mike's murder investigation. What do you want from me?"

Royce's eyes narrowed. He then turned to glare at Cameron, who cocked an eyebrow in his direction while waiting for an answer.

Joshua folded his arms across his chest. With questions about the true motivation of Royce's visit, his expression changed from perplexed to suspicious.

The tension in the room became so thick that it was suffocating.

Royce spun on his heels and stomped out of the kitchen. Seconds later, they heard the front door slam.

After a long silence, Cameron asked, "Has he always been like that?"

"Strange? Yes," Joshua murmured while replaying Royce's unusual visit in his mind. "That strange? No."

Cameron turned to the box resting on the kitchen table. "Mike was missing for how long? Why did Hunter just bring this box of stuff from his desk *now?*"

"What?" Her question startled Joshua out of his stare at the spot Royce had been standing.

Cameron pointed with the spoon from her grapefruit to the box resting on the table. "Hunter brought that over this morning when he picked up Tracy. It's his father's stuff that his mother gave him from his desk. Where has it been all these years? Why didn't Belle give it to you before?"

It was the first time Joshua had noticed the box. "Good question."

Cameron abandoned her less-than-satisfying grapefruit to join him at the other end of the kitchen table.

Joshua tossed the top aside and peered inside at stacks of folders filled with papers. "Maybe we'll get lucky and Mike's notebook will be in here," he said. "I doubt it. Officers carry their notebooks with them to take notes while interviewing witnesses. It would have been in the cruiser."

"But this was his own personal case." Cameron reached into the box to remove a stack of used yellow legal pads that had been placed upright on their side against the long side of the box. "He may have kept his notes at home, especially if he didn't want the sheriff to know that he was working on a murder case involving Dolly's."

A slow grin crossed her face when she noticed the blank page on the top of the used notepad. "He did the same thing I do." She flipped back the first page to reveal handwritten notes. "I leave the top sheet blank and start on the second page. Then, when I'm done, I flip it over so that someone walking past my desk can't read what I've been working on."

She flipped the top sheet back over. "But this top sheet isn't blank. There's a note scribbled on it." She turned it around for Joshua to read. "Friday, four pm T R Park."

"T R Park is Tomlinson Run Park. He disappeared on a Friday." He took the notebook to observe that the "4" had a single slash through it and a "1" written in the line above it. "Looks like the meeting was originally scheduled for four o'clock and then changed."

"I wonder which of them changed it," she asked. "Maybe the confidential informant got nervous that someone was on to him and that's what got Mike killed."

"We need to find that CI." Joshua flipped through the stack of folders. "These are copies of reports from case files." He read the name across the top of the page. "It's an accident report for a single car accident. The driver was killed. A woman. Her name was Sabrina Collins."

"Died March tenth, nineteen eighty-two," Cameron said. Joshua looked at her.

She turned the notepad around for him to read. "It's a list of names, followed by a 'D' and a date." She counted the list, which totaled eight names. The last one, listed as "Rachel," had no date beside it.

Joshua set the folder aside and went to the next one on the pile. "This is a suicide in Columbus, Ohio. Drug overdose for a woman named Morgan Bates."

"December eighteenth, nineteen eighty," Cameron read from the list.

Their eyes met.

He went to the next folder. "Fatal stabbing during a mugging in an alley in downtown Pittsburgh. The victim's name is Jaclyn Jones."

"Died July sixteenth, nineteen seventy-nine."

Joshua tossed the folder aside to move on to the next. "Bambi Crawford died in a home fire."

"On January fifth, nineteen eighty-two."

"In Newark, New Jersey, Farrah Monroe was beaten to death and strangled," he told her. "Her boyfriend swore he came home from a night out with the guys and found her dead. Detectives suspected he did it, but there was not enough evidence to prosecute him."

"October twenty-third, nineteen seventy-nine." Cameron ticked on the name to find only two left. "We have Ava Tucker already. Do you have a Bianca there?"

"Bianca Stephens was found with her wrists slashed in a bathtub at a hotel in Charleston, West Virginia."

"She died on September twenty-fifth, nineteen seventy-six," Cameron said. "The only woman listed here that doesn't have a death date is Rachel." She gazed at him. "There's eight names here. Dolly had eight girls. Rachel Hilliard is the only one who's still alive."

"All of these women were dead when Mike started looking into Ava's murder," Joshua said. "He must have started out trying to contact them for statements about what happened the night Ava was murdered and realized that they had each died suddenly."

"Except the one with the most to lose if it had come out that she had been a common call girl," Cameron said. "That would be a very heavy motive for her to kill him."

The doorbell prompted Admiral to race up from the family room downstairs and for the foyer. Irving rolled over from where he had almost fallen asleep in the sunbeam and scurried after him.

"I guess Curt is here," Joshua said.

CHAPTER NINETEEN

"Well, let's get the worst part over with," Curt replied when Joshua asked which envelope and tape they wanted to listen to first.

The envelopes were bundled together with rubber bands into two packages. Congresswoman Rachel Hilliard's and Colonel Henry MacRae's envelopes were bound together. Russell Null and Philip Lipton were bound together as well. A cassette tape was attached to each package.

The old-fashioned cassette tape prompted Joshua to dig through the desk drawers in his study for a dusty cassette player on which to listen to the recordings.

While Cameron slipped Hillard's tape into the player, Joshua referred to the transcript that was written out in an ink pen. He recognized the elderly woman's penmanship from numerous cards and notes she had sent him throughout the years.

A call to Dolly's lawyer confirmed that she had given him the package to mail several years earlier—shortly after Joshua had returned to Chester and was elected Hancock's prosecuting attorney.

"The date on this transcript is February thirteen, nineteen seventy-six." Joshua handed the transcript to the sheriff.

"That's the date that Ava Tucker and Virgil Null were killed," Curt said.

"We also know that Dolly bugged the parlor at the gentleman's club," Cameron said. "Let's see what she got on the congresswoman and police superintendent. How much do you want to bet it's an affair?"

"Now let's not make assumptions," Joshua said.

"According to this transcript, they start out kissing," Curt said.

"See," she said with a smug grin before hitting the start button on the cassette player and turning up the volume. As indicated by the transcript, the tape started out with several moments of kissing and moans of pleasure along with the rustle of clothes.

"Oh," a man's voice groaned, "I missed you so much. I couldn't wait to be with you."

There were more sounds of heavy kissing.

"This is the only thing that keeps me going, darling," she said. "Being with you, like this—when I'm with him, I picture you holding me. When we are together, I pretend that it is you I am with. Otherwise, I'm afraid that he would see the disgust in my eyes."

"Don't talk about him." He kissed her again. "I can't bear the thought of him having you this way."

"Neither can I … anymore."

Silence.

"You aren't thinking of divorce, are you?" There was fear in his tone. "Your plans—"

"Our plans," she said. "I can't wait anymore. I don't like waiting in the wings to have what I want while playing the dutiful wife." Her tone was cold.

"If you divorce Rod, then you'll get nothing—we won't get anything. All of our hard work will be for nothing. You'll end up back here at Dolly's—flat on your back."

"I'm not talking about divorce," she giggled. "What kind of fool do you think I am? The solution to our problem is simple. Instead of waiting for this overweight old man to kick the bucket naturally, he has an unfortunate, horrible accident. With all the years that he has served this state in Washington, to die suddenly, then there will be a lot of publicity, which will put me in the spotlight to show the voters what a formidable, intelligent woman I am. By the time I am through, Rod's friends in the capital will be begging me to take his place, finish his term, and then run for his seat."

Her voice dropped seductively. "And then, I can use my new influence to bring my favorite man in blue down to Charleston to take a position of power with the state police. No more patrolling around in your cruiser, my love." She kissed him.

"How do you propose to do it?" he asked in a rasping voice.

"I was thinking about—" She kissed him. "—A plane crash. Rod thinks he's so cool flying in his own private plane to Washington. It should be easy enough to make that aerial go-cart drop down out of the sky and go boom, don't you think, darling?"

Henry laughed. "I used to fly in the air force. Do you know that a simple break in the seal on the door could cause a problem with the pressure in the cabin that can knock everyone, including the pilot, out and bring the plane down in the Appalachian Mountains—"

Joshua snapped off the recorder. "That's how it happened. Congressman Roderick Hilliard and two assistants crashed in his private plane in the mountains. If I recall, the FAA called it a mechanical failure."

"Caused by Henry MacRae and Hilliard's wife tampering with the plane," Curt said. "This is a case for the feds. They conspired to kill a United States Congressman."

"I know some people at the FAA," Joshua said. "Before we go throwing accusations at a congresswoman, let's make sure we have all of our facts straight. For one, the date on this tape is February thirteen, nineteen seventy-six. Congressman Hilliard died in the fall."

"People like Congresswoman Hilliard don't go acting rashly," Cameron said. "According to this recording, they seem to be just hatching this plan. It's conceivable that they spent six months planning and making sure they had all their ducks in a row."

"MacRae is a former state trooper," Curt said. "He would have known everything necessary to pull this off."

"Except for a madam with a tape recorder," Cameron said.

"But why kill Ava Tucker?" Curt asked.

"Maybe she overheard their plan," Cameron suggested. "She happened to be going by the doorway—"

"No," Joshua said. "Congresswoman Hilliard is not that sloppy."

"According to Mike's files, it looks like Hilliard has been killing off all of her former co-workers," Cameron said. "Why not start that night with Ava?"

Joshua ejected the cassette from the recorder and slipped in the next one. "Before we go slapping cuffs on killers, let's take a listen to this tape that's marked for Russell Null and Philip Lipton."

"Russell is Virgil Null's brother," Cameron said.

"He's also on the board of county commissioners," Curt said.

"More dirty politics?" Cameron cocked an eyebrow in Joshua's direction. "Am I sensing a theme here?"

Ignoring her, Joshua referred to the transcript. "It starts with Russell Null."

"What are you doing here?" a hushed voice demanded.

They heard a door slam in the background while a younger man's voice answered, "This is a bordello. What do you think I'm doing here? How did you know I was coming?"

"That's Virgil Null," Joshua said hurriedly while sitting down to move his ear closer to the player's speaker.

"Be serious," a third male voice said.

"That's Philip Lipton," Curt said. "I recognized his voice. What's—"

Joshua hushed him.

"Do you have any idea what you're doing?" Russell asked.

"He knows exactly what he's doing," Philip said. "He's sneaking around behind our backs to ruin our whole lives because of one stupid mistake we made on one stinking night, that's what."

"Yeah, that's what I'm doing," Virgil said. "I'm making things right—once and for all."

"Why?" Philip Lipton squawked.

"Because it's the right thing to do," Virgil said. "Do you have any idea how many lives we've ruined? Ava. Toby."

"We didn't ruin anyone's lives," Philip said. "They did. They made their decisions on their own for how they wanted to live—or not live—their lives." He added forcibly, "It's not our fault."

"Like we made our decision to not take responsibility for the mistake we made," Virgil said.

Philip made a noise, but was cut off by Russell. "You want to talk about ruined lives. Then here's a count of how many lives you'll ruin if you go upstairs. Yours. Mine. Philip's. How about Dad's life when his two sons go to jail? And then, what about Suzie? She and I were planning to get married in three months. Think about that."

There was silence on the tape before Virgil said in a low voice, "It was an accident. We know that. We need to tell everyone the truth about what happened. Otherwise, Toby's death will be for nothing."

There was the sound of movement, followed by the sound of a punch and a yelp.

"Stop it, Phil!" Russell yelled. "Let him go!"

The sound of a struggle stopped.

Philip Lipton's voice was low and threatening. "If you go up those stairs with her, I swear you'll be dead before morning. I'm not going to let you rip everything I've built out of my life because of one stupid night a decade ago! Do you hear me, Null! You tell her what we did, and you're a dead man!"

Joshua hit the stop button. "And he was dead before morning."

"Ava was Ava Tucker," Curt Sawyer said. "Who is this Toby guy?"

"Someone whose life Russell and Philip ruined because of one night of stupidity," Joshua said.

"Both Toby and Ava made a choice that ruined their lives because of something they did." Cameron fingered the bruise that was still tender on her forehead. "I heard a Toby somewhere in this case. Where do I know a Toby from?"

"Toby Winter." Joshua sat up straight in his chair. "Toby was tight with Virgil Null—and Toby hung himself out at Raccoon Creek."

"Which is where Douglas O'Reilly was killed in nineteen sixty-six," Cameron said. "That's a decade before the night of this recording."

"How does Doug O'Reilly figure into all this?" Curt asked. "His name isn't mentioned in either of these recordings."

"What about this?" Cameron jumped to her feet. "Douglas O'Reilly got a flat tire while on his way out to see Ava Tucker, who was pregnant. He's changing the flat tire. It's late and dark. Philip, Russell, and I guess Virgil and Toby had to be with them—probably drunk, doing whatever it is teenagers do on a weekend night, and then they hit Douglas with the car and killed him. They panic. They're young. They have their whole lives ahead of them. So drunk and stupid—"

"One night of stupidity," Joshua quoted.

"—they dump the car and body in Raccoon Creek, intending for it to look like an accident—like he drove into the lake," Cameron said. "However, as circumstances would have it, everyone assumed that Douglas O'Reilly killed himself because of his pregnant girlfriend. Out of guilt, Ava turns to prostitution."

"And Toby hangs himself," Joshua concluded.

"Out at Raccoon Creek where his life went to hell," Cameron said.

"After his best friend's suicide," Joshua said, "Virgil decided to make things right and went to tell Ava the truth. Douglas did not commit suicide because she had gotten pregnant—he was killed."

"I think Virgil was trying to make things right before that," Cameron said. "The O'Reilly's were receiving cash payments for years after Douglas' death. They needed the money, so they said nothing. The money stopped coming the same time that Ava and Virgil were murdered. I think it was Virgil who was sending the money to try to make up for his role in taking their son away."

"Good story," Curt said. "But we can't prove any of it. All we have is this tape with an argument that's pretty vague." He referred to the written transcript. "Douglas O'Reilly's name isn't mentioned at all on this recording."

"I think we have enough to shake things up," Joshua said. "This tape proves Philip Lipton and Russell Null were on the scene the same night that Virgil and Ava were killed. This argument, plus Lipton's threats, prove motive."

"Not to mention the blackmail that they have been paying Dolly to keep their secret quiet," Cameron turned to Joshua. "You know Russell Null. I assume you know Philip Lipton, too, since he's the head of the crime lab in Weirton. Were you aware that they were friends?"

"No," Joshua said with a shake of his head.

"That's the advantage in cold cases," she said with a low laugh. "Loyalties shift. Maybe Russell Null ended their friendship after his brother got killed. Maybe he even suspects Philip Lipton carried out his threat."

"And is willing to talk about it now?" Curt asked. "Now that would be an ideal interview."

Joshua agreed. "Let's bring them in for questioning about Virgil's and Ava's murders and see what they have to say."

"Let's not forget about Dolly's murder," Cameron said. "They all have reason to see her dead, and three out of the four of them were at Cricksters on the same day she was killed."

"Don't worry, Cam," Curt said, "I haven't forgotten about that for even a second. Who's going after the congresswoman?" The sheriff looked directly at Joshua.

"Does the congresswoman scare you?" Cameron asked the sheriff with a wicked grin.

"I'm not proud. She scares the dickens out of me."

"She doesn't scare me," Joshua said. "I'd go up against her any day."

"Just don't plan to go up in a plane with her and her toy boy around," Cameron warned.

CHAPTER TWENTY

Joshua was still out on the front porch with the sheriff going over their plans for interrogating Philip Lipton and Russell Null when Cameron, on a whim, brought up the website for Null Landscaping on her laptop.

A family-owned business for over fifty years, she was certain that they had a theme color, like green—the same color found in the paint transfer on Douglas O'Reilly's car.

When Joshua had walked out of the study with Sheriff Sawyer, Irving scurried in and jumped up onto the desk to rub the side of his head against the corner of the laptop monitor while she typed "Null Landscaping" into the search engine.

"Scare anyone today, Irv?" She scratched him behind one of his ears while scanning the listings that came up in her search.

After climbing up onto a stack of case files, Irving lay down with his front paws tucked under him. He was so large that he spilled over all four edges of the stack of folders.

Cameron clicked on the website for Null Landscaping. A home page came up with a picture of Russell Null posing in front of a big green four-wheel-drive truck with a magnetic sign on the door that read, "Null Landscaping, local family-owned business, celebrating 80-plus years in business."

Green.

The grin of satisfaction was still stretched across her face when Joshua came back into the study. "What do you think are the chances that an insurance company would keep accident claim records going back to nineteen sixty-six?" she asked.

"Slim to none," Joshua replied with a smirk. "But it's worth a shot." He went around the desk to see the homepage she had displayed on the computer screen. "Green truck. O'Reilly was hit by a green truck."

"A decade before the time of the recording would be nineteen sixty-six," Cameron said. "If they smashed into Douglas and his car, then there had to have been damage to the truck. Wouldn't they put in a claim with the insurance company? If I can get a copy of that claim—"

"Call Dirk Reed," Joshua interrupted her to say. "He was the main insurance guy in these parts back then. He knows everyone and everything—"

"More than Tad?"

Joshua chuckled. "Dirk has a memory like a bank vault. He never forgets anything. If Null Landscaping put in a claim for one of their trucks about that time, Dirk will re-member it."

Her brow furrowed with doubt. "We're talking nineteen sixty-six, Josh. How old is this guy?"

"He's got to be in his nineties."

"Where will I find him? Fox's Nursing Home?"

"What's today?" He checked the calendar for the answer to his question. "Wednesday. You'll find him at the bowling alley."

Tri-State Lanes was located in East Liverpool, Ohio. Even though she was on medical leave, Cameron clipped on her badge and strapped on her gun to go looking for Dirk Reed, the source for everything pertaining to insurance in the Ohio Valley, according to Joshua. She expected the ninety-plus-year-old man to be sitting passively next to a lane with a hearing aid, and maybe, if he was perky enough, a beer next to his elbow.

Since Joshua had said that everyone knew Dirk Reed and he was a regular at the bowling alley, she went up to the front desk to ask where to find him.

The pretty young woman in tight faded jeans and big blonde hair smiled broadly. "Oh, yeah, everyone knows Slim. He's on lane seven." She pointed into the alley. "He's up now."

Cameron turned to see an extremely tall and very thin man running up to the lane and letting loose with a bowling ball that went flying down the alley to knock over all the pins, at which point he threw both fists up into the air while those on his team cheered loudly.

"Tur-KEY!" Slim Reed cheered before tucking his thumbs under his armpits and dancing a jig back up the alley while gobbling like a turkey.

"Turkey?" Cameron muttered.

Hearing her, the clerk behind the desk explained, "That's his third bowling strike in a row. It's nothing new for Slim, but he still cheers like a little kid when he gets one."

The group of elderly men and women on his team were still bumping fists and giving high fives when Cameron approached them. Spotting her badge and gun, they let out a mocking "ooh" and made jokes at Slim's expense when she asked for him.

"Looks like they finally caught up with you, Slim," said a man with a handlebar mustache and suspenders over his plaid shirt.

"My momma always said it will all catch up with you eventually," Slim said.

"Are you allowed to question Slim here when you're from Pennsylvania?" a woman with dark hair and a suspicious expression asked Cameron.

"I only have a few questions," Cameron replied. "Slim isn't in any trouble."

"Rats!" Slim slapped his thigh. "And here I was hoping that you would take me for a ride and spank me for whatever it was I did."

There was a round of naughty laughter among the old-sters while Cameron ushered Slim to a table in the dining area off the lanes.

Once they were out of earshot, Slim said, "I hope I didn't offend you with that shot about spanking." The naughty-lit-tle-boy sparkle in his eyes was replaced with a sincere gentle-manly tone. "I have a tendency to get carried away when I'm with the gang."

"I can understand that," she replied before adding in a whisper, "I'm the same way."

"Good." He sat up in his seat. A business-like expression came across his face. "What do you need, Detective?"

"Null Landscaping."

"My insurance company handled all of their business for half a century," Slim said. "My grandson is still handling their accounts."

"Nineteen sixty-six—"

"Baltimore Orioles swept the World Series over the Los Angeles Dodgers with four games," Slim interjected. "France withdrew from NATO. Lyndon Johnson was the president. Hubert Humphrey was the vice president. The United State

Supreme Court decided on the Miranda rights in *Miranda versus Arizona*, and Brandon Null filed one damage claim in that whole year—his sons had taken one of his company trucks out on a joy ride and hit a deer before slamming it into a tree." With a roll of his eyes, he chuckled.

"You don't believe that that's what happened?"

"Not unless that tree was painted red. There was red paint and what looked like blood on the grill and fender of the truck," Slim said.

Cameron felt her heart beat faster. *Red. The same color as Douglas O'Reilly's car.* She had to swallow before she could get out her next question. "Did you pay the claim?"

"Brandon Null was a good customer, just like Russell is," Slim said. "He paid his policy on time and in full and rarely put in a claim. The story the kids told was that they had hit a deer and then lost control of the truck and slammed into a tree. I figured it wasn't a tree, but another car, and Brandon paid for the guy's repairs off the record. But then since so much work had to be done to the truck, they put in a claim." He shrugged his shoulders. "No one ever put in a claim for damage to the other car, so who was I to quibble?"

"I don't suppose you remember when they hit this deer?" Even though Slim's memory was exceptional, like Joshua had told her it was, she assumed it was too much to ask. But it was worth a shot.

"First Tuesday in September," Slim said. "I don't remember the exact date. My old memory isn't what it used to be. But it will be in my records."

Cameron blinked. "Records?"

"Of course," Slim said. "What kind of businessman doesn't keep good records? It will all be in there, along with my pictures of the truck and the damage."

"You have pictures?" Cameron's voice went up an octave.

"Sure." His eyes disappeared into a face filled with wrinkles when he flashed her a broad smile. "Do you want to see them?"

In a small county like Hancock where everyone knew everyone, it took less than five phone calls for Joshua to uncover that Henry MacRae was staying in a VIP suite at the Mountaineer Resort. The hotel manager confirmed that Congresswoman Rachel Hilliard had also been staying there in a separate suite but had left that morning for a flight back to Washington.

"By the way," the hotel manager said as an aside before Joshua hung up the phone, "MacRae and the congresswoman had a big fight in the lounge last night before she left suddenly this morning."

"Would you by any chance know what it was about?" Joshua asked him.

"Nope," he said. "They tried real hard to keep it under control, but the congresswoman had the same expression she got on her face when the head of that ethics committee was questioning her last year about that little fiasco with some of her campaign funding being traced back to a union with mob ties."

"You mean that expression she had right before she blurted out, 'Who the hell cares!'"

"Yeah," the hotel manager chuckled. "That interview video went viral."

Joshua stopped laughing when he recalled that the senator who had been head of that ethics committee died less than two weeks later of a sudden heart attack.

After confirming that Rachel Hilliard was gone and MacRae was alone, Joshua strolled into the lounge and took a seat at the table next to his. After ordering a cognac, he cocked his head at the police superintendent. "Hank?"

Colonel MacRae jerked his head from where he was watching the horse races on the closed circuit television. He slowly shook his head until recognition crossed his face.

"Joshua Thornton." Joshua rose and shook his hand. "Hancock County Prosecuting Attorney."

"We met at the governor's inaugural dinner a couple of years ago," he said. "Surprised to see you here. From what I've seen on the news, crime has been hopping in Hancock County. The body of a deputy turning up after being missing twenty years.—"

"And now my neighbor got murdered two days ago," Joshua said. "I'm sure you heard about that."

"No," MacRae said quickly, "I don't believe I did. I've been focused on the deputy. We don't want it to look like law enforcement in West Virginia will roll over and play dead—especially when the victim is one of our own."

"I'm glad to see you and I agree on that." Joshua mouthed a thank you to the server who delivered his drink.

"Of course we do," MacRae said while Joshua took the first sip of his drink. "Neither of us would be in this business if it wasn't for the love of justice. We certainly aren't in it for the fame and riches," he added with a chuckle.

"Well, some of us may be in it for other, more sordid reasons," Joshua said over his glass.

MacRae hesitated to study Joshua, who stared directly into his eyes. "Are you talking about power?"

"Maybe," Joshua said. "I haven't decided if it was that, or maybe love, or maybe an even mixture of the two."

"What are you talking about, Thornton?"

"I told you that my neighbor was murdered the other night," Joshua said. "You didn't ask me who she was."

"Is it someone I know?"

"Dolly Houseman."

Colonel MacRae's face turned white when the color drained from it. He swallowed.

"She used to be the madam at Dolly's, which was located right out here." Joshua jerked his thumb in the direction of the long country road down from the resort. "But I believe you know that already."

Eying each other, the two men drank in silence. MacRae almost drained his drink in one gulp before ordering another. Joshua still watched him.

MacRae rubbed his face with his hands. "You didn't just drop in here by coincidence."

"No."

"You heard the tape?"

"Of course I did."

MacRae moved over to Joshua's table. As he sat down, he said in a low voice, "I can explain."

Sitting up, Joshua crossed his arms on the tabletop. "I'm listening."

"Congressman Hilliard's plane crash really was just an accident," MacRae said.

"Which happened exactly the way you and his wife planned six months earlier during your rendezvous at Dolly's?"

"Listen, I'm going to tell you what I told Dolly when she tried to blackmail me," MacRae said. "Bring it on. I had nothing to do with Rod Hilliard's death. I was in Huntington that weekend and the week before working a double homicide, and I have a whole team of police officers and detectives to alibi me."

"So you paid someone to do it for you while you were wrapped up in a case," Joshua said. "Like you said, I heard the tape. You and Rachel Hilliard conspired to kill her husband in what appeared to be a plane crash so that she could take over his seat, and then she used her influence to get you into Charleston, which is exactly what happened six months after that conversation was recorded."

"Six months," MacRae said. "A lot can happen in six months."

"Like what?"

"Like I came to my senses," MacRae said. "That's right. I went along with it during the conversation, in the heat of passion, wanting her like I always want her. Have you ever heard about addiction?"

"Yes."

"Well, it's possible to be just as hooked on a woman," MacRae said. "Sometimes I wish my drug was cocaine. I've been Rachel Hilliard's lapdog ever since that night I busted her for possession of pot and she batted those eyelashes at me and offered me a carnal bribe." He took a big gulp of his drink. "With one hit, I was hooked and have been sorry ever since." He looked over at the prosecutor. "Is Congresswoman Hilliard a conniving, power-driven, manipulator? Yes. Do I love her? No. Sometimes I don't even like her." He shook his head firmly. "But I'm hooked on her."

"Is your addiction strong enough to make you kill for her?" Joshua asked.

"No," MacRae said with certainty. "Yes, we talked about killing Rod to clear the way for her to get to Washington, but when it came to actually doing it, I couldn't. I've done a lot of things for that woman that I'm not one bit proud of. But murder?" He shook his head. "That was where I drew the line."

"If you didn't do it, why did you pay blackmail to Dolly Houseman all these years," Joshua asked.

"I didn't," he said. "I told Houseman to take the tapes to the police if she wanted because I didn't do it. She never did. I know she took the tapes to Rachel, and Rachel has been paying her off."

"Do you think Rachel Hilliard arranged her husband's murder without you?"

"Why else would she pay the blackmail?" MacRae replied. "But she wouldn't do the dirty work herself, I know that." He chuckled, "Rachel's too smart to get blood on her hands."

"Even if Dolly had enough evidence to destroy her?" Joshua asked.

"Do you know how many friends Rachel has collected throughout the years?" MacRae asked. "Dirty friends. Those rumors about mobsters funding her campaign with dirty money aren't just rumors. You wouldn't believe all the scandal that's continuously brewing around her. But does the media ever even hint about it? No." With a chuckle, he shook his head. "There's a reason for that."

"Like her enemies having sudden and fatal accidents?"

MacRae's face was void of emotion. "You've been doing some research."

"Were you aware of the number of former call girls who used to work with Rachel Hilliard who died suddenly within years of Dolly's closing its doors?" Joshua asked. "It's like Rachel made sure her past got completely deleted ... maybe to pave her way to the governor's mansion. How well are you going to sleep at night knowing that you played a role in putting her there?"

"You're preaching to the choir, Thornton," MacRae said. "I know more than you what Rachel Hilliard is capable of." After glancing around, he moved in closer to Joshua. "She does not do her own dirty work. The weekend Rod Hilliard's plane went down was the same weekend that a senator's daughter was getting married. Rachel had three hundred witnesses in Hawaii to alibi her. Do you think that timing was a mistake?" He held Joshua's gaze. "Sure, I can say with certainty that if—and I mean if—someone brought that plane down, Rachel was running things behind the scenes to make it happen. And as for the sudden deaths of all of Dolly's girls? If that's what it took to pave the way for Rachel to get ahead? Yeah, most likely she was behind that, too. But it wasn't me who did it for her. Who's her guy? I have no idea, and I don't want to know."

"What if I told you that forensics found two blood types at Dolly Houseman's murder scene?" Joshua asked. "What if I told you that forensics says the DNA from the killer's blood type came from a woman? Would that make you consider Rachel Hilliard a hands-on killer? Maybe if she got desperate enough to protect her political career?"

MacRae stared at him in silence, which answered more than any words could. The server brought his check. He took the pen and wrote down his room number.

Joshua waited until the server left before continuing their conversation. "If you aren't her guy," he asked him in a low voice, "then who is?"

"I said I didn't know."

"You've been with her for over forty years," Joshua said. "You know her better than anyone. You have to have some suspicion of who it would be."

With the pen that he had kept from the server, MacRae wrote on the cocktail napkin and slid it across the table in Joshua's direction. He said in a low voice, "Rachel hasn't deleted everyone from her past—yet." He then got up from the table and walked out.

Joshua picked up the napkin and read the name that Henry MacRae had written across it.

Larry Van Patton.

The former bartender at Dolly's, who was then the bar owner Dolly had called after realizing she was dying.

Joshua glanced up from the napkin in time to see Henry MacRae waiting for the elevator to take him downstairs to his room from the VIP lounge on the top floor. A movement near the bar caught Joshua's eye. The name on the napkin connected with the familiar face.

Larry Van Patton waited for Henry MacRae to board the elevator before making his way through the crowd to the stairwell.

After depositing a twenty-dollar bill on the table for his drink, Joshua reached across the table to see what room number Henry MacRae had written on his bill to charge his drink to.

Suite 214.

It was one floor down.

A group of executives with a convention was coming off the elevators at the same time that Joshua hurried out of the lounge. Ducking and dodging the crowd, he forced his way through the bottleneck to reach the door leading to the stairwell.

The sense of urgency roaring in his ears was drowning out the party noises from the conventioneers. Joshua ran down the stairs to the next floor and threw open the door in time to hear the sound that, to anyone else, resembled that of a car backfiring. But with the situation at hand, he recognized it for what it was—

Gunshots.

At the sound of the gunshots, a busboy in the corridor dropped a serving tray that he was picking up from outside a room door to put onto the cleaning cart.

While Joshua ran down the corridor in the direction of the gunshots, the server ran toward him in his haste to escape on the elevator from whatever was happening. When Joshua grabbed him by the arm, he pulled away. "You need to let me in that room."

"Are you crazy?"

The sound of a crash came from inside the room followed by shouted cursing.

"I'm the county prosecutor! If you don't unlock that door to let me in, someone is going to die!"

Another gunshot prompted the server to thrust his keycard into Joshua's hand before running down the stairs.

Joshua ran to the room and pounded on the door. "This is Thornton! Van Patton, I know you're in there, and I know what you came for! Give yourself up! I'm coming in!"

The next gunshot sounded close to the door.

Joshua dropped down to grab the gun he wore in his ankle holster and used the keycard to open the door. Keeping low, he pushed his way inside. He was halfway through the door when the two men fighting in the room rolled along the wall to crash into the door and pin him against the doorframe.

Larry Van Patton had Henry MacRae in a headlock. MacRae twisted in his grip to jab Larry in the ribs. The blow was enough to make Van Patton collapse onto the floor with MacRae under him.

Joshua squeezed through the door, stepped over them, and aimed his gun at the former bartender. "It's over, Van Patton. Give up."

"Never!" Larry Van Patton jumped up and grabbed Joshua's arm with the gun.

Fighting to keep from accidentally firing it at Henry MacRae, Joshua elbowed Van Patton in an effort to fight him off.

Meanwhile, MacRae swung his legs around and kicked Larry Van Patton directly behind the knee. Van Patton buckled and dropped down onto the floor. As soon as he was down, the police superintendent slugged him to knock him out. "Now stay down!"

The suite was a wreck with overturned and broken furniture. The mirror over the dresser was shattered where one of the men had been slammed into it. Joshua spotted a semi-automatic on the floor at the end of the entrance hall and another next to the bed. He also spotted bullet holes in the walls. How neither man had been shot was a mystery to him.

Gasping and moaning, Larry Van Patton rolled on the floor. Equally exhausted, Henry MacRae climbed up to sit on the edge of the bed.

There was a loud knocking on the suite door. "Hotel security! Open up in there. Police are on the way."

"You're going to jail, Van Patton," Joshua said while making his way around the overturned furniture to open the door.

"You've got nothing on me," Van Patton grunted.

Joshua threw open the door and introduced himself. "The man you want to arrest is on the floor. His name is Larry Van Patton. The charge is attempted murder."

"I bet I know who sent you." MacRae said before looking up at Joshua. "What'd I tell you? Tying up loose ends."

"I have no idea what you two are talking about," Van Patton said. "I came here to the Mountaineer to have a few drinks, but I got lost and walked into this room. This guy, who I happen to know from long ago, got paranoid and started shooting at me. I haven't talked to Rachel in decades. I know nothing about her wanting to tidy things up."

Joshua knelt down to peer into Larry Van Patton's face. "Who said anything about Rachel?"

Realizing his blunder, Larry Van Patton glanced from Joshua to Henry, and then back again to the prosecutor, who narrowed his eyes while he studied him. "I want a deal," Van Patton said.

"What do you have to offer me?" Joshua asked.

"A congresswoman."

CHAPTER TWENTY-ONE

"Are you kidding me?" Cameron said by way of greeting Joshua when she found him in the observation room at the sheriff's department. "Larry Van Patton is *handing* Congresswoman Rachel Hilliard over to you for hiring him to kill her husband and all of her sisters in prostitution?"

"Good evening to you, too, beautiful," he replied with a tone heavy in sarcasm.

Her abrupt entrance brought to her attention, she tossed the valise in which she carried her folders and notes, wrapped her arms around his shoulders, and kissed him fully on the lips while taking time to taste his mouth before letting go. "How's that for a how do you do?"

"Much better," he replied before kissing her again. "And yes, he is rolling over on the lethally ambitious congresswoman."

"I thought he was the one who pointed you and Sawyer in the direction of MacRae and Hilliard in the first place," she said.

"Haven't you ever heard of honor among thieves?" he said with a wink. "It's worse with killers."

"Why insinuate Hilliard if he was her guy?" Cameron asked him. "Wouldn't he realize that the trail would lead right back to him?"

"Because Dolly was dead," Joshua said. "All of her black-mail victims had to know that those tapes are now in the hands of the authorities," Joshua said. "When we walked into his place, he knew that if we had not already heard that tape, we would."

"He wasn't on that tape," Cameron noted.

"But MacRae was," he said. "So Van Patton pointed us in the direction of MacRae. Since the idea of him being the killer was already planted in our minds by the recording, it wasn't hard for us to take his tip and run with it. Then Hilliard sent him to kill MacRae to keep him quiet about all of her other dirty dealings—which includes accepting bribes and all of the other assorted dirty games that she has immersed herself in during her long career in politics."

"Is MacRae going to help bury her?" she asked.

"MacRae took this attempted hit personally," Joshua said with a laugh. "It's going to be hard to shut him up."

Delighted, she grasped his arm. "Then do you even need Van Patton's testimony to convict her? If I were you, I'd tell him to forget any deal and throw the book at both of them."

"Van Patton has killed half a dozen ex-call girls and a congressman, plus the two assistants who were on that plane with Hilliard," Joshua said. "He's never going to see the light of day again." He patted a stack of case files on the table next to him. "While Van Patton has been conferring with his lawyer, Sawyer has been busy. He's doing a full back-ground check on Van Patton and his club. Since we showed Mike Gardner's notes to him this afternoon, Sawyer has col-lected reports on every one of those call girls' murders and is going to compare them to Van Patton's statement. Van Patton claims he's recorded every meeting he's had with

Hilliard where they discussed each hit going all the way back to Rod Hilliard, her late husband, and up to tonight's hit when he was supposed to kill Henry MacRae."

"They both wanted to pin her husband's murder on MacRae," she said.

"According to Van Patton," Joshua said. "Rachel Hilliard wanted MacRae full time. When he refused to kill Rod Hilliard, she hired her good friend from behind the bar at Dolly's. It was Hilliard, not Dolly, who gave him the seed money for his own bar as payment for getting her husband out of the way."

"And the superintendent of the West Virginia State Police knew that the wife of a United States Congressman had her husband killed, and he did nothing to arrest her?" Even though she had seen a lot of outrageous things in her career as a police officer and detective, she was still shocked.

"Suspected, not knew." Joshua nodded his head. "He didn't want to know."

Cameron turned to the two-way mirror to watch Larry Van Patton in the interrogation room where he was meeting with his attorney. "Do these two men know enough to take Hilliard down?"

Joshua nodded his head. "MacRae told us that when he heard Dolly Houseman had been murdered, he confronted Hilliard. They had a huge fight last night at the Mountaineer and she suddenly took off for Washington, which sent up a red flag to him. She's smart enough to make sure she's nowhere in the local area when a hit is going down." He held up a finger. "However, he did say that she was in town the night Dolly was murdered, and forensics says that they have not completed the profile on the second blood sample left at the scene. However, they have determined that it was left by a woman."

"If the killer's blood didn't come from a man—"

"If it didn't come from a man, it had to have come from a woman," Joshua interrupted Cameron to whisper into her ear. "What else is there?"

"A mutant." She narrowed her eyes before giving him a playful jab in his ribs. "You know what I'm saying. That clears Anthony Tanner. Maybe he's telling the truth—as outrageous as it sounds. He was hired to kill Dolly—"

"By a woman," Joshua said, "but not Rachel Hilliard, because Larry Van Patton claims he was her go-to guy."

"Maybe Rachel Hilliard went to Dolly's to coerce her into turning over the tapes, things got out of hand, and she ended up killing her. Tad says it was a crime of passion."

Joshua shook his head. "That would be stupid."

"Most killers are stupid."

"Not all of them," Joshua said. "Rachel Hilliard is very smart. Larry Van Patton is copping to more than ten kills on her command—ten kills that she has never even been on the radar for being behind. After all these years, she's too smart to hire an unknown quantity like Anthony Tanner to kill Dolly Houseman, especially before she got out of town. She would have made very sure that she was in Washington or Charleston, and with witnesses to alibi her for the time of the murder."

He made sense. Cameron lowered her eyes. She thoughtfully gritted her teeth. "Josh, think about it. Why kill Dolly now? Even if Rachel was planning a bid for the governor's mansion, killing Dolly, who had that recording, would be stupid because she had to know that Dolly had insurance. If anything happened to her, it would get into the hands of the authorities, which is exactly what happened. *No way* would she want anything to happen to Dolly before making sure she had that tape in her own hot little hands."

Joshua agreed. "Rachel had every reason to want Dolly to stay alive."

"But she's our only female suspect," Cameron said.

"I know." He shrugged. "There's only one way to find out for sure. Ask Hilliard for a sample of her DNA to compare to the blood left at the scene."

"She'll refuse to give it up."

"We'll get a court order," Joshua said. "We have probable cause now. MacRae confirms that Dolly was blackmailing her. Not only do we have her for ten counts of murder conspiracy, counting the attempted murder of Henry MacRae, but we have a burn phone with her fingerprints that was found at the scene."

"Ten?" Cameron did a quick mental count. *Seven call girls, Virgil Null, Mike Gardner, Congressman Rod Hilliard and the two assistants on his plane, and Dolly makes thirteen.*

"Van Patton's lawyer says he's copping to ten counts of conspiracy to commit murder," Joshua said.

Sheriff Curt Sawyer came into the observation room. "Josh, we're ready."

"But—"

Joshua interrupted her objection with a kiss on the cheek. "Watch and you'll get the answer to all of your questions." He went out into the hallway with the sheriff directly behind him.

Clutching her valise against her chest, Cameron turned to watch Joshua and Sheriff Sawyer go into the room next door. *Is Van Patton saying Rachel Hilliard was not behind all those murders? Maybe she is, but he didn't commit them all. Maybe she did some on her own.*

Larry Van Patton's defense attorney didn't offer to shake Joshua's or Sheriff Sawyer's hands. Instead, he started off the meeting by stating that Larry Van Patton was making his confession completely against his advice. "Before he tells you anything else about what he knows, we want to know what type of deal you're offering him in exchange for the evidence that he has to offer."

"I'm not offering your client any deals until I see exactly what he has," Joshua said. "He has already made statements confirming that he killed six women who Congresswoman Hilliard had worked with, plus her husband and his two assistants. The fact that her late husband was a congressman makes this a federal offense."

"We've already contacted the FBI," Sheriff Sawyer said. "They're on their way."

"We're prepared to turn that case over to the feds," Joshua said. "So your client can talk to them about any deal he's looking to make. As for the call girls, we're in the process of contacting each of those jurisdictions. We're going to have a full house here pretty soon with detectives and prosecutors fighting to get their hands on your client."

"Over a bunch of dead hookers?" Larry Van Patton laughed. "I don't think so."

"Don't worry," Joshua said, "I'm not turning you over to anyone until I get the facts about the cases in my jurisdiction. Let's start at the beginning." He flipped open his notepad. "Ava Tucker and Virgil Null."

Larry Van Patton shook his head.

"You told me you were going to cooperate." Joshua turned to Sheriff Sawyer. "We're through here. We'll turn him over to the feds and let them put a needle in his arm." They both stood up.

"I am being straight with you," Larry said. "Rachel had nothing to do with those murders. She had no reason to want them dead. Neither did I."

Joshua regarded him for a long moment before slowly lowering himself back down into his seat.

"She seemingly had reason to kill the rest of her fellow call girls."

"After I killed Rod Hilliard for her," Larry said. "Ava and that john were killed way before I killed Rod. It was after I killed Rod Hilliard that the problems with the girls started. Turns out this green-eyed little redhead, and I don't mean her eyes were green in color, but she was filled with envy for Rachel—her name was Bianca—she had been listening at the door when Rachel and Henry were talking about offing Rod. Bianca didn't know that MacRae didn't have the stomach for killing. As soon as Rod was dead, Bianca went running to Charleston and started threatening to ruin everything. She even set herself up in a penthouse suite at some fancy hotel and told them to bill Rachel for it. She had grand plans to bleed Rachel dry. So I went over there to party with her. She never saw it coming. In no time, I had drugged her, put her in the bathtub, and then slashed her wrists and made it look like a suicide. Rachel called in favors from her friends to close the case fast, and—" He snapped his fingers. "The case was closed faster than you could say cover up." He shook his head. "After that, Rachel thought it would be best to simply take care of all of them, just in case any of the others got any bright ideas. It was actually pretty easy. After Dolly's had closed, none of them wanted to stay in touch with each other. Dolly had given each girl fifty thousand dollars cash to start all over, and they scattered into the four winds. Not one of them had any idea what was coming when I came a-knocking on their doors and suggested that we get together to catch up on old times."

His grin reminded Joshua of the type of smile the serpent may have flashed at Eve in the Garden of Eden when convincing her to try the forbidden fruit. He felt ill to his stomach when he thought of each of those young women embarking on a new life only to have it snuffed by the self-serving, power-hungry Rachel Hilliard, who had once been one of them. "If Rachel wasn't behind Tucker's and Null's murders, then who was?"

Larry said, "I have no idea who killed them. Dolly was convinced it was Rachel even though I told her that it wasn't. I think it had to be someone connected with the guy Ava was with. I had seen him arguing with two other guys before he went upstairs with Ava that very night. I told the sheriff, too. But nothing came of it." He flashed a telling glance in Sheriff Sawyer's direction.

Curt Sawyer's eyes narrowed. Neither he nor Joshua had seen any reference in the case file to Larry telling the sheriff any such thing.

Joshua wondered if Russell's father, Brandon Null, a man of influence in the county, had anything to do with deleting all record of his son being on the scene and arguing with Virgil shortly before the murders.

Of course, Brandon would have had no power over Dolly Houseman and her recording of Philip Lipton and Russell Null threatening Virgil. While she must have been convinced that Rachel had killed Ava, she probably held onto the recording because of their reference to the mistake ten years before. Maybe—recalling the bouncer's statement, Joshua asked, "Didn't you run into a woman in the kitchen?"

The nod of Larry's head turned into a shake. "But she had nothing to do with those murders."

"What makes you so certain?" Joshua asked.

"She was the wife of one of the members."

"Which one?" Joshua asked.

"I don't know," Larry replied, "but that used to happen all the time. We would get jealous or suspicious wives sneaking in to get a peek at their husbands fooling around with the girls. Some would even take pictures to use in divorce court."

"Had you ever seen this woman there before?" Joshua asked.

"No, and considering that the club was closed six weeks later, not since either."

"Could you give us a description?" Sheriff Sawyer asked him.

Larry shrugged. "Maybe."

Curt said, "We'll get a composite artist in here to do a drawing."

Joshua moved on. "Tell me about Mike Gardner."

"Never heard of him," Larry replied.

Joshua slammed both of his hands down on the tabletop. "Now is not the time to play dumb, Van Patton! What's the matter? Confessing to killing a bunch of hookers is one thing, but a cop—"

"Cop?" Larry held up his cuffed hands. "Whoa! Are you talking about the deputy that was found in the lake?"

"Yes, that cop," Sheriff Sawyer said.

"I didn't kill him," Larry said.

"Come on," Joshua said. "We know he was investigating Ava Tucker's and Virgil Null's murders. So he must have contacted you because you were a bartender at the club. We found his notes. He had uncovered the sudden deaths of each of Dolly's girls—"

"Yeah, I heard from him and told him nothing," Larry said. "He contacted Rachel, too. Yeah, you're right. He figured it was suspicious that all of them died suddenly the way they did. That's true. He told me so. He even thought that Ava was killed by the same killer, which isn't true because I did the rest of them, but I didn't do her."

"And Rachel didn't get nervous with a deputy poking around?" Joshua was doubtful.

"Oh, yeah, she was more nervous than a cat in a room filled with rocking chairs," Larry said. "So she told me to do him and make it look like an accident. So I called him and suggested that we meet out at Tomlinson Run Park late in the afternoon, shortly before it closed to make sure we were alone. But he never showed. The next thing I hear on the news is that a deputy went missing."

In a flash, Joshua recalled meeting with Mike during lunch at Allison's diner. *He was picking up his lunch on his way out to the park. It was much earlier than late afternoon. Then there was the note Mike had made in his notepad. He had scratched out four and changed it to one.*

"Did you change the meeting time?" Joshua asked him.

"No," Van Patton said in a firm tone.

"Maybe he changed it," Joshua said more to himself than to Van Patton.

"If he did, he didn't tell me about it."

"Could Congresswoman Hilliard have taken care of him herself?" Sheriff Sawyer asked.

"That's what she pays me for," Larry said in a firm tone.

"Who else knew about your meeting with Mike Gardner?" Joshua asked.

"No one," Larry said. "That's how we've been able to get away with it all this time."

"Someone else had to know," Joshua said. "When you called Mike, did you call him at the police station?"

"No, his house. This was before cell phones." With a start, he added, "When I first called to set up the meeting, I had left a message with his wife—at least I assumed it was his wife. I left the number for the bar for him to call me back. She may have known about it."

Staring at the wall behind Larry, Joshua was still digesting the possibilities when the sheriff asked, "What about Dolly Houseman?"

"She was off limits," Larry said. "That woman knew her stuff. Heck, she learned from the best. Al Capone was her Uncle Al. She knew how to keep Rachel in line. Why else do you think Rachel paid her five thou every month to keep her happy? But Dolly was fair. I mean, she was a woman of honor. She never raised her rates. She was decent. I think over the years Rachel even came to respect her. I mean, it got to the point that when Rachel was passing through the area, she would even take Dolly out to lunch once in a while and give her the pay off herself. As long as Rachel paid her, then Dolly was cool."

"But you did lie to us about Dolly calling you," Joshua said. "Henry MacRae never came into your bar looking for a hit man, and you didn't set him up with Anthony Tanner, and you didn't give Dolly a heads up. So now tell us the real story."

"Hey, I did nothing illegal there," Larry said. "Really. I had nothing to do with it, and I had nothing to do with killing Dolly. Just take a look at what's happened in the last few days because Dolly got offed. Those recordings ended up in your hands. You guys looked up MacRae, who is going to roll on Rachel, who is going to try getting a deal by rolling on me. Like I didn't know this was going to happen the second I saw her name in the newspaper?" He shook his head vigorously while waving his hands. "Dolly dying was the last thing we wanted to happen."

The more Larry talked, the more Joshua was convinced that he and Rachel Hilliard had every reason to keep Dolly alive. Scratching his head, he asked, "Why did Dolly call you?"

"You really want to know?"

"I wouldn't be asking you if I didn't."

"She wanted me to set her up with a hit man," Larry said. "But I had no idea who the target was. I swear."

"So you set her up with Anthony Tanner?" Joshua said.

"I gave her Anthony's burn phone number, and she called him and dropped my name. I know nothing else. She never gave me the name of the target."

Joshua leaned across the table at him. "Did Rachel have a burn phone?"

"That was what she used to call me on, yes. Do you think we were stupid? We didn't want to be connected to each other."

"Did she lose her burn phone recently?"

Larry stared blankly at Joshua.

The corners of the prosecutor's lips curled.

"Yes, I believe she did mention that to me. She said not to accept any calls from that phone. She was afraid it had been stolen."

"My client has been cooperating fully," his lawyer interjected. "What kind of deal are you prepared to offer him?"

With a single knock on the door, two federal agents entered. In contrast to Joshua's easy-going demeanor, the agents had stern expressions on their faces.

Joshua rose from the table. "He's all yours, gentlemen."

"So what do you think?" Curt Sawyer asked Joshua as soon as they were outside the interrogation room and down the hall.

Before Joshua could answer, Cameron came rushing out of the observation room. "You don't actually believe him, do you? Dolly called him to hire a hit man? For who? Who would she want dead?"

While Curt and Cameron gazed at him, Joshua waited to allow a grin to work its way across his face. "Think about it." He folded his arms across his chest. "If we put Larry's statement and Anthony's together, they do kind of match. Especially when you pair them up with Tad's autopsy results."

"Dolly was dying," Cameron gasped. "She gave me those albums the same day that she died and said something about justice."

"Are you saying she hired Tanner to kill herself?" Sawyer asked.

"If we ask Hilliard, I'll bet we find out that she had met with Dolly recently, at which time her cell phone and a pendant necklace belonging to her disappeared," Joshua said.

"Dolly used that phone, making sure she was careful not to lose Hilliard's fingerprints on it, to coordinate with Tanner," Cameron said. "Then, she arranged for him to come in to kill her using the same MO for how Ava and Virgil were killed. She held Rachel's locket in her hand to make it look like she had ripped it off her killer. With the tapes coming to you, she bet on burying Rachel for her murder."

Sheriff Sawyer said, "Van Patton just told us that Dolly was convinced Rachel killed Ava and Virgil."

"But she also didn't have any proof of it," Joshua said. "That's what she wrote in her letter to me when she sent that package."

"Framing Rachel for her murder was the justice Dolly was looking for," Cameron said.

Joshua turned to Curt. "Let's dig around to see if we can get a recording of Dolly's voice anywhere and then do a voice lineup with Tanner. If he can identify the voice of the old woman he spoke to as Dolly, then we'll know who hired him."

Sheriff Sawyer grabbed his cell phone from his belt.

"But he didn't kill Dolly," Cameron said. "A woman's blood type was on the knife."

"If Larry told the congresswoman about Dolly hiring a hit man, Hilliard may have feared that she was the target," Joshua said. "That may have motivated her to set up a face to face with Dolly to hash things out."

"I'm going to go start looking for audio recordings for that voice line up." Curt turned to trot down the hallway.

Joshua stopped him. "Hey, Curt, can you do a favor for me?" The prosecutor wrote a name on a blank yellow sheet of paper on his notepad, tore it off, folded it in half, and handed it to the sheriff. "Can you run a DMV check on this name and see if you can find a black Bonneville registered to him?"

Once Curt was gone, Joshua asked Cameron, "Have you had dinner yet?"

"Are you asking me for a date?"

He chuckled, "No, I was hoping that you'd go home and cook something."

She pinched his arm. "Think again."

"Cricksters?"

"Great!" She kissed him on the lips. "Then we can go over the evidence I collected from Slim. I'll go order our sundae and meet you there." She whirled around and headed down the hallway to the exit.

"I said dinner," Joshua corrected her.

"That will be my dinner." She shot back over her shoulder.

CHAPTER TWENTY-TWO

Crickster's was *their* place.

When Joshua walked in the door, the hostess grinned at the regular customer. "Your C & J Lovers' Delight Sundae is already on its way, Mr. Thornton, and your bride is waiting."

As was often the case when he entered a crowded room and laid his eyes on her, Joshua felt a surge of excitement in seeing that Cameron Gates, his wife, was the prettiest lady in the room—even with a black eye, which was now a nice shade of purple.

When he attempted to sneak up behind her, he got only within four feet of her when she said, without turning around to face him, "It's not a good idea to sneak up on a woman packing a nine-millimeter semi-automatic."

He grasped both of her shoulders from behind, bent over the back of the booth, and kissed her on the top of the head. "Clearly that concussion didn't affect your observation skills." He went around and slid into the booth across from her. Spotting the sundae in the middle of the table, he picked up the spoon that she had set at his place. "Ladies first. Dig in."

"I thought you'd never ask." She snatched the cherry resting on top of the whipped cream. After dropping it into her mouth and chewing it, she said, "You weren't kidding about Slim."

"I hope my mind is half as sharp as his when I'm his age." With a shake of his head, he scooped up a spoonful of the chocolate ice cream. "Did you know he bowls three times a week? Plus, he jogs on alternate days."

"Stays active," she said.

Spotting a folder on her side of the table, Joshua asked, "Is that from Slim?"

She nodded her head. "Claim filed by Russell and Virgil Null's father for a wrecked truck that happened the first weekend in September in nineteen sixty-six." She slid the folder across to him with one hand while continuing to eat the sundae. Between bites, she said, "Russell and Virgil were out gallivanting around on Friday night with two other friends, Philip Lipton and Toby Winter."

"Toby Winter? Lorraine's son."

"And Virgil referred to Toby in that recording," she said.

"I think we're on to something. Maybe Larry was telling the truth about him and Rachel Hilliard having nothing to do with Ava's and Virgil's murders."

"Oh, it gets better," she said. "According to the claim, Russell was driving—"

"Wait a minute," Joshua said. "All four of them were in the truck?"

"Virgil and Toby were in the back in the bed of the truck," she explained. "In the statement, their father says Russell hit a deer. Then, he lost control of the truck and hit a tree. The truck was still drivable, so they took it home and their father filed a claim first thing Tuesday morning on September sixth. It was Labor Day weekend and Slim's office was closed on Monday." Reaching across the table, she flipped open the folder. "Take a look at the pictures of the damage. Tell me what you see."

Joshua studied the images of the crumbled passenger side front and side fender of the big green pick-up truck. Even in the yellowed pictures, he could make out red paint.

"Slim said he saw blood, too," she said. "That's where the deer comes in—to explain the blood on the front grill."

"Did he believe they hit a deer?"

She shrugged her shoulders. "Because of the paint transfer, Slim was convinced they hit another car when they lost control after hitting the deer. He thought Brandon Null paid the owner of the other car out of pocket so that it wouldn't go on his driving record with the insurance company. People do that all the time." She added, "O'Reilly's car was red, by the way."

Joshua peered at the image of a close up of the smashed in fender. The image of the tire was clear in the picture. "I'm assuming the truck is gone."

"Long gone," she said, "But this picture shows the tread of the tire. We're reaching, but don't you think our forensics people should be able to compare this tread pattern to that on the hubcap for Douglas O'Reilly's car? They probably won't be able to be conclusive in determining if this is the actual truck that struck him. What do you think?"

Joshua closed the folder and slid it across to her. "It's worth a shot."

She slipped the folder into her valise. "You're not going to talk me out of it? Tell me that I'm wasting my time on a case that no prosecutor in his right mind would want to pursue?"

"Your case and mine are now connected," Joshua said. "In order to prove motive for Russell and Lipton killing Virgil and Ava, we need to prove that they were involved in the hit and run that killed Douglas O'Reilly. Their motive for the double murder was to prevent Virgil from spilling the beans about their cover up to Ava, O'Reilly's girlfriend."

"Considering that all of the physical evidence is gone, that's a pretty tall order, Mr. Thornton."

"I think you're up to the challenge." Joshua picked up his spoon again. "Assuming you're right that forensics will be unable to conclusively match the tread of the truck tire to the tread mark on O'Reilly's hubcap, what's next?"

"Old fashion gum-shoeing," she said. "Four young men killed an innocent bystander changing a flat tire on his way to meet his girlfriend. By covering it up, they inadvertently made it look like a suicide? Obviously, two were feeling a lot of guilt about it. One committed suicide." She shook a finger at him. "Remember I told you Toby Winter hung himself in Raccoon Creek. There had to be a significance to that place. It was where his life changed forever—and where he ended it."

"And after he died, Virgil decided to make things right," Joshua said.

"All those years, all that guilt building up," she mused, "Toby had to have talked to someone about it. I'm going to need to talk to his mother."

"Lorraine Winter?" Shaking his head, Joshua sucked in a deep breath. "I wouldn't go talk to her without a backup."

"Like you?" she asked innocently.

"Maybe Tad," he said. "He does have a way with women. Even the most hostile soften under his spell."

"Based on what I've seen of Lorraine Winter, she's immune to any charm," Cameron said. "But don't worry. I can handle her. Since Toby committed suicide in my jurisdiction, I have access to the original police report. They would have had to have talked to her and taken her statement at the time. You would think that if he had told her anything about the hit and run that she would have mentioned it."

"Unless she was too ashamed of her son being involved in something like that," Joshua said. "I remember hearing that

Toby did leave a suicide note, but Lorraine never told anyone what was in it."

"Maybe it was a confession about the cover up of the accident," Cameron said. "I'll go through Toby Winter's file and then interview his mother to see what he may have told her or left in his suicide note. If she doesn't know anything, do you remember anyone else who Toby was close to?"

Joshua slowly shook his head. "He really kept to himself. I remember that Virgil was the only friend he had."

"Well then, after Mrs. Winter, that leaves Russell Null and Philip Lipton," she said. "Considering that Virgil was his brother, maybe I can get Russell to turn on Lipton for being the bad guy. Lipton certainly appeared to be the aggressor in that recording."

She sensed, rather than saw, the man making his way to them through the doorway and the crowd coming. Joshua saw the figure making a beeline for him, and at the same time he saw Cameron raise up out of her seat to grab the gun she wore on her hip.

"Thornton!" Philip Lipton blurted out while grabbing Joshua by the shoulder. "Who do you think you are?"

Joshua threw his hand straight up in an order for Cameron to stand down before turning to the enraged chief of the West Virginia state crime lab bureau in Weirton. In contrast to Lipton's fury, Joshua was extremely calm. "I'm doing my job, what the voters elected me to do. Ensuring in every way possible that justice is carried out to the full extent of the law."

"By going behind my back?"

"If that's what it takes, Lipton."

"Listen, Thornton." Lipton threatened to poke Joshua in the chest with his finger. "I was nailing killers with my microscope while you were still figuring out how to woo cheerleaders with those baby blues of yours. I've always gone to bat for you, no matter how crazy your cock-eyed requests have seemed, and now this is how you pay me back? Sending in the FBI to take over my lab?"

"I didn't send them in to take over your lab."

"They came in with a warrant to collect every piece of evidence we have on four murders! Are you saying I'm dirty?"

"Are you?" Joshua asked. "Why didn't you tell us that you were connected with the Ava Tucker and Virgil Null murders and had a conflict of interest?"

"I'm not!"

"You were there the night Virgil Null and Ava Tucker were killed," Joshua said.

Philip Lipton's mouth dropped open.

"As soon as you became head of the crime lab, you also checked out their evidence boxes," Joshua added. "Makes me wonder what you did to that evidence."

"Virgil Null was a friend! His brother had been my best friend! I wanted to see if I could uncover anything to find out who did do it."

"But you failed to mention in all these years that you were on the scene right before the murders?"

"You have no idea what you're doing!" Lipton grabbed Joshua by the front of his shirt.

Her hand on her gun, Cameron stepped forward.

"Stay back, Cam!" Joshua ordered her before peering into Philip Lipton's angry eyes. "I know exactly what I'm doing, and so do you." He lowered his voice to a whisper. "I got the tape. I heard it all. The whole conversation between you, Russell, and Virgil Null—right before Virgil and Ava Tucker were murdered."

Slowly, Philip Lipton released his hold on Joshua's shirt.

A collective sigh was heard throughout the restaurant.

Lipton's expression switched from fury to fear.

"The FBI is the least of your problems, Lipton," Joshua said.

"What a day." Cameron and Joshua had driven home in separate cars, and when she arrived home he was waiting for her on the porch. With a sigh, she slipped into his arms.

He hugged her tight. "Yeah, well we're getting close. We'll get these cases closed out and then I'll take you away for a nice long weekend."

"Right now, all I want is a nice long bath."

"Alone?"

Giggling, she looked up at him.

"I think I can accommodate that." Placing his hand under her chin, he tilted her head up to kiss her softly on the lips. She pulled him in tight against her. When he pulled back, he whispered, "Consider that a preview."

Rowl!

Startled, Joshua whirled around.

With his back arched and his fur standing on end, Irving bounced along the edge of the porch, leapt up onto the railing, and jumped down over into the rose bushes.

"I guess he saw a squirrel," Cameron said.

"You know he hates me."

Cameron opened her mouth to argue. Deciding against it, she shook her head. "He'll get over it."

"What if he doesn't?"

"He will," she insisted.

"He never got over my moving his cat treats to the upper cupboard."

"You know, there are people who can't accept change." She placed her hands on her hips.

"What does that have to do with it?"

"Just saying." She went inside.

Joshua could see Irving glaring at him from the dark bushes. Like those of an unearthly creature, his emerald green eyes glowed with a fiery fury directed at him. "She's mine," Joshua told him in a harsh whisper. "Get your own girl."

"He can't," Donny's voice came out of the darkness. "He's fixed. Cameron's it."

Startled to be caught arguing with Irving, Joshua tried to look innocent when Donny came up the steps from where he had walked home from a friend's house.

"Betcha feel bad now for stealing his girl, huh?"

"Not really," Joshua replied.

Inside the house, they found Cameron in the kitchen with Tracy and Hunter. Squeezed in between the two of them, Cameron was admiring pictures on Tracy's cell phone.

"We have pictures of my engagement ring." Tracy ripped the phone out of Cameron's hand to run over and show her father.

"Why didn't you bring it home?" Donny asked her.

"They have to size it," Tracy said. "It won't be ready for two weeks. So Hunter is going to bring it up to New York to give me later on this summer. That's when we'll set a date for the wedding." She squealed with delight when she said the word 'wedding.'

"It's a custom design. One of a kind." Hunter explained that they had found a custom jewelry shop in Pittsburgh. "The diamond is a whole carat."

"Sounds pricy and looks expensive," Joshua said. "Will Dolly's lawyer release the money for that from her estate?"

"He says he will," Hunter said. "He also agreed with you that it'll be best to sell her house and for us to buy our own place. He'll even help us find a place out of town."

Cameron contained the sigh of relief threatening to work its way to her lips.

Noticing that the box he had left for Joshua that morning was now in the study, Hunter asked if he had a chance to go through it. "Did you find anything that can help us?"

While inviting Hunter to sit down, Joshua pulled out a chair from the kitchen table. "Something very interesting."

"What?"

They all sat around the kitchen table.

"Your father was on to something," Joshua told them. "He was on the brink of uncovering a murder spree involving Congresswoman Rachel Hilliard. She used to be a call girl at Dolly's and had all of her co-workers killed to cover up her past."

"Do you mean Congresswoman Hilliard had a deputy killed?" Donny gasped.

Tracy's eyes were wide.

"I don't think so," Joshua said.

"Why not?" Hunter asked.

"Because we got the hit man she tasked to do the job and he says he had a meeting set up, but your father didn't show."

"And you believe him?" Hunter asked in a tone filled with doubt.

"Actually, I do," Joshua said. "He was straightforward about committing several murders on her behalf, including a capital offense of killing Congressman Rod Hilliard and two innocent passengers on his plane. Why not confess to killing a deputy?"

Cameron said, "He stated that he had an appointment to meet your father in the park at four o'clock. We found your dad's note about the appointment, and he had the time set for four, but then crossed it out to make it one."

"The hit man denies changing the time," Joshua said. "I met your father at Alison's diner a little bit before one o'clock when he was picking up his lunch and on his way to the park to meet his CI. I think someone who knew about that appointment moved up the time in order to get Mike out there earlier and kill him before he met with the person he thought was his confidential informant."

"Actually, it was someone else who was planning to kill him," Donny pointed out. "Talk about irony."

Joshua said, "Most likely, whoever moved the time didn't know that, which tells me Mike's killer may not have had any connection to the case he was working on."

"Have you eliminated Russell Null and Philip Lipton as suspects?" Cameron asked Joshua.

"I don't think they did it," he said. "Remember Larry stated that he told the sheriff at the time about seeing Russell Null and Philip Lipton at the club and about them arguing with Virgil. Well, that is nowhere in the police report. I'm convinced Russell's father used his influence to have that kept out of the case file, so Mike wouldn't have had any reason to suspect them."

"The only way we knew about the confrontation was Dolly's recording," Cameron said. "That may have been why Lipton checked that evidence box and case file as soon as he came to work for the state lab here. He wanted to make sure Russell and him were in the clear."

"Unless Dolly told him," Joshua said, "Mike would not have known they were at the club on the night of the murder. They would have been nowhere on his radar."

"He would have questioned Russell because he was the brother of one of the victims," Cameron said. "But if Mike didn't suspect anything, Russell would have had no reason to panic."

"Then who killed him?" Hunter asked.

"I want to talk to your mother again," Joshua said. "According to the hit man, he had left a message with her. So she knew about that appointment. I want to know who she may have told."

CHAPTER TWENTY-THREE

Belle Fontaine uttered a gasp of pleasant surprise when she answered the doorbell to find a horde of visitors standing on her doorstep. "Well," she demurred, "I guess I should have been expecting a visit from all of you eventually." She opened the door wider to allow Hunter, Tracy, Donny, Cameron, and Joshua to enter. "We're going to be family, but I was planning to invite you all for dinner." With a wave of her hand, she ushered them into the living room. "We can have drinks."

Contrary to Royce's insistence that his wife was too distraught to answer questions about the case, Belle appeared elegant in lilac-colored lounging pajamas with a form-fitting-floor-length-robe over them. She clutched a cup of tea in her hand.

Joshua kissed her on the cheek. "You look lovely, Belle." He called into the living room where her husband looked like he had just sucked on a very sour lemon. "Not at all what I expected, Royce."

"Why not?" she asked Joshua. "Oh, you mean about Mike. Well, that is all a shock, but I'm getting over it. I had a talk with Tad today and he'll be releasing the body. Finally, we can give Mike a proper burial. Did you find anything helpful in that box that I gave Hunter?"

"What box?" Royce asked in a sharp tone.

"I remembered a box I kept in the back of my closet that I had put everything from Mike's desk into," Bell said. "I gave it to Hunter to take over to Joshua's."

"Yes," Joshua said, "it was very helpful." He noticed Royce move over to the bar.

"Royce," Belle said, "I believe we have a bottle of champagne in the fridge. Why don't we break that open to toast Hunter and Tracy's engagement?"

"I don't need any," Cameron said. "Thank you, Belle." In response to their host's questioning expression, she explained, "I don't drink alcohol. A soda will be fine for me, please."

"I'll have what Cam's having," Donny said, "especially if you can put a scoop of ice cream in it."

"Oh, please come into the living room and tell us," Belle said. "I want to hear all about what Josh has uncovered. I swear, if it turns out I had the answer in that box all these years, I'll kill myself." Slipping her hand through his arm, she escorted Joshua into the living room and pulled him down onto the sofa to sit next to her.

In the recliner across from him, Cameron arched an eyebrow at the sight of Belle with her hands clasped on Joshua's elbow. Royce's jealous expression brought a smirk to her lips. After a long stretch of silence, Royce cleared his throat.

"Did you find the champagne, dear?" Belle asked him.

Royce broke his glare from where his wife had another man by the elbow. "I'll get it." He poured a short glass of whiskey, straight up.

"What was in that box that I overlooked, Josh?" Belle asked.

"Mike's notepad," Joshua said. "On the top sheet, he had written out his appointment for that afternoon to meet someone at Tomlinson Run Park at four o'clock."

"Yes," she said. "I remember that. We actually got into an argument about it."

"You did?" Hunter asked. "I didn't know that."

Belle's gaze dropped to the floor. Her eyes became teary. "I tried to forget about it. I was so ashamed."

"Why?" Cameron asked.

"Because it seemed so silly after what happened," she said. "I was mad because Mike had set that appointment for four, but he was supposed to pick up Hunter from the babysitter at five o'clock. He wanted me to take off work early to go pick Hunter up. He didn't used to do that to me. But suddenly, out of the blue, Mike was working on this case that I knew nothing about and he refused to talk about it. He was keeping secrets from me and I was mad about it. It all seems so petty now."

"Did you know that the appointment time had changed?" Joshua asked her.

Her face was blank.

"That was very long ago, Josh," Royce said. "How could she be expected to remember a tiny detail like that?"

"Because that was the last time she saw and spoke to her husband," Cameron answered. "I remember every single detail, every instant, every second of the last time I saw my husband before he was killed." She cocked her head at Royce. "If Belle knew, she'd remember."

"I don't remember the appointment changing," Belle said. "Mike would have let me know because then he could have picked up Hunter."

"Someone changed that appointment," Joshua said, "and it was not the man he was planning to meet. It was someone else, someone who lured Mike to the park so that he could kill him."

"Do you know who?" Bell asked.

"Someone who wanted to get Mike out of the way," Joshua said. "Someone who knew about the appointment. The man who made the original appointment didn't tell anyone. So who did Mike tell? We know he told you, Belle. Who did you tell?"

"No one," she blurted out.

"What are you implying, Thornton?" Royce demanded in a loud voice.

"You two were fighting," Cameron told Belle. "You just admitted it."

"Are you saying I killed my husband?" Her eyes were filled with tears.

"You were a young mother," Cameron said. "You were working. It had to be hard. Stressful. You needed to talk to someone. Think, Belle! Who did you talk to? Who did you tell about that appointment that interfered with your schedule, forcing you to leave work early to go pick up Hunter because your husband was obsessing over a case that he refused to talk to you about?"

Her eyes widened.

"Belle?" Royce said in a tone that was an eerie mixture of an order and a plea.

She rose to her feet and turned to him.

"They're manipulating you, Belle," he said. "Don't listen to them."

"It was you, Royce." Her voice was low and harsh. "You were my boss, but you made me think you were my friend. I told you everything."

"Was Royce at work that afternoon?" Joshua asked in a quiet voice.

She hesitated to think. "No, he had gotten a call from someone—I don't remember who, but suddenly he had to leave for a meeting and—I had to leave early to pick up Hunter and had to close up the whole office early because Royce wasn't there."

There was a crash of broken glasses behind the bar when the champagne bottle overturned and smashed several of them. Everyone was startled to their feet.

Royce stared at his hand, which was cut and dripping blood from the broken glass.

"It was you," Hunter said in a menacingly low voice. When he stepped forward, Tracy grabbed him by the arm. Joshua held him back with a hand pressed against his chest.

"This is ridiculous!" Royce picked up a dishcloth and wrapped it around his bleeding hand. "You can't prove anything."

"I saw you following Mike in your Bonneville," Joshua said. "We ran a DMV check on your vehicle registrations. You had a black Bonneville registered in your name at the time of Mike's disappearance. You changed the appointment time, followed him out to Tomlinson Run Park, and killed him to clear the path for you to move in on Belle."

"Playing the devoted, compassionate friend there for her in her hour of need," Cameron said.

"That's why you had a fit about my digging into the case," Hunter said. "Because you knew we'd find out if we kept on digging."

"You can't prove any of this!" Royce said. "My wife knows the truth." He gazed at the woman he loved. "Tell them, Belle."

Instead, she stared at him. Her face was white.

The room was filled with silence.

Suddenly, Royce reached down under the bar and came back up with a handgun. "Everyone stand back."

Hunter pushed Tracy behind him. Donny stepped forward to give his sister an extra layer of protection.

Enraged, Belle moved forward, but Joshua yanked her back.

Her gun already drawn, Cameron stepped in front of everyone.

Casually reaching behind his back for the gun he had tucked into his waistband, Joshua said, "Calm down, Royce."

"No!" Tears rolled down Royce's face.

"You killed my father," Hunter roared, "for what? To win a woman who loved another man?"

"She loves me!" Royce argued. "Tell him, Belle!"

Belle's eyes were wide with disbelief. Her face was pale and filled with rage, not only directed toward her husband, but also inwardly for not having seen it all before.

"Just tell us what happened," Joshua said in a calm and low tone while easing Belle back behind her son.

"You already know," Royce cackled while waving the gun. "After Belle told me about her fight with Mike, and how furious she was about being left to take care of Hunter all the time while he was investigating this case that he refused to even talk to her about—it was suddenly so clear. It came to me in a flash. Hey, he was a cop. Cops die or disappear in the line of duty every day. So, I called Mike. He didn't even recognize my voice. I told him that I was an associate of his four o'clock appointment and he had a schedule conflict and wanted to know if they could meet earlier, at one o'clock in same place. I had no idea where that place was and I thought that if I suggested the place, Mike would suspect something. But I had it figured out."

Royce tapped his temple with the barrel of the Colt handgun that Joshua recognized as a former standard police issue. "Mike said sure," Royce told them. "Then, I went to their house and waited for him to leave and followed him.

When we got to the park and he saw me get out of the car, he was confused, but—"

"Since he knew you, he had no idea that you had lured him there to kill him," Joshua said.

"I had the tire iron tucked behind my back," Royce said. "Mike was a big guy. I knew I had to get the jump on him. That first hit had to count. He hit the ground. He was still shaking the stars out of his eyes when I grabbed his gun off him and shot him between the eyes."

"No!" Belle screamed. "You monster! I can't believe—" She tried to shove through her guests to take her husband on—armed or not. Tracy threw her arms around her to take her into a bear hug, not only to comfort her, but to hold her back.

"I did it for you," Royce called to Belle.

"You did it for yourself!" Hunter fought to force Joshua's arm out of his path to get to Royce. "Because you wanted to have her, like a possession, like a prize. You wanted to own her and you couldn't stand to see another man, a man who was twice the man you ever were, have a woman who has always been too good for you, and always will be."

"Look at the life that I gave her!" Royce said. "See this house? Look at the cars and the places that we've been!"

"I'd give it all up to have Mike back for just one day," Belle sobbed.

"No!" Royce yelled.

"Yes, you …" Belle searched for the word. "Son of a bitch! You hear me? You're a monster!"

Cameron interjected, "Do you really think we should be calling an armed crazy man names, Belle?"

Sobbing hysterically, Royce looked down at the gun he was holding in his hand.

Joshua tried to ease up toward the bar. "Royce, is that the gun you used to shoot Mike?"

"I didn't realize that I still had it until I was halfway back to Pittsburgh." Royce nodded his head. "You know, if you had asked me an hour ago if killing Mike was worth it, I would have said it was—to have the woman I loved and to give her everything she ever wanted …"

"But you took away the only man I ever loved," she sobbed. "I never loved you. I only married you because I knew that love would never come my way again after Mike. He was it. I can't ever love like that again. How could you take that away from someone you said you loved?"

"Because I wanted you so much," Royce said. "Don't you see? You were my Mike. Without you, I had nothing. But now—seeing that look of horror on your face—directed at me—like I'm …"

"A monster," Hunter said. "That's what you are."

"We are trying to talk him into putting down the gun," Cameron whispered to Hunter. "Insulting him isn't helping."

"Do you think I'm a monster, Belle?" Royce asked her.

"Belle, don't—" Cameron ordered, but she was too late.

"Yes," Belle said. "I despise you."

"Well, then, that does it."

Reaching for the gun, Joshua dove over the bar. Royce fell back against the wall so that Joshua's reach fell short by a mere inch. Before Joshua could make another attempt to grab the gun, Royce pressed the barrel of the gun up under his chin and pulled the trigger.

258

CHAPTER TWENTY-FOUR

"How are you doing?" Cameron went over to the SUV to talk to Tracy, who was leaning against the fender of the car alone after finishing her statement to one of Sheriff Sawyer's deputies.

"Shaking like a leaf," she said. "I've never been in a situation like that. Dad went charging toward a man with a gun. I can't believe Royce held on to the same gun that he used to shoot Hunter's dad all those years ago. How crazy is that?"

"Extremely crazy," Cameron said.

"He was obsessed with Hunter's mom," Tracy said. "I can't believe nobody saw it—except Dad."

"He's sharp like that." Cameron shrugged her shoulders. "But I think someone else suspected as well."

"Belle." Tracy peered through the dark to where Hunter was consoling his mother. "All those years she held onto her late husband's notes and then—suddenly she remembered them and gave them to Hunter. Why didn't she give them to Dad when he first talked to her about reopening the case?"

"Denial," Cameron said. "I have found that those closest to a killer only see what they want to see. But then, eventually, the truth will bubble up to the surface and they'll unexpectedly see what has been there all along. I think that happened when Mike's body was discovered earlier this week. Belle gave us that box because she wanted us to find proof of what she may have already suspected deep down. It may have been buried so deep in her mind that she wasn't even aware of those suspicions being there."

"But you and Dad saw it," Tracy sighed before dropping her gaze down to her feet. "That's what makes you two a great team … lovers in crime." She flashed Cameron a soft smile. "I hope Hunter and I can be like you and Dad—I mean, a good team."

"Aw, shucks," Cameron said with mocking gratitude.

"I mean it." Tracy sucked in a deep breath. "I owe you an apology."

Cameron was suspicious. *Is this a trap?* "What for?"

"All the nasty things I thought about you," she said. "I knew that it wasn't Dad who didn't want a wedding. He wouldn't have shut all of us out on that—unless the woman he was marrying wanted to shut us out."

"This is an apology?" Cameron asked.

"Yes, it is," Tracy said. "I didn't know the whole story. You see, I was so hurt, that I didn't care to hear it. But now I know it and I understand. I'm sorry for jumping to conclusions about you."

Cameron felt a burn start in the pit of her stomach. *What did Josh*—"Did your father—"

"No, Donny explained it all," Tracy said. "How you and your late husband had a big Catholic wedding and then, four months later, you were in the same church, before the same friends and family, for his funeral. That's why you don't do weddings or funerals."

"But I never told Donny about that."

Tracy giggled. "You'd be surprised by how well Donny picks up on things." She took Cameron into a warm hug.

"I'm glad he picked that up and told me, and I'm glad you're my stepmother." She kissed Cameron on the cheek. As she pulled away, she added, "I hope you can make an exception to your no wedding rule to come to mine."

Smiling softly, Cameron whispered, "We'll see."

"I need to go check on Belle," Tracy said before hurrying away when Joshua and the sheriff came up to the SUV.

"Did I just see Tracy hug you?" Joshua asked. "Or was she strangling you?"

"That was a hug. We need thicker walls in our house." Cameron turned to the sheriff. "Did you check the registration number on the gun Royce used to shoot himself?"

"It was Mike Gardner's gun all right." The sheriff nodded his head. "Can you believe it? Belle knew he had a gun, but she had no idea that it was Mike's gun. She only thought it looked like Mike's gun." He asked both Joshua and Cameron, "What are your feelings? Do you think Belle knew her current husband killed her first husband?"

They shook their heads in unison. "She was completely stunned," Cameron said. "I think if we hadn't been there she would have killed him herself."

Joshua agreed. "Totally caught off guard. I'm not going to press charges."

"Good," Curt said. "That's my sense as well."

"At least Royce Fontaine saved your county money on a trial and putting him up in prison." Cameron saw Hunter and Tracy in a group hug with Belle Fontaine. "Can you imagine the guilt Belle is going to go through knowing that she was married and sleeping with the same man who killed her husband?"

"A nightmare," Joshua said.

"Well, speaking of making progress on murder cases," Curt said, "right before your call came in, the FBI picked up Hilliard in Washington for questioning on her husband's murder. We'll be getting her DNA to compare to the blood found at Dolly's murder scene. Forensics said they should have the DNA profile from the blood left on the knife in the morning."

"Good," Cameron said. "Maybe we can get this wrapped up tomorrow after we interrogate Lipton and Null and after I go talk to Toby's mother. I'd like to deliver some good news to Douglas O'Reilly's mother."

"Oh, you mean the news that she has a great-grandson isn't enough?" Joshua asked.

Chapter Twenty-Five

"Detective Gates, what are you doing?" Lieutenant Miles Dugan asked Cameron when she answered her cell phone.

Looking through the two-way mirror into the interrogation room where Russell Null was conferring with his attorney, a white haired man with a handle-bar mustache who she recognized from defending suspects she had arrested before, she replied, "I'm watching a killer lawyer up, sir."

"Yeah, I know," the lieutenant said. "I just got a call from our prosecuting attorney saying that you wanted two arrest warrants for vehicular homicide that took place in nineteen sixty-six. Are you serious? What part of 'time off' are you having trouble understanding?"

"These two men's bad decision from almost fifty years ago ruined numerous lives, including the life of the man they killed," Cameron said. "Here in Hancock County, they're suspected of a double homicide to cover up that hit and run."

There was a long silence on the other end of the line before Dugan let out a deep sigh. "Do you have any evidence to connect them to the hit and run that took place here?"

"Circumstantial," she replied. "But once I get a go at them, I'm sure I can get one of them to confess and flip on the other."

"Make sure you dot all your i's and cross all your t's. I'll work with the prosecutor to get you those arrest warrants."

"Thank you, sir." She tried not to grin when she hung up the phone.

Sheriff Curt Sawyer came into the observation room with Joshua, who was carrying two case files.

"No surprise," Joshua told her, "Philip Lipton is in the other room with his lawyer. Based on his body language, he's ready to do battle. He's got a lot to lose. If he cops to covering up that hit and run by dumping O'Reilly's body, his reputation as a criminalist will be ruined—not to mention the possibility of jail time." He stepped up to the mirror to study Russell Null, who was holding his head in his hands. "Russell is another story. His brother is dead. He knows there's no stopping the truth from coming out now. For him, a confession may be a welcomed relief."

She stepped up to his side. "Then let's start with Null."

Joshua turned to her. "Ava Tucker's and Virgil Null's murders belong to us since they happened here in Hancock County. But the suspected motive is the hit and run in Raccoon, which is your turf. You're going to have to take the lead since that's where it all started."

"I can do that." She smiled broadly at being in charge of the interrogation of what was, after all, her case.

"Don't get cocky," Sheriff Sawyer warned with a good-natured grin while opening the door for them to move on to their interviews. "This is still my county."

"Didn't your mother ever tell you to be nice to guests?" She trotted ahead of Joshua out into the hallway, where she turned around to ask them, "Does Lipton know his old friend Russell is here?"

Sheriff Sawyer answered, "We've been keeping them separated."

"I'd like to try something," Cameron said. "It may help to move things along."

"You have nothing to worry about, Russell," his lawyer was telling him. "It doesn't matter what that old woman recorded thirty-something years ago. You had no reason to kill your brother. Without any proof—"

The door flew open.

Philip Lipton and his lawyer started to enter, only to find Russell Null and his lawyer already sitting at the table.

Lipton and Null locked eyes.

While a series of emotions filled both of their faces, Sheriff Sawyer stepped in to apologize to Lipton. "They told me that this witness was in room three. Let's try the one across the hall." Urging Philip Lipton and his attorney backward into the hallway, the sheriff closed the door.

Russell Null's face was white and his hands were shaking by the time the door opened again and Cameron and Joshua entered. They each carried a case file. Joshua also had a cassette player tucked under his arm.

"Russell, thank you so much for coming in this morning," Joshua said in a cordial tone. Even though Russell Null was a suspect in two serious crimes, he could not forget that he was a county commissioner and they knew each other casually. Politics demanded that Joshua treat him with respect, which was something Cameron struggled with. "Have you met my wife, Cameron Gates?"

Russell shook her hand. "I heard you got married."

While they took seats across the table, Joshua announced, "Cameron is a homicide detective with the Pennsylvania State Police."

"Why is she here?" Russell's attorney asked in a blunt manner.

"I'm investigating a homicide," she replied. "We think that maybe your client might have some information pertaining to it."

"In Pennsylvania?" the lawyer looked over to Joshua. "I thought this had to do with the double homicide of Russell's brother and that hooker he was with at Dolly's back in seventy-six."

"It does," Joshua replied. "I'd like for you to listen to a tape that was delivered to my home a couple of days ago. The date on this tape is February thirteen, nineteen seventy-six." He pressed the button to play the tape.

"What are you doing here?"

"That's your client," Cameron told the lawyer.

A door slammed in the background while a younger man's voice said, *"This is a bordello. What do you think I'm doing here? How did you know I was coming?"*

"That's Virgil," Joshua said before turning to Russell, "but I think you know that."

"Be serious."

"That's Philip Lipton," Cameron said, "an old friend of your client."

"Do you have any idea what you're doing?" Russell asked.

"He knows exactly what he's doing," Philip said. *"He's sneaking around behind our backs to ruin our whole lives because of one stupid mistake we made on one stinking night, that's what."*

"Yeah, that's what I'm doing," Virgil said. *"I'm making things right—once and for all."*

"Why?" Philip Lipton asked.

"Because it's the right thing to do," Virgil said. *"Do you have any idea how many lives we've ruined? Ava. Toby."*

"We didn't ruin anyone's lives," Philip said. *"They did. They made their decisions on their own for how they wanted to live—or not live—their lives. It's not our fault."*

"Like we made our decision to not take responsibility for the mistake we made," Virgil said.

"You want to talk about ruined lives," Russell cut off Philip to ask. *"Then here's a count of how many lives you'll ruin if you go upstairs. Yours. Mine. Philip's. How about Dad's life when his two sons go to jail? And then, what about Suzie? She and I were planning to get married in three months. Think about that."*

After a long hesitation, Virgil said, *"It was an accident. We know that. We need to tell everyone the truth about what happened. Otherwise, Toby's death will be for nothing."*

There was the sound of movement, followed by the sound of a punch and a shriek.

"Stop it, Phil!" Russell yelled. *"Let him go!"*

Joshua said over the sound of the struggle, "Philip Lipton attacked your brother here, didn't he? Shortly before he and Ava Tucker were murdered."

Philip Lipton's eerily low voice came out of the speaker, *"If you go up those stairs with her, I swear, you'll be dead before morning. I'm not going to let you rip everything I've built out of my life because of one stupid night a decade ago! Do you hear me, Null! You tell her what we did and you're a dead man!"*

Joshua hit the stop button. "And he was … dead before morning, just like Philip Lipton said he would be."

"What did Virgil tell Ava Tucker that got him killed, Russell?" Cameron asked. "What wrong did your brother die trying to fix?"

Russell's eyes filled with tears.

"Russell Null had nothing to do with those murders," the lawyer said.

"But he knows who did," Joshua said.

267

"It wasn't Philip," Russell said.

"You don't need to protect him anymore, Russell," Joshua said.

"He killed your brother," Cameron said.

"No," Russell said.

"Don't tell us it was you," Joshua said.

"No, it wasn't me either," Russell said. "I was afraid Philip was going to kill him. Really. Yeah, he was serious when he grabbed Virgil. I thought he was going to break his neck. So when Virgil went upstairs with Ava, and Philip was so mad, I got him out of there. We came down here to New Cumberland to a bar and we drank to our lives coming to an end. Man, it was over as we knew it. I made sure I stayed with him because I didn't want him going back to kill Virgil. We closed that bar, which I now can't remember the name of—" He sucked in a deep shuddering breath. "Then we went our separate ways. When I got home, I found out Virgil was dead anyway. I stuck with Philip trying to protect him—" He swallowed, "and still he died. Somehow, I felt like it was—" With both hands, he wiped the tears from his eyes and face. "When Toby killed himself, Virgil was convinced that it was God punishing us for what we had done. I thought he was crazy. I mean, we took this guy from those he loved, so God was now taking away those we loved." His voice squeaked. "Virgil could be such a pain, but I loved that little guy. And he was only doing what we should have been man enough to do in the first place—and still someone killed him."

"What wrong was Virgil trying to right?" Cameron asked him again.

"Don't say anything," the lawyer warned him.

"We killed a man," Russell said. "The first weekend in September back in nineteen sixty-six. It was like the last weekend of summer. Philip Lipton and I were best friends then. He was from Hookstown, and I was from here. We had met at a Boy Scout camp. Virgil and Toby Winter were only fifteen. They were in the back of the truck. We were all drinking and smoking weed out at Raccoon Creek. We were higher than kites. Philip was doing wheelies with one of the company trucks, whipping those two lunatics around in the bed of the truck. We were all laughing like a bunch of hyenas on one of those dirt roads cutting through the park, when suddenly, the truck smashed into something and it happened so fast. This body hit the hood of the truck and bounced over on the other side."

The room was filled with silence.

"That sobered us up real fast," Russell said.

"What happened next?" Cameron asked.

"Philip and I were both seniors in high school," Russell said. "We had our whole lives in front of us. Philip was planning to be a doctor. My dad wanted me to be a lawyer. And there we were, all drunk and we had marijuana on us and we reeked of it. Toby and Virgil wanted to take him to a doctor, but we could tell by looking at him that he was already dead. Blood was all over. Philip said there was nothing we could do. We were right there at the lake, and with the sharp turns in the dirt road, people were wiping out their cars all the time and hitting trees. He made it sound so simple. Put the guy in the car and push it into the lake. Everyone would assume he had an accident."

"Only that wasn't what happened," Cameron said. "Everyone assumed Douglas O'Reilly had committed suicide because his girlfriend was pregnant. He was a young man with a whole world of promise, too. His family was left destitute. His mother's heart was broken. The girlfriend's reputation was ruined, and she ended up becoming a call girl. The guilt drove Toby to commit suicide at the same lake where it all started."

Collapsing onto the table, Russell sobbed into his arms.

Cameron leaned across the table. "Russell, Virgil said in this recording that he wanted Toby's suicide to mean something. Don't you want Virgil's murder to mean something? Finish what he started. It's not too late to make things right." She slid her notepad across the table to him. "Write down what happened that night."

When Russell reached for the notepad, his lawyer's hand came down onto the pad to stop him. "What's he going to get in return for his confession?"

"How about peace of mind?" she replied.

Joshua and Cameron met Sheriff Curt Sawyer out in the hallway.

"Did seeing Russell Null shake up Philip Lipton any?" Cameron asked Curt.

"Yeah," Curt said. "How did Russell Null react? He looked like he was going to pee his pants."

"Just about," Cameron replied. "He confessed to Douglas O'Reilly's vehicular homicide."

"But he claims he and Lipton were together getting drunk while Virgil and Ava were being killed," Joshua said.

"They must have compared notes on that," Curt said. "Because Lipton is singing the same song. He says they were closing Marie's lounge here in New Cumberland after Virgil told them he was coming clean with Ava."

"Russell couldn't remember the name of the bar," Cameron said. "If they had compared notes, he would have known the name of the bar."

"We've run out of suspects for Ava's and Virgil's murders," Joshua said. "It has to have been them."

"Maybe they did it together," Curt said.

"I can't believe Russell would have killed Virgil," Cameron said. "He is genuinely distraught about it, and he's rejecting his lawyer's advice and coming clean about O'Reilly's death."

"I agree," Joshua said.

Curt folded his arms across his chest. "What's his story for killing O'Reilly?"

After Cameron reported what Russell had told them and written in his statement, the sheriff chuckled. "That's not the story Lipton told."

"Oh, yeah? What's he saying?" Joshua asked.

"It was the same about them going to Raccoon Creek. Smoking weed and getting drunk. Then, when it comes to getting behind the wheel, Lipton claims Russell let Virgil drive and that it was Virgil who killed O'Reilly. Lipton also says it was Russell's idea that they dump the body and car in the lake because he was afraid of what his father would do. When Lipton said he wanted to tell the truth, Russell threatened him with bodily harm."

"One of them's lying," Cameron said. "I think it's Lipton, because he was the aggressor in that recording."

"Problem is," Joshua said, "you have no proof of who was driving."

"They were all there," Cameron said. "I say I take them both in."

"They're pointing their fingers at each other," Joshua said. "Without being told who was driving and who made the decision for the cover up, the jury isn't likely to convict either one."

"With both Virgil and Toby dead, you have no other witnesses to confirm either man's statement," Curt said. "I don't envy you."

Shaking her head, Cameron stuffed her notepad into her valise. "There is one other witness I can talk to. Toby Winter committed suicide over this. He had to have told his mother why. You said there was a suicide note."

"No one knows what he wrote in that note," Joshua said. "It's been forty years, and Lorraine's told no one. What makes you think that old biddie is going to tell you?"

"You're not the only one who's an artist at manipulation," Cameron said. "Even if she won't tell me what he put in the note, he must have told her something about what had happened to have made him so distraught. Maybe when he did that, he told her who was driving."

"I doubt it," Joshua said.

"It's worth a shot." She kissed him quickly on the lips. "I'm going to go see her. Wish me luck. I'll call you after I talk to her." With a wave of her hand, she ran down the hallway. At the door, she stopped to call back to Joshua, "Love you," before heading out the door.

"She really is a firecracker," Sheriff Sawyer told Joshua with a sigh.

Fighting the grin on his lips, Joshua replied, "She most certainly is." Arching an eyebrow, he turned to the sheriff. "How are things with Tiffany, the pole dancer?"

The sheriff's chuckle held a wicked note. His cheeks turned pink. "She's a firecracker, too."

CHAPTER TWENTY-SIX

"… Do you hear me, Null! You tell her what we did and you're a dead man!"

Once more, Joshua hit the stop button on the cassette player. He had listened to the recording four more times in hopes of uncovering some clue of who killed Ava Tucker and Virgil Null.

Larry Van Patton had a point. Rachel Hilliard didn't have a motive at that time to kill Ava, unless there was a motive no one knew about.

Russell Null and Philip Lipton alibied each other. Unless they did it together.

They were holding Russell Null and Philip Lipton while waiting for the arrest warrants from Pennsylvania. But if either or both of them had committed murder on his turf, he wanted to know.

Could Russell Null be playing us? Won't be the first time a killer played the inconsolable relative of a victim.

With a deep sigh, he collapsed his head into his arms and closed his eyes.

I'm missing something, and I think it's on this tape.

"I guess you're waiting here for this." Sheriff Sawyer came into the conference room where Joshua was playing the tape. After draping a leg over the corner of the table, he gave Joshua a copy of the message they had received from Washington. "The FBI got the warrant for Rachel Hilliard's DNA. They're running a comparison to the blood from the knife now." He handed Joshua another report. "In the meantime, forensics had already run the blood from the crime scene through the database. No match."

"Why am I not surprised?" Joshua picked up the run down on the analysis of the blood. "It's from a female. So that eliminates Null and Lipton as suspects for Dolly's murder." He lowered the report. "It's very suspicious that Lipton checked out the evidence box for Ava's and Virgil's murders as soon as he became head of the forensics lab, especially since he seems to have an alibi for the time of the murder."

"He says it was because Virgil Null was a friend and he wanted to see if he could find something," Curt said.

"And a jury will buy that." With a groan, Joshua slumped in his seat. "It could very well be true. Working on murder investigations all the time, even if he had bad feelings toward Virgil, curiosity could have made Lipton want to look into the case."

"Dolly was blackmailing him and Null," Curt said. "He probably thought that if he could find the real killer, it would get him off the hook."

"Which brings us back to who killed Dolly." Joshua picked up the forensics report on the blood and the DNA profile. Reading the toxicology report, his eyes narrowed. "That's interesting."

"What is?"

"Drugs they found in the blood," Joshua said. "They found a mixture of drugs commonly used to treat osteoporosis and dementia." He glanced up at the sheriff. "Could Rachel Hilliard suffer from dementia?"

"I thought it was a job requirement when running for political office," Curt replied with a grin.

"Crazy? Yes," Joshua shot back. "Dementia? Not so much."

"Suffering from dementia is not the type of thing you publicize," Curt said. "Want me to call Washington to see if we can get someone to ask the congresswoman?"

"It would save time."

While Curt hurried out the door, Joshua pressed the button to play the tape again. This time, he rewound it to the beginning to catch any phrase that might have escaped him before.

It started to come together.

" … How did you know I was coming?"

"Be serious."

"Do you have any idea what you're doing?"

"He knows exactly what he's doing. He's sneaking around behind our backs—"

Joshua sprang up from his chair and out into the hallway, where he collided with the sheriff who was on his way into the conference room.

"Well, it's not Rachel Hilliard," the sheriff announced with a grumble. "She has neither osteoporosis nor dementia."

"I didn't think so." Joshua pushed past Curt and ran down the hall to throw open the door to the interrogation room where Russell Null was cooling his heels with his lawyer. "Null!"

Russell Null and his lawyer jumped at Joshua's abrupt entrance. They both looked frightened when Joshua slammed his hands down on the table. He was breathing hard when he asked, "On the tape of you and Lipton confronting Virgil that night at Dolly's, Virgil asked you a question that neither of you answered. How did you know he was going to see Ava? Virgil didn't tell you that he was going there because Lipton said so himself on the tape. Virgil was sneaking behind your backs—because he knew you two, especially Philip, would stop him. So who told you? How did you know he was going to tell Ava about killing Douglas O'Reilly?"

Uncertain of where Joshua was going, Russell stammered out his answer. "Toby's mom told us."

"She knew about Douglas O'Reilly?" Joshua asked.

Russell nodded his head. "Toby told her about it right away. He wanted to go to the cops but she wouldn't let him— she kept saying that we had all made a mistake and now we had to live with the consequences like men. She thought Toby was weak when he killed himself because he couldn't live with the guilt."

"And when Virgil decided to come out with the truth?"

Russell slowly shook his head. "She called me and told me to stop him because Toby had shamed her enough by killing himself. If it came out that he had killed a man—"

Joshua was on his way out the door when he met Curt in the corridor outside the sheriff's office. "Is Larry Van Patton still in the holding cell?"

Sawyer nodded his head. "Waiting for the feds to transport him to a federal prison."

"Get me Lorraine Winter's picture from the DMV!"

Larry Van Patton was eating his lunch when Joshua suddenly appeared at the door to his cell and held up a color photograph of an elderly woman. "Is this the woman you saw in the kitchen at Dolly's the night Ava Tucker and Virgil Null were murdered?"

"That was a long time ago," Larry argued while setting aside his lunch tray and shuffling to the door.

Shaking the picture, Joshua ordered, "Look at it!"

Larry took the photograph. He studied the image for a matter of seconds before nodding his head. "Yep, that's her. I'm certain of it. I had forgotten her wild eyes. She had this crazy look." He handed the picture back to Joshua. "That's her. No doubt in my mind."

Joshua whirled around on his heels to find Curt Sawyer pressing the button on his radio to call his deputies to Lorraine Winter's home. "I need to call Cameron."

While waiting for what seemed like an extremely long time on the porch of Lorraine Winter's small, run-down home built into Chester's hillside, Cameron strolled over to peer into the backyard. She figured that maybe Lorraine hadn't heard her knocking on her door because she was outside.

That was when the detective noticed that Lorraine's backyard was adjacent to Dolly Houseman's backyard. Only a broken-down privacy fence separated the two lots. Her brow furrowed. *Why didn't I notice that before? They're neighbors.*

"What do you want?" Lorraine demanded from the other side of the screen door.

Forcing a smile on her lips, Cameron went back to the door. She was taken aback when she saw the elderly woman.

When the detective had met her earlier in the week, Lorraine Winter had been dressed in clean, pressed clothes. Her hair was brushed without a strand out of place. She was as neat as a pin.

This time, her unkempt gray hair fell lose down to the middle of her back. Her flabby frame was encased in a worn housedress under a tattered robe that hung open. Her feet were nestled in shabby blue bedroom slippers.

"I'm sorry to bother you, Mrs. Winter," Cameron said once she regained her composure, "but I had some questions for you about your son, Toby."

"He's dead," Lorraine announced in a matter-of-fact manner.

Even through the screen door, Cameron was unsettled by Lorraine's wide eyes. They were filled with a fury that seemed to pierce through the screen barrier between them.

"I'm sorry for your loss, Mrs. Winter," Cameron said gently. "But, I understand he committed suicide at Raccoon Creek—"

"Hung himself," Lorraine said.

"Did he tell you why he wanted to die?"

Lorraine stared at her. "Why are you asking?"

"Because there's another family who lost their son, and I believe Toby may have been involved. If your son told you what happened that night, and the truth could finally come out, then maybe things could be set right—or at the very least, this family could have closure."

While Cameron waited, Lorraine's lips pursed.

Cameron could feel the hatred boring into her from the old woman's eyes.

A slow smile worked at the corners of Lorraine's lips. Finally, she pushed open the screen door. "Come in," she invited Cameron in a crackly voice that oozed with unnatural sweetness.

Cameron stepped into the small living room filled with tan furniture devoid of cushions or warmly colored throws. The pictures on the walls were old and yellowed. The less-than-homey décor sent a chill through her. She was so busy taking note of the décor that she was startled when she heard the click of the lock on the door.

"Come into the kitchen." The corners of Lorraine's lips curled into a grin that appeared out of place. She flashed Cameron a smile that revealed discolored and uneven teeth.

While following her out of the room, Cameron asked, "Did Toby ever mention the name Douglas O'Reilly?"

In the kitchen, Cameron felt as if she had been transported back in time to the home of her nasty aunt who had despised her. The appliances and cupboards that had once been white were yellow with age. The black and white tiled floor was chipped.

The only freshness in the dreary room was a breeze that swept in from the backyard through the screen door.

Lorraine went over to the cupboard across the room and reached up to take out a teacup.

Standing behind her, Cameron noticed Lorraine's bandaged right hand as she reached into the cupboard. Nodding toward the gauze wrapped injury, she asked, "What happened to your hand?"

"Cut it on a butcher knife." Carrying two teacups, Lorraine turned around and flashed that odd-looking smile at her again. "You look like you take sugar in your tea."

"Yes, I do." She jerked when she felt her cell phone vibrate on her hip. Taking it from the case, she checked the screen to read the caller ID, which said, "JOSH."

Pressing the button to take the call, she turned around. "Yes, hon?"

"It's her!" Joshua called out.

"What?"

"Lorraine! She killed them!"

Hearing a movement behind her, Cameron turned around in time to see the flash of the cast iron frying pan before it made contact with the side of her head.

Everything went black.

CHAPTER TWENTY-SEVEN

"Isn't that Cameron's cruiser?" Hunter Gardner rolled his car to a stop in the middle of the street when he noticed the white Pennsylvania State Police cruiser parked in front of the little house in the middle of the block.

They were on their way to his grandparents' home, two doors down from Lorraine Winter's house, where his mother was staying while recovering from the trauma of the night before. So far, Belle Fontaine was insisting she didn't ever want to return to the home she had made with Royce Fontaine.

Her feelings were compounded after a long night of comparing notes with her former in-laws. For years, the Gardners had believed their former daughter-in-law was pulling away from her late husband's family—possibly painful memories of her loss or shutting the door on her past to enjoy the life of being a rich man's wife.

Hours of heart-to-heart conversation revealed that it was Royce Fontaine who had cut Belle off from Mike's family. Numerous messages and attempts to reach out had been intercepted and concealed in his continuing effort to have the object of his obsession all to himself.

By morning, Belle had made the decision to legally change her name back to Gardner.

There were many decisions to make.

"The doctor told her not to drive, but Cameron insisted on picking it up yesterday," Tracy said in response to Hunter's question. "That's Cameron for you."

"What's it doing in front of Lorraine Winter's house instead of at your place?" Hunter asked.

"She's working on Ms. Houseman's murder," Tracy said. "Maybe she's questioning Mrs. Winter to see if she saw something. She lives right behind her. If the killer went out the back door, she may have seen him."

Staring at the cruiser in front of the broken-down house, Hunter eased the car forward a few feet before stopping once again. The driver in the car behind him honked his horn.

"What's wrong?" Embarrassed to be a part of the traffic hold up, Tracy said, "Cameron is a trained detective. She can take care of herself."

"Have you met Lorraine Winter?" Hunter pressed his foot on the gas pedal. "I swear the Brothers Grimm based the wicked witch in *Hansel and Gretel* on her."

"Every neighborhood has one nasty old woman." She picked up her cell phone, which was vibrating on her hip. The caller ID indicated that it was Sheriff Sawyer. "Curt, are you calling to put in your dinner order?"

"Tracy, it's me," Joshua said. "Are you with Hunter?"

"Sure—"

"Are you two at his grandparents' house or ours?"

Shooting a look of concern across at Hunter, Tracy pressed the speaker button. "We're on our way to the Gardners. Why?"

"Lorraine Winter killed Dolly," Joshua said. "She also killed Ava Tucker and Virgil Null. Cameron is with her now, and when I called her I heard a crash and scuffle. The phone is still on and she's making noises like she's hurt. Police are on their way, but Hunter, you were with military police. Can you—"

"I'm on my way." Hunter was already making a U-turn in the middle of the narrow street. The driver behind him blasted his horn while swerving to avoid a collision "Tracy, get my gun out of the glove compartment."

"I just want you to see if Cameron is okay," Joshua said. "Backup units are on the way."

The room was spinning. No matter how hard Cameron pressed her eyes shut, every time she opened them, the room continued to swirl around her.

The floor felt gritty on her face and hands. Pushing herself up onto her knees, Cameron dropped face first back down onto the floor when nausea overcame her. Something warm and moist dripped into her eyes. Thinking it was sweat, she wiped it away to realize that she was losing the feeling in her fingers. In spite of the numbness, she could recognize the feel of it.

Too sticky. Nope, it's not sweat.

Squinting, she peered at her fingertips. Even through the blur, she could recognize it as blood.

The sound of running water roared in her ears. Footsteps resembling that of an oncoming gorilla across a tile floor echoed inside her head.

A pair of dirty blue slippers stopped in front of her.

Shoot her! Cameron heard inside her head. *Get your gun and shoot the old witch dead. Now! Before it's too late.*

"What are you doing here?" she heard Lorraine ask in a puzzled voice.

With numb hands, Cameron groped for her gun in its holster strapped to her hip. With effort, she unsnapped the holster and fumbled around to grab the grip and remove the gun. Rolling over onto her back, she aimed it up at the figure standing over her. The gun shook in her hand.

Shoot!

She pressed her finger on the trigger, which didn't move.

Pull on the trigger. Harder. Why aren't you firing, you dumb—the safety! Turn off the safety!

Clumsily, she lowered the gun and felt for the safety to unlock it.

"What are you trying to do?" Lorraine took the gun out of her hand and peered at it. "Stupid girl. You could hurt someone with this thing." She tucked the gun into the pocket of her robe. "There. That's better." Rising back up to her feet, Lorraine went over to the knife block and removed the butcher knife. She studied the blade in her hand. "Now I remember what I was going to do." She opened the cabinet under her sink and took out a garbage bag.

Joshua stared at the clock on the dashboard of the sheriff's cruiser. "What's our ETA now?"

"Thirty seconds less than the last time you asked," Sheriff Sawyer said. "I wish you hadn't called Hunter."

"He's right there," Joshua said.

"He's not even a rookie! Every deputy in the county is on his way. Chester's police are right down the road. She's going to be all right."

"Lorraine Winter has killed three people." Joshua held up his cell phone. "Cameron is hurt."

"And what are you going to do if your daughter's fiancé gets hurt—or worse—because you ignored police procedure and sent him in to save your new wife?"

Joshua bowed his head and closed his eyes to say a prayer.

"Stay in the car," Hunter told Tracy.

Even as he gave the order, she trotted down the steps to Lorraine Winter's small porch. "Cameron is my stepmother and I love you. No way am I staying out here and letting you go in there alone to save her."

"I thought you didn't like Cameron." Holding his gun up and ready to fire, he moved up to the front door.

Keeping close behind him, Tracy followed. "She's growing on me."

"You want to help?" Hunter said. "Stay out here. Tell the officers when they arrive that I have gone in. That way I won't get shot. If you see Lorraine coming around from the back, scream bloody murder. Don't try to stop her. Tell me that you understand and will do what I said."

"I understand."

"Stop kicking me, you stupid girl."

In spite of the old woman's command, Cameron delivered another kick that planted the heel of her foot to Lorraine's nose. She heard the crack when her nose broke. The old woman dropped Cameron's other foot to grab her face, which was covered with blood from the blow.

Cameron was too heavy for the old woman to drag easily into the bathroom where she intended to cut her up in the bathtub, which she was filling with water. Her struggling made it even more of a chore.

Upon her release, Cameron attempted to fight the nausea and crawl up to her feet to scurry to safety on the other side of the screened back door. She made it only halfway to the door before vertigo plunged her face first down onto the floor.

"Bitch!" Lorraine screamed when she saw the blood. Grabbing up the knife that she had placed on the floor with the garbage bag, she lunged for the young woman's back.

"The door's locked," Tracy said.

"No kidding," Hunter replied.

"Bitch!" they heard Lorraine Winter curse from inside the house.

"Stand back." Hunter delivered a kick to the old door, which broke free from its lock. It swung open as if to invite him inside. "Cameron! It's Hunter Gardner!" he announced while rushing inside with his gun drawn. "Are you okay? Police are on the way."

The sound of the door being kicked in roared in Cameron's head.

"Cameron! It's Hunter Gardner! Are you okay? Police are on the way."

In the distance, Cameron picked up the sound of sirens growing closer.

Lorraine Winter heard them too. Her wild eyes grew wider. With a sadistic grin that stretched across the width of her face, she scurried out of the kitchen and through a door leading down to the basement. Placing a finger to her lip, she gestured to Cameron to be quiet before closing the door behind her.

"Cameron, are you okay?" Hunter Gardner rolled her over and quickly examined her. "Oh, dear God, look at you! What did she hit you with?" She felt his hand on her neck. "Where's Mrs. Winter?"

Cameron opened her mouth to speak, but only unintelligible noises came from her lips. Her jaw shook. Her teeth chattered.

"You're in shock. EMTs are on their way." He glanced up at the screen door leading outside. "Did she go out the back door?"

With a gleeful light in her eyes, Lorraine eased open the basement door and crept forward. Like a child sneaking downstairs to shake presents on Christmas morning, she tiptoed into the kitchen.

Seeing her, Cameron tried to force a warning from her throat. All that came out was a high-pitched shriek.

"It's okay, Cameron." Hunter tucked his gun into his waistband. "We'll find her."

But you'll be dead before they come in. There she is. Turn around. Hoping he could understand her fear, Cameron grabbed Hunter's arm and squeezed.

Seeing her cell phone on the floor, Hunter picked it up. "Mr. Thornton, are you there? … Yeah, I'm in. She's got a wicked head wound, but she's alive…Mrs. Winter appears to have escaped out the back …"

Lorraine covered her mouth with her hand to stifle the giggle bubbling to her lips in anticipation of her next brutal murder. Taking Cameron's gun out of her bathrobe pocket, she tiptoed across the kitchen toward her next victim.

The warning failing to come, Cameron's eyes pleaded with Hunter to grasp their message.

In the sheriff's cruiser, Joshua let out a deep sigh and gave Curt Sawyer a thumbs up. "We're coming up Fifth now," he told Hunter into the phone. "Dispatch says units have just arrived on the scene. Where's Tracy?"

"She's—" Hunter's response was broken off by a loud scream that almost pierced Joshua's eardrum. He felt his heart skip a beat as a series of gunshots erupted through the phone's speaker.

"Hunter!" Joshua shouted into the phone. "What's happening? Who's shooting?"

Curt cringed when he heard an officer reporting across the police channel. "Shots are being fired from inside the house."

"Oh, dear Lord," Joshua clutched his stomach with his hand with the realization that his worst nightmare was coming true. He made one last attempt to contact him on the phone. "Hunter? Are you all right?"

The cruiser fishtailed when the sheriff turned off Rock Springs Boulevard onto the little street and came to an abrupt halt. Joshua threw his cell phone onto the seat and ran down the steps to where the officers were still making sense of the situation. The front door was wide open.

Recognized as the prosecuting attorney, Joshua ran inside without anyone attempting to stop him. "Where are they? What's happened? Gunshots were fired?" he asked a deputy he recognized as a senior officer.

"MacMillian is on the way," the deputy said.

Joshua felt sick to his stomach. *Tad? They called the medical examiner? Oh, dear God …*

"She's back there." The deputy jerked his head in the direction of the kitchen. "Your daughter is with her."

Joshua's whole body felt numb. Afraid of what he would find, he slowed his pace but at the same time hurried to get to Cameron and Hunter.

He only took a few steps before clearing the threshold into the kitchen where he found Tracy kneeling over Cameron. With Tracy blocking his view, he could only see the lower half of Cameron's body covered in a blanket.

"Well, at least this time you didn't jump off a roof," Tracy was saying.

Cameron's voice trembled when she said, "It was a fire escape."

"Whatever."

In the middle of the floor, there was another body that Joshua recognized as Lorraine Winter's, lying in a quickly growing pool of blood. Her body was riddled with bullet holes.

"Mr. Thornton," Hunter called to him from the corner of the room where he was being questioned by another senior deputy, "I'm sorry we got cut off, but suddenly things got really busy here."

The senior deputy shot Joshua a grin. "Looks like your son-in-law-to-be is a real hot shot. Hasn't even been to the police academy one day and he's already broken his cherry." He gestured at Lorraine Winter. "His first kill."

Hunter didn't look as thrilled as the deputy did. "Not really such a hot shot," he said. "I screwed up. I saw the open door and assumed she had gone out the back while I was coming in the front. I let my guard down and almost got killed. If I hadn't seen the look in Cameron's eyes warning me, we'd both be dead."

Joshua clasped Hunter on the shoulder. "You did good, son. I'm proud of you, and your father would be, too."

Sheriff Sawyer came around the corner to shake Hunter's hand. "You're going to be a fine addition to the department. Let's get you outside to get your statement."

Behind Hunter's back, the sheriff fired off a glare in Joshua's direction.

Joshua didn't need to hear the words to understand what was going through Sawyer's mind. The sick feeling he had in his own stomach said it all. Joshua had sent a civilian in to save his wife and Hunter wasn't just any untrained civilian, he was Tracy's fiancé. It could very easily have been Hunter bleeding out in the middle of the kitchen floor.

Tracy moved aside to allow Joshua room to kneel next to Cameron. "She must have a hard head," she whispered with a grin. "Most people would be dead with a blow like that from a cast iron skillet."

"Just like every other woman in my life." Joshua lifted Cameron into his arms. The blood that covered the side of her head smeared onto his clothes, but he didn't care. She was safe, and he was holding her. The feel of her breathing against him confirmed that she was alive, and that made everything okay.

She opened her eyes and gazed up to him. "Josh," she murmured as best she could with a numb tongue.

"I've got you," he whispered to her. "You're going to be okay, baby. You scared me half to death. You know that, don't you?"

Caressing his face, she squinted into his blue eyes. "No need to worry. You're not burying this wife. I promised. Remember."

"Yeah, I remember." He stroked her blood soaked hair off her forehead. "I love you, Cam."

"I know." Closing her eyes, she rubbed her face against his chest and drifted off.

Epilogue

Sheriff Deputy Michael Gardner was buried with full military and police honors. The front row was filled with his widow, his son and his fiancé, his adopted family, and members of his family who he had never met: his grandmother, Eleanor O'Reilly, and his aunt Flo.

Police officers from every district in the area, including many from Ohio and Pennsylvania, turned out to honor the young deputy who died while trying to solve the case of the murdered hooker, who no one seemed to care about except him.

But one detective was not in attendance. She wanted to go, and had even dressed in her uniform in an effort to work up her courage. But instead of going to the funeral, Homicide Detective Cameron Gates ended up in Crickster's drowning her grief in hot fudge.

Joshua Thornton stayed the minimally required amount of time at the reception that followed at the church home of the Gardner family before meeting his wife at their place. Seeing that she had eaten enough, he ordered his own sundae.

"What did you tell everyone?" she asked him.

"I think everyone understands." Joshua reached across to stroke the side of her face, which was bruised from her forehead and down her cheek to her jaw. Tad claimed it was a miracle that Cameron hadn't died from the brutal blow to the side of her head, which had fractured her skull.

He told her, "Between your second concussion and the doctor tacking another two weeks on to your sick leave … you're excused."

She slowly shook her head. "I owed it to Mike, and to Hunter, to be there as an officer and show my respect."

"That's something for you to work on." Joshua forced a grin. "The O'Reillys were there. Douglas' mother and sister. You should have seen how they looked at Hunter, who has already made arrangements to have their farmhouse renovated."

"Renovated?" she asked. "The whole house?"

"For wheelchair access," Joshua said. "Tracy took him out there to meet them, and he's going to make good on his grandfather's promise to take care of them. Tad was talking to them at the reception. He's going to recommend a good motorized wheelchair for Eleanor. They're also going to look at a wheelchair lift so that she can come down from the second floor on her own. Everyone was crying with joy when I left." He grinned. "I think Hunter is going to fit in well with our family."

The corners of Cameron's lips tugged in a grin while she fought to push away the memory of her first husband and his police funeral.

"Good news." Joshua sat back to allow the server to place his sundae in the middle of the table. By habit, she gave him two spoons, one for him and one for Cameron. "Forensics had gotten a fingerprint from the duct tape used to killed Ava Tucker and Virgil Null. There was never any match for it until now. It was a match for Lorraine Winter."

"So she did kill them," Cameron said, "Because Virgil was going to confess to their killing Douglas O'Reilly, and she didn't want her family shamed by what her son had done." She let out a chuckle. "Ain't it ironic?"

Joshua was unsure of what she was commenting on. "What?"

"Lorraine Winter murdered Ava Tucker," Cameron said. "In the end, who killed Lorraine?" She waited a beat before answering her own question. "Ava Tucker's grandson."

While his mouth was hanging open in surprise, Joshua spooned some ice cream and whipped cream into it. "I never realized that, but it's true."

"Which proves what goes around, comes around."

"Ain't it the truth?" Joshua nodded his head. "Lorraine's DNA was also a match to the blood left on the scene at Dolly's house."

"Which clears Rachel Hilliard of Dolly's murder." Cameron propped her chin on her hand. "I so wanted it to be her."

"Oh, her career is over," Joshua said. "She's got a dream team of lawyers, but by the time the media gets ahold of all those tapes that Larry Van Patton recorded throughout the years, plus the tape with Henry MacRae's testimony about what he knows—even if she doesn't go to jail, she'll never get re-elected."

"Speaking of media getting ahold of tapes ..." With a mysterious grin, she looked at him out of the corner of her eyes. "Exactly how did Dolly's tape of Rachel and MacRae make its way to *The Review* and the Associated Press? Somehow Jan Martin-MacMillan got her hands on it? Do you know how?"

With mock innocence, Joshua rolled his eyes. "Gee, I have no idea. You know Jan. She didn't make it up to editor at *The Review* playing by the rules. She smelled something and refused to stop until she got to the source. Why, I wouldn't be surprised if she didn't sneak a copy of that tape out of our own home in T. J.'s diaper."

"You wouldn't?"

With a chuckle, he returned to his sundae.

"You know how I hate unanswered questions," she said.

"What ones do you still have?"

"*Why* did Lorraine kill Dolly?"

"I thought it was because she didn't want you reopening the investigation into Ava's and Virgil's murders," he said.

"I thought so, too," she said. "But then, I guess after the stars cleared from my head, I remembered that Lorraine was in the car when Dolly and I were talking about Ava's murder. I didn't know about Virgil until we were at Dolly's house—after Lorraine had gone home. Did Lorraine even know Ava's name?"

"Why else would Lorraine kill her?" Joshua asked.

"Because she was just plain crazy," Cameron said. "She and Dolly had an altercation here at Cricksters that day. It wasn't the first time. They were adversaries and neighbors. They had been fussing for years. Lorraine could have gone off the deep end on that very day and decided to do something about her deep-seated hatred for Dolly—that could have been her motive." She frowned. "For all we know, the fact that Dolly was enlisting my help to solve a double-murder that Lorraine had committed was nothing more than a coincidence."

"Is that what you think?" Joshua cocked his head.

"We'll never know," she replied in a soft tone. She uttered a deep sigh. "I hate cases that end like that."

"So do I." Wishing he could bring a wider grin to her face, Joshua stabbed at the ice cream with his spoon. *Maybe it's best to just give her time.* He was aware of her watching him while he ate his ice cream in silence.

"You are such a good man, Joshua Thornton."

"Really?" His heart leapt to see her smiling at him when she sat forward and leaned her elbows on the table.

"You didn't say, 'You were wrong, Gates.'"

"What were you wrong about?"

"Don't you remember when I told you and Sawyer that Mike Gardner's, Ava Tucker's, and Douglas O'Reilly's murders had to be connected? What are the odds that three people, all from the same family, get murdered separately, and that they're not all connected?"

"But they were," Joshua replied.

"No, they weren't," Cameron said. "Philip Lipton ran down Douglas O'Reilly while driving under the influence—"

"Lipton says Virgil Null was driving," Joshua said.

"I believe Russell Null when he said it was Philip Lipton," she said. "He was the most aggressive in the recording. Besides, Russell isn't fighting the charges brought against him by Pennsylvania. I think that with the remorse he's feeling, if it had been Virgil, he would have said so by now. Even if the prosecutor chooses not to prosecute, which I don't think he will, at least the O'Reillys have closure."

"I tend to agree with you."

"Only because you're a nice guy," she said. "The fact is, none of these murders were connected."

"Ah, but there was a connection." Joshua laid down his spoon.

"What?"

"Have you ever heard of the domino effect?"

Fearing that he was going to start a discussion that was destined to go over her head, she sat back in her seat. "I've heard of dominos."

"It's the same idea," Joshua said. "Only instead of talking about a toy or game, it is a real-life occurrence. A linked sequence of events that's set in motion by one single—" He held up a single finger. "—even small—action."

Narrowing her eyes, Cameron cocked her head at him.

"Ava Tucker made the bad decision to get pregnant, which would have forced Douglas to marry her," Joshua said. "That decision put him on the road that night to go see her, which resulted in his death."

"Then Lipton and Null made the bad decision to cover up the accident, which resulted in Toby's suicide," Cameron said. "If you want to, you can trace it back to Ava's bad decision. Otherwise, O'Reilly would not have been out on that road for them to kill accidentally."

Joshua said, "Since they covered up his death, Ava thinks her boyfriend committed suicide, so she blames herself and becomes a call girl. Toby's suicide causes Virgil to come clean, which drives the already-insane Lorraine Winter to murder him and Ava, which, years later, brings Mike Gardner, Ava's illegitimate son, into the case."

"Because he was investigating Ava's murder," Cameron picked up the domino, "he has a fight with Belle, who tells Royce, who uses the opportunity to kill Mike."

"If Ava hadn't decided to get pregnant and trap Douglas into marriage," Joshua said, "Mike would never have been born—or murdered."

"But if Mike had never been born, then he would not have had Hunter, who is now marrying your little girl," Cameron said with a wide grin.

"Which proves that God does have the power to turn tragedies into blessings," Joshua said. "Which leads to my bad decision." He dropped his eyes in shame.

"What decision was that?"

"I never should have sent Hunter in to save you," he said with a sigh. "I broke police regulations and procedure, which I know. But I let my emotions for you override everything. What if Hunter had been hurt or killed saving you? Tracy would have been so heartbroken—"

"I know the feeling."

"How would I have ever earned my little girl's forgiveness?" Sickened by the thought, he pushed the sundae aside.

She reached across the table to take his hand. "You wouldn't have."

Caressing her fingers, he noticed the light catching both of their wedding bands to send sparks of light in the middle of the table.

"That is why you are never going to ever do anything stupid like that ever again, Josh." She squeezed his hand. "Promise me."

He squeezed her hand back. "Promise."

"Do you have stock in this place?" Sheriff Curt Sawyer's booming voice interrupted their moment. They had been so wrapped up in their discussion that they had failed to notice when the sheriff came in and sauntered up to their booth to show off that he was not alone. His date was clinging to his arm like self-adhesive wallpaper.

"Cameron, Joshua, I believe you met Tiffany from that hostage situation in Weirton." Curt's pride was evident by how he held her slender hand tipped with long manicured nails in both of his hands.

In contrast to how Cameron and Joshua had previously seen her, she was dressed in a backless summer dress that fell modestly down to her mid-calves, and high heeled sandals. Still, in spite of the long dress, her sensuous appeal oozed from every curve. She was the type of woman who could look sexy in a flour sack.

"Tiffany, you remember our county prosecutor Joshua Thornton, and Detective Cameron Gates," Curt introduced them.

Apparently, Tiffany was too distracted by her attraction to her handsome date. She barely glanced in their direction before telling Curt, "Not really." She wrapped both of her arms around the sheriff to take him into a tight hug. "All I remember is you sweeping me up in your big strong arms to save my life." She sighed a deep breath filled with adoration.

Caught up in their own bubble filled with love, the two of them strolled to the other side of the restaurant to cuddle up in a booth.

As soon as they were out of earshot, Cameron leaned across to table to ask Joshua in a harsh whisper, "Was that the stripper from the Blue Moon?"

"She's not a stripper," Joshua said. "She's a *dancer*—"

"She's a pole dancer," Cameron replied. "She dances half naked for drooling men."

"Curt insists that she's a professional—an artist," he countered. "He says she studied under Abby Lee Miller."

"Who's that?" Cameron shot back.

With a combination of a shake of his head and a shrug of his shoulders, Joshua spooned the last bite of the sundae into his mouth before answering, "Some VIP, I guess."

"I never heard of her." Cameron squinted at him. "VIP in what?"

"I have no idea," he confessed. "My guess, she's a Very Important Pole-dancer."

Her laughter signaled a lightening of her mood.

Setting the spoon down next to the empty bowl, Joshua said, "Tracy really wants you to come to the wedding, and Hunter did save your life. He thinks that means you owe them."

Instead of answering, she grinned across the table at him. Arching an eyebrow, she said, "I guess that's our next mystery."

The End

For The Lovers in Crime's Next Case—

KILL AND RUN

A Thorny Rose Mystery

Five women of various ages and backgrounds are found brutally murdered in a townhome outside Washington, DC. Among the many questions surrounding the massacre is what had brought these apparent strangers together to be killed.

Taking on his first official murder case, Lieutenant Murphy Thornton, USN, believes that if he can uncover the thread between the victims, then he can not only find out why they were killed, but who is behind their horrible deaths.

The investigation takes an unexpected turn when Murphy discovers that one of the victims has a connection to the late husband of his stepmother, Homicide Detective Cameron Gates.

When the FBI reveals that a recently arrested hit man has confessed to killing her husband, Cameron sets out for Washington to learn the truth about why someone would put out a contract on a Pennsylvania State trooper working a night shift on the turnpike.

In this first installment of the Thorny Rose Mysteries, the Lovers in Crime join newlyweds Murphy and Jessica Faraday to sift through the a web of lies and cover-ups. Together, can the Lovers in Crime and detectives of the Thorny Rose uncover the truth without falling victim to a ruthless killer bent on ambition?

Available Now!

About the Author

Lauren Carr

Lauren Carr is the international best-selling author of the Mac Faraday and Lovers in Crime Mysteries. Lauren introduced the key detectives in the Thorny Rose Mysteries in *Three Days to Forever*, which was released in January 2015.

The owner of Acorn Book Services, Lauren is also a publishing manager, consultant, editor, cover and layout designer, and marketing agent for independent authors. Visit Acorn Book Services website for more information.

Lauren is a popular speaker who has made appearances at schools, youth groups, and on author panels at conventions. She also passes on what she has learnt in her years of writing and publishing by conducting workshops and teaching in community education classes.

She lives with her husband, son, and three dogs on a mountain in Harpers Ferry, WV.

Visit Lauren Carr's website at www.mysterylady.net to learn more about Lauren and her upcoming mysteries.

CHECK OUT LAUREN CARR'S MYSTERIES!

Order! Order!

Numerous readers have asked the order of Lauren Carr's titles. All of Lauren Carr's books are stand alone. However for those readers wanting to start at the beginning, here is the list of Lauren Carr's mysteries in order. The number next to the book title is the actual order in which the book was released.

Joshua Thornton Mysteries:

Fans of the *Lovers in Crime Mysteries* may wish to read these two books which feature Joshua Thornton years before meeting Detective Cameron Gates. Also in these mysteries, readers will meet Joshua Thornton's five children before they have flown the nest.

1) A Small Case of Murder
2) A Reunion to Die For

Mac Faraday Mysteries:

3) It's Murder, My Son
4) Old Loves Die Hard
5) Shades of Murder (introduces the Lovers in Crime: Joshua Thornton & Cameron Gates)
7) Blast from the Past
8) The Murders at Astaire Castle
9) The Lady Who Cried Murder (The Lovers in Crime make a guest appearance in this Mac Faraday Mystery)
10) Twelve to Murder
12) A Wedding and a Killing (September 2014)

Lovers in Crime Mysteries

6) Dead on Ice
11) Real Murder

Made in the USA
Middletown, DE
22 July 2021